CARNIVAL QUEEN

Also by Roland P. Joseph:

Prose in the Key of Life—Four Short Stories from Trinidad and Tobago

Amazon.com

CARNIVAL QUEEN

ROLAND P. JOSEPH

iUniverse, Inc.
Bloomington

CARNIVAL QUEEN

iUniverse books may be ordered through booksellers or by contacting:

iUniverse
1663 Liberty Drive
Bloomington, IN 47403
www.iuniverse.com
1-800-Authors (1-800-288-4677)

Because of the dynamic nature of the Internet, any web addresses or links contained in this book may have changed since publication and may no longer be valid. The views expressed in this work are solely those of the author and do not necessarily reflect the views of the publisher, and the publisher hereby disclaims any responsibility for them.

Any people depicted in stock imagery provided by Thinkstock are models, and such images are being used for illustrative purposes only.

Certain stock imagery © Thinkstock.

ISBN: 978-1-4759-4835-6 (sc)
ISBN: 978-1-4759-4836-3 (e)
ISBN: 978-1-4759-4837-0 (dj)

Library of Congress Control Number: 2012916474

Printed in the United States of America

iUniverse rev. date: 10/17/2012

For my mother and late father

Chapter I

....

1993

The red Mazda coupe travelled dangerously fast along the narrow, tortuous road of the island's east coast, precariously negotiating the sharp bends and wooden bridges. The driver's gauzy white scarf fluttered about in the breeze as she rushed through the alternate single-lane bridge, ignoring the queue of eastbound traffic which was about to enter the bridge. She knew she acted uncouthly, but she had to get to Ricardo quickly. The letter alluding that he was on his deathbed was already three weeks old when she opened it. It was a race against time. Pulses of excitement raced through her body like a loaded electrical wire dangling in a storm. Her thoughts were a fusion of distant memories and wishful imaginings of a faint and misty world—a world she had to embrace again before it faded into obscurity. Her dwindling sanity depended on it.

Forty-five years was a long time—a very long time. What if …? She quashed any negative thoughts that emerged in her mind. As far as she was concerned, everyone and everything lay frozen in time, waiting to unfurl when she arrived. She was as nervous as a child anxiously awaiting the results of an important exam, but highly optimistic. This had to be her reward for the seemingly good deeds she had done in her life. She had already paid in full for her bad deeds, she pacified herself. An aura of sadness came over her as she recalled her father saying to her as a child whenever she was sad, "No situation is permanent; time heals all wounds." Oh, how she wished he were still here to hold her and tell her it would be okay.

Darkness had descended as she approached the village of Manzanilla. The white, distant breakers of the long stretch of beach came into view as she cleared the sharp bend. The car tyres against the loose planks of the Bailey Bridge dispatched a volley of clattering echoes into the serenity of the evening. A dark canopy of clouds posed a threat to the October moon which waited on its cue from the fading sun. A chilly breeze periodically rustled the copious stretch of coconut palms, which formed a revolving panorama in the rear-view mirror.

Her left hand moved away from the steering wheel to the back seat, groping around for a black leather handbag. She glanced quickly to the back to navigate its location, but as she redirected her focus onto the road, she frantically grabbed the steering wheel with both hands. Her heart pounded loudly; she had to make a snap decision. The dark outline of a bison appeared out of nowhere and stood statuesque in the middle of the road. She was driving too fast to stop, and both sides of the road were lined with coconut palms. As she approached the animal, she closed her eyes and fidgeted with the steering wheel, slamming on the brake pedal with enormous force. Her head remained down, her eyes closed. After a few seconds, she slowly raised her head, took a deep breath, and exclaimed loudly, "Thank you, God!" She reached into her handbag and retrieved a packet of cigarettes, lighting one with trembling hands. She took a deep pull and exhaled slowly.

The loud screech of the brake interrupted a group of gossiping women who sat on the steps of a cluster of small, craggy cottages of the nearby coconut estate. Bare-breasted men attending to small, scattered fires of burning sticks and leaves abandoned their chore. Children of varying sizes attired in ragged hand-me-downs left their game of hide-and-seek to investigate the commotion. With the assistance of two of the men, she managed to reposition the car onto the roadway. The right fender was damaged, but she would worry about that tomorrow. For now, her only concern was to get to Ricardo.

Night was approaching swiftly. The large, luminous moon peered through streamers of dark clouds with a shimmer of violet and purple. A cool sea breeze caressed her face and stroked her mussed hair, sending a refreshing sensation through her body. The thick growth of coconut palms was now a mass of dark shadows sprinkled with silver splashes. The peaceful ambiance emanating from the hamlet she now approached triggered her into a nostalgic mood.

The flickering light of candles and kerosene lamps peered through the windows and crevices of the squalid cottages. The serenity comforted her like the arms of her pa. It reminded her of the world she was once a part of, a direct contrast to the harsh world which had adopted her. It was as though the wind of change had spared this village from its cruelty—to her, this was a good omen. The cacophony of croaking frogs and buzzing insects overpowered the distant roar of the ocean and occupied her consciousness for a fleeting moment.

Joyanne? What will she think of me? Will she think that I had abandoned her? She must know the truth. The memory of the little baby girl she kissed goodbye forty-five years ago brought tears to her eyes.

Sparkles of lights through teary eyes were her first vision of Mayaro. But she was too engulfed by thoughts and filled with excitement to become nostalgic over the town which filled her childhood memories. Her old school and other familiar sights did, however, manage to flash through her mind, if only for a moment.

She was now a short distance away from the hamlet of Bristol Village—her home. There were other places she had called home in her lifetime, but to her, this was her ultimate home. She felt safe and comforted there. Memories of her father saddened her. She had disappointed him and was denied the opportunity to make amends. She was not going to be denied the opportunity to make amends to Ricardo. Fate would not rob her of that chance again. If only she had taken heed of the haunting presentiment which assailed her, she would have been home to respond to the letter right away. The flight from New York was delayed by almost four hours. It was an unrewarding trip. Her business deal went sour; nothing substantive was achieved. If only she were there to have immediately responded to the letter, she scolded herself.

While in New York, she had a gnawing premonition to return home. It made her uneasy and sad. But it was a dream, a recurring nightmare that convinced her to abort her stay in New York. The first time she had had the dream was about a year ago, and it was a long time since she'd had the dream, only this time it was more vivid, more intense. It petrified her.

She was walking along a road with Ricardo, and he was holding a baby in his arms. Although she didn't see the baby's face, she instinctively knew it was Joyanne. No words were spoken between them. It was dark, pitch-black. They walked without seeing where they were going. Then suddenly, she realized that they were way ahead of her; she was being left behind. She grew scared and began walking faster and faster, but she could not reach them; then they disappeared from sight, and she was left alone in a sea of darkness, scared to death. At this point, she sprang from her sleep, sweating profusely. The dream was the same as the previous times, only this time it lasted longer. Usually, she awoke at the point where she realized they were slightly ahead of her.

That very morning, she'd called the airline, adamant that they book her on the next flight home. She scrambled her belongings and bundled them into the suitcase, ran into the shower, dabbed on some make-up, twisted her hair into a roll, and called a cab. But this had to be the worst day of her life. Thinking that nothing else could go wrong, an announcement that the flight was delayed—due to technical problems with the aircraft—came through the airport's paging system. Half an hour turned into an hour, two hours, three hours, and four hours. By now, she was seething with anger and anxiety.

The announcement that the flight was now boarding snapped her out of a catnap and into a moment of disorientation. She straightened up her slouched body and passed her hand through her hair in a combing motion. After an agonizing six hours, she felt a sense of relief as the aircraft hit the runway. She was home at last!

She suddenly realized that there was no one to meet her at the airport, for in her haste to leave New York, she forgot to telephone her chauffeur, Lionel. She waved for a taxi and placed herself in a lounging position in the back seat as the car departed from the airport.

The voice of the driver asking for directions to her home woke her from a slumber. Talking through a yawn, she directed the driver to her home in the posh suburbs of Port-of-Spain.

It was an enormous white house with a steep green roof, set in a sprawling, well-manicured garden. The woodwork was intricate, bequeathing the island's colonial past. The driver observed that the house looked like an iced wedding cake.

"Oh, where is Lionel!" she muttered. She turned to the driver and said, "Could you pop the horn?"

"I wonder where Lionel could be!" she mumbled to herself.

Moments later, the front door was flung open. "Madam, I … I did not expect you home until next two weeks. Sorry I take so long to come to the door, but … I was, I was," Lionel said with a mortified expression on his broad, dark face, buttoning his shirt as he approached the car.

"Help me with the luggage," she said.

She followed him into the foyer as he hobbled with a suitcase in each hand.

"You can leave them here; I'll take care of them in the morning," she said.

She flung her shoes off her feet as she entered the large living room and jumped onto the sofa, sighing loudly. "Could you please get me a cold drink of water?" she asked.

She guzzled down half the water and stared curiously at Lionel. "Who's in the shower?" she asked.

"Well, ma'am, that's what I wanted to explain to you outside. I invited a friend to stay over for the night," he replied.

"Do you always do this while I'm away?" she asked.

"No, ma'am, this is the first time," he replied through a sheepish grin. "Oh, ma'am, there's a whole lot a mail for you on the piano."

"I'm sorry if I sounded a bit terse; I'm so frazzled," she said. She retrieved a small box from her handbag. "Oh, here, this is for you."

Lionel opened the box with an eager smile on his face. "Ma'am, it's the watch from the magazine," he said, excited.

"Oh, it's nothing. I know I can be a bitch at times, but we go back a long time," she said.

He left the room, smiling broadly.

She riffled though the envelopes, casting each one aside. "Bills! Business! I'm too tired for this," she lamented.

But a hand-addressed envelope caught her interest. She set down the glass and curiously opened the envelope, an intense look of concern on her face.

She sprang from the sofa, putting on her shoes with haste, and called out to Lionel.

"Open the gate right away. I have to go!" she exclaimed.

"Where are you going, ma'am?" Lionel asked.

"Just open the gate!" she shouted.

She hurried to the car, reversed it hastily onto the road, and sped away.

The windscreen wiper smudged the soft droplets of rain, leaving arches of white frost across the glass, partially impairing her vision as she negotiated the narrow silver bridge of the Ortoire River. She was mere minutes away from forty-five years. She could no longer contain her emotions as chills ran through her stomach. She felt a mixture of infallible joy and presentimental sadness. Her mind was a kaleidoscope of memories.

Imbued with excitement, she accelerated. She was ready to face anything. But her optimism was short-lived. As she cleared the corner and her old home came into view, she cried, "Oh no, this must be a cruel trick! This cannot be happening."

A gush of blood rushed to her head. A dizzy feeling overwhelmed her. She was on a merry-go-round moving at an excessive speed, suddenly slowing down. She was fighting a losing battle with her dwindling consciousness.

Chapter 2

· ·

A sullen silence penetrated the rural hamlet of Bristol Village. The hot afternoon sun peered through gauzy clouds, inciting a sultry atmosphere. An occasional breeze was the only respite to the gloomy ambiance. The trickling movement of people clad in funeral attire ruffled the stillness as they made their way to the small cemetery situated on a slight prominence, overlooking the solitary roadway that connected the fishing village of Mayaro in the east and the agricultural town of Rio Claro in the west. The sylvan enclave of trees surrounded the sporadic stretch of hamlets along the road.

A stone's throw away from the cemetery, a green tarpaulin tent cantilevered from a crude wooden house, under which a funeral service was taking place. The booming voice emanating from a tall, thin figure of a balding man commanded the attention of the gathering, inducing an instantaneous silence as he recited the twenty-third psalm, as though to impose his moral authority on the naive villagers. Everything about the afternoon appeared melancholy through the eyes of these mourners, as though life was viewed through a veil of grey.

The faint, poignant strains of "What a Friend We Have in Jesus", sung in a discordant tone, wafted on the wind to the small crowd in the cemetery who chose to eschew the religious service. Some sought shelter under the small shed at the crest of the hill, among a herd of goats which were chewing their cuds, while others stood chit-chatting beneath umbrellas or propped against headstones.

Funerals were an occasion for the women to don their Sunday best and catch up on the latest gossip. The men relished the rum-shop lime—a tradition in the rural villages, almost like the commemoration of the final funeral rite. Their faces reflected impatience and affected grief as they waited on the cortège: men attired in worn suits of varying fashion eras topped with fedoras; gaudily dressed women in styles and fashions unsuited to their plump figures—some in hats, others in black or white mantillas.

The village seamstress was all too eager to tell of the disagreement between her and the women of the village. They would bring her photographs of models and movie stars decked in exquisite clothing from which to fashion their dresses. At the fittings, they would express dissatisfaction at her craftsmanship, comparing their images in the mirror to that of the photographs.

"I ain't a magician; I is just a seamstress!" she regaled with a comical lilt.

Sighting of the cortège making its way to the cemetery roused the languid crowd; they hurried up the incline and encircled the freshly dug grave. All eyes were trained on the procession as it made its solemn trek to the cemetery. The hearse, topped with colourful wreaths, travelled slowly to keep pace with the mourners who sauntered behind.

The crowd at the graveside receded to make room for the hearse, which came to an eventual stop alongside the open grave. The pallbearers retrieved the coffin from the hearse and delicately positioned it on a gurney.

The wistful cries of a village woman pierced the silence as the coffin was opened for viewing and recital of the final funeral rites. The noise attracted the attention of some grazing goats, which lifted their heads in the direction of the commotion. "Oh Gawd! Oh Gawd!" she shouted before fainting in the arms of a stout woman.

A dragging rendition of "Rock of Ages" followed the reading of the scriptures. As the singing of the final verse commenced, the pastor gestured the pallbearers to carry the coffin to the grave. The pine box was hoisted on two strands of rope, held firmly in place by four shirtless men whose burly bodies shimmered in sweat. All heads followed the coffin as it was lowered in the grave. The raspy voice of a man swayed the mourners into singing "Blest Be the Tie that Binds" against the hollow echoes of earth sounding off the pine box as mourners threw the symbolic handfuls of dirt in the grave.

Suddenly, an unanticipated turn of events shifted focus from the burial to a commotion at the bottom of the incline. Everyone abandoned the pastor as he recited, "From ashes to ashes, dust to dust ..." and turned in the direction of a tall, exquisitely attired woman who appeared exceedingly conspicuous amid the staid ambiance. That morning, Annabelle, accompanied by Joyanne, with whom she was reunited, went to Rio Claro to purchase the best clothing she could find at the store, to wear at the funeral. She chose a royal-blue, double-breasted suit and a frilly lace blouse that clearly complemented Annabelle's fair complexion. A blue felt hat and large gold earrings framed her face with its red, chubby cheeks, oblong eyes with black, runny lashes, a straight, well-defined nose, and thin lips lined with red lipstick. She gently patted her eyes with the white handkerchief and after neatening herself, she stepped gingerly toward the pastor in her high-heeled shoes.

In a soft, cultured tone she said, "Oh, please, don't bury him, please; I must see his face for the last time. Oh, please, I must see my Ricardo." Her voice faded into a teary whisper. She covered her face with her hands.

An instantaneous silence ensued. The crowd gawked at her with shocked and perplexed expressions. She removed her hands from her face and grabbed the pastor by the hand.

"Please, sir, I must see his face. I must see my Ricardo," she pleaded.

She buried her face in the pastor's chest and cried hysterically. Puzzled and confused, he reluctantly placed his hand on her shoulder and patted her. He looked into the crowd, hoping that someone would come forward and take her away, but instead, they all stared blankly at him.

The gravediggers resumed their task of throwing dirt into the grave with added haste as though to deter any notion by the pastor to accede to the woman's request. But the pastor gently removed the woman's arms from his shoulder and in a soft, compassionate tone, whispered, "I'm so sorry, madam, but you're too late."

The silence was again rudely disturbed, this time by a loud, vengeful cry from the woman who had fainted—a fat, drably attired villager. She arose quite clumsily from the back seat of the Austin Cambridge, where she had been placed to recuperate. She shouted in a gauche tone,

"Get that bitch out of here! Get her out!" Her voice grew louder and more spiteful. "She killed him! She is to blame for his death! She abandoned him and her child! What the hell did she come back here for?"

Two men restrained her as she moved closer to the well-dressed woman as though she was going to slap her. The eventualities were too much for the exquisitely attired stranger; she fainted in the arms of the pastor.

The placing of the wreaths on the grave prompted the dissemination of the crowd. The scent of fresh earth permeated the cemetery as groups of people trickled down the earthen track, some stopping to extend final condolences to family and friends of the deceased. Others extended colloquial greetings to old acquaintances: "We only meet at funerals"; "I hope next time we meet, the occasion is more pleasant"; "Yuh doh need ah invitation to visit me house, you know."

A slim man in a white shirt clapped his hands with all his might to attract the attention of the driver of a blue Cortina. "Boss," he said, "you could take me wife home for me? I want to go with the boys for a li'l' drink."

The wife—a plump, short woman—reluctantly got into the car, but not before issuing a stinging warning to him. "Yu better eh drink and get drunk!"

The rum shop was located within walking distance from the cemetery, in the downstairs of a small blue house. An L-shaped counter in one corner of the choked room provided a makeshift bar around which were six barstools. Four tables with rusted metal chairs strewn around them stood on the other end of the rugged concrete floor. The caustic scent of urine, which emanated from the nearby urinal, aroused no discomfort; neither did the flies nor the cockroaches.

The rum shop was instantaneously transformed into a noisy confusion, as men decked in funeral attire poured in and occupied every chair and stool while others leaned against the wall. The hot topic of conversation was the commotion in the cemetery involving the exquisitely attired woman.

"Who the hell was that woman?" one man asked, directing the question to anyone who might have an answer.

"She had a hell of a nerve, disrespecting the dead like that!" another man said with a voice slurred from rum.

A stuttering voice directed the question to an old man in a black suit and brown stingy-brim fedora with a cream band and small feather.

"Grandpa Philly, you seem to know everything about the village. Who the hell was that woman?" he asked.

A silence followed as all eyes turned toward this slim old man who was considered the village sage. He took up his glass with trembling hand and gulped down the contents. He paused for a while with a grin on his face as he shook his head from side to side. As if to inject a sense of authority on the topic, another man interceded.

"That was the same woman who car did hit the light pole on the night of the wake. Rumours say that she is the rich sister of Ricardo wife. And I hear she was the dead child mother."

A man in high temper interrupted the discourse, "Nobody eh ask you nothing; jus shut yuh mouth! We waiting on the true story from Grandpa Philly."

After clearing his throat, Grandpa Philly replied, "That is one long story. There is some truth to the rumours, but sometimes the truth doh always be good to talk. But the lady was Annabelle Castello."

He retrieved his walking stick and tediously lifted himself from the chair.

"Fellas, I have to go. Enjoy the rest of the night." He waved his hat and hobbled out of the bar.

The silence was retained until he disappeared into the night.

Chapter 3

· ·

Strong winds from the gathering storm ruffled the dense growth of coconut palms, the ocean dispatching sprays of water high into the air as violent waves slammed against the coastline. The ebbing tides formed crescents of white foam on the wet sand. It was inconceivable for anyone in the locale to ignore this unfolding drama, but Annabelle Johnson Reed sat on the porch of the beachfront villa, totally oblivious to the evening's eventualities. She stared as though she could see infinity. Her eyes focused on the burning torches of the oil rigs, which appeared to float on the horizon. Their flames illuminated the darkening sky and penetrated the grey blanket of ocean. The full, ominous moon, entangled in streamers of dark clouds, fought with the raging fires for prominence.

The pale gas lamps of the fishing boats moved slowly toward the horizon, riding the waves in a dipping movement that resembled a two-step waltz. The weather might not have been encouraging for an all-night fishing expedition, but it was their livelihood. This too did not occupy Annabelle's consciousness; she gazed meditatively through her mind's eyes at the shadows of her past. The occasional sentimental smiles and bewildered expressions on her face suggested this.

The drama of the past few weeks was too much for her to endure—she was confronted with radically contrasting situations and emotions: optimism to disappointment; joy to sorrow; hope to despair. Her only shimmering light in this sea of darkness was Joyanne. She was not quite sure what the nonchalant look on Joyanne's face meant when she eventually told Joyanne that she was her real mother. She hoped it did not mean resentment.

Was Father Perez right? Maybe she should have followed her gut feeling and told Joyanne the truth a long time ago. She could still hear his cold, raspy voice.

"Miz Castello, this child, Joy—um, Joyanne—was a product of lust. No? You blame her for your father's demise. No? You resent her, perhaps subconsciously. But you do resent her. Your life is unstable and unrighteous. Sordid! Why would you even think of bringing her to live with you here? Guilt, perhaps? That is very selfish of you. She has a stable life back home with your sister and her father. Not forgetting that this man, Ric—Ricardo—with whom you fornicated, is now in a relationship with your sister. Do you believe that material things will make your daughter happy over love and a stable home? No, I don't think you believe that, Miz Castello. If you love the child as you profess you do, think about her welfare, not your own selfish needs. Leave her with her father and your sister. Don't attempt to contact her. Leave her alone if you love her. Let's pray ..."

Amid the anxiety which rankled her mind, a moment of solace came rushing through like a cool breeze as she recalled the voice of her father comforting her as a child: "Give it some time, Belle. Time heals every wound." Oh, how she wished he were still here, if only to embrace her. Tears gathered in her eyes.

The brightly coloured scarf which held her long, curly hair responded to the wind by fluttering over her head, while the long white dress sailed in the breeze. Her crossed hands, which rested gracefully on her lap, looked regal in a pair of thick gold bracelets. Large hoop earrings accentuated her distinctly Spanish features and framed her oblong face with straight nose and slightly flared nostrils. Red smudged lipstick contoured her thin lips, and a light veneer of red rouge on her chubby cheeks contrasted elegantly with her fair complexion. Her tall, medium frame slouched forward against the banister. She looked younger than her sixty-three years, with a trace of childlike innocence in her mature features. She was a picture of sophistication.

It was just a few days ago that she was filled with profound hope as she journeyed from Port-of-Spain to Bristol Village. But her optimism was reduced to anguish in that one cruel moment, which she replayed over and over in her mind. She was totally unprepared for the sight which confronted her: the tarpaulin tent, the crowd of people. She instinctively knew it was a sign of death—Ricardo's death.

The crash of the car against a utility pole attracted the attention of mourners at the wake. Men abandoned their game of cards, some gulping down their last drinks of rum, others taking their glasses with them. A group of women stopped their singing of "Safe in the Arms of Jesus" in the middle of a bar, and children jumped out of bed. Before long, the entire wake had relocated to the crash site.

The night was cool and tranquil. The three-quarter moon played hide-and-seek among the clouds, occasionally illuminating the dew-laden trees and balls of swirling sand flies. The bluish lights of candle flies manifested in the darkness as everyone stared at this woman, whose body was slouched over the steering wheel of the chic sports car.

"Is she dead?" a woman asked.

"Like she unconscious," another said.

"You is a doctor?" a woman sarcastically asked a man who approached the car and attempted to feel for a pulse.

Just then, a police vehicle pulled up.

"Everyone move aside. Give us room to do our job!" a strapping policeman exclaimed. But no one moved. Clapping his hands to gesture the crowd away and in a louder and sterner tone, he demanded, "I said to move. Can't you people understand?"

As the crowd reluctantly receded, the policeman approached the car and called out to the woman, "Madam! Madam! Can you hear me?

"She's breathing faintly. We'd better get her to the doctor," he said to the other officers.

Before they proceeded to move her, one of the policemen enquired, "Any of you know who she is?"

The only response he got was the shaking of heads from side to side.

As they were about to lift her from the car, the sound of clattering footsteps grew progressively louder, and all eyes turned toward a medium-build woman whose dress blew behind her as she hurried toward the crowd.

"It's Joyanne!" a woman exclaimed.

She paused for a while to catch her breath before stating, "She's my aunt Annabelle." She again paused to catch her breath. "From Port-of-Spain."

A deafening silence followed her disclosure. The crowd dispersed into small groups, and everyone had his own story to relate.

The delicate kiss of dawn consumed the senses. The soft morning sun emerged from the horizon, soothingly stroking its subjects like the gentle hands of a mother and bathing them in a wash of yellowish gold. Tides were low; the distant waves broke lazily and running toward the shore like playful children. The fresh scent of fish wafted on the strong northeast trade winds.

The sound of rustling coconut palms and a warbling chorus of birds greeted Annabelle as she awakened in a state of disorientation. She lay supine on the bed of the beach house staring up at the ceiling, slowly gathering her thoughts. She had regained consciousness the night before in the health centre, where she was taken after the accident on the night of the wake. Not wishing to remain in the centre, she remembered pleading with the nurse to help her locate a beach house. Joyanne stayed with her until she recovered.

The strong aroma of coffee incited her senses like an alarm clock. She languidly got out of bed, trying hard to fight off a dizzy spell. She threw a duster coat over her nightgown and shuffled to the kitchen. She stood in the doorway for a moment, pondering whether it was an opportune time to tell Joyanne.

She twitched as she approached the kitchen table, startling Joyanne, who was preparing breakfast.

"Oh, Annabelle, I wasn't aware that you got up," Joyanne said. Taking her gently by the arm, Joyanne suggested that they retreat to the porch for breakfast. "Some fresh air might do you well," she told Annabelle.

The sun was already high in the sky when they settled themselves around a white cast-iron table. The interaction which followed was clumsy; after all, they were virtual strangers. Joyanne's first recollection of Auntie Annabelle was perhaps over three decades ago during one of Annabelle's infrequent visits to Bristol Village. She remembered how Grandma Rosey hated when she visited, and she grew up with the notion that Auntie Annabelle was a bad person. Then again, when she was nineteen and Ricardo arranged for her to spend some time with her auntie in Port-of-Spain, she cried and begged him not to send her, but he insisted that it was for her own good. Her mother, Rosabelle, had just died, and Grandma Rosey was recovering from a mild stroke. Ricardo feared that Joyanne would have no one in the world should anything happen to him and was anxious for her to develop a relationship with Annabelle.

When she arrived in Port-of-Spain, Joyanne felt alone and depressed and begged Auntie Annabelle to send her back home. She wanted to be left alone. She was embarrassed at the ordeal she had endured a year ago and begged Ricardo not to say anything to Auntie Annabelle or anyone else. Annabelle reluctantly agreed to send her back home when she saw how withdrawn she had become. Joyanne heaved a sigh of relief when she reached home. She ran to her room, locked the door, and pledged never to leave her room again.

A year earlier, Joyanne gazed with excitement in the mirror, affixing the long white veil to her elegantly styled hair. It was as though she was in a fairy tale and was magically transformed from an ugly duckling to a princess. She was not an attractive girl, but her warm smile and effusive nature were alluring. She slathered powder on her large, broad face for the second or third time, lined her pouty lips with red lipstick, and blotted beads of perspiration from her round nose. She had fantasized about this day for most of her life but never thought it would really happen. Ricardo was even happier than his daughter. For him, it was a dream come true. But in the midst of his gratifying feeling, he felt sad that Rosabelle could not attend her daughter's wedding, as she was confined to hospital. He was perturbed that Annabelle was not attending the wedding; Joyanne was dead set against her being there. She remembered how ill at ease she felt around Auntie Annabelle the few times she visited Bristol Village and how much her mother and Grandma Rosey hated her.

Joyanne's fiancé, Peter, was a good boy from a respectable and well-to-do family, Ricardo thought to himself. Peter would take good care of her, and she was quite fortunate to find someone like him, but then again, Peter was also fortunate to find her. She was a good girl and would take good care of him and their children. But deep inside, Ricardo harboured distressing thoughts—he wondered why a handsome, educated, and wealthy boy who could have any girl chose his daughter.

Joyanne and Peter had met a mere five months earlier at a church bazaar. Although they had seen each other on numerous occasions before, it was the first time they actually spoke to each other. Joyanne always took a second look at him, as she was attracted to his good manners and handsome features, but she dismissed any thought of a relationship between them. She felt she was too plain and unattractive for his taste, and besides, he was from a rich family, and she—a poor girl.

She was sitting alone at a table in the tea stall. He came up from behind and asked, "Is this seat taken?" He startled her and caused her to spill tea all over her skirt. He was overly apologetic, kneeling on the bare ground and attempting to wipe her skirt with his handkerchief.

"Don't be silly. Get up from the floor. It was just an accident," she said.

They spent the rest of the evening together, participating in games and buying candies and novelties from the gaily decorated bamboo stalls. He won a small teddy bear which he playfully kissed before presenting it to her. She responded by placing its face to his lips, gesturing a long smooch.

Ricardo glanced at his watch constantly as he paced the floor of the living room, calling out to her for the seventh or tenth time, "Joyanne, hurry up, dear; we'll be late."

This time, she refused to answer. He wanted everything to be perfect; nothing must go wrong on his daughter's wedding day. Lighting another cigarette, he called out again, "Joyanne, we're already thirty minutes late. We have to leave right away."

She shouted at him from behind the closed door, "Papa, they say it's bad luck for the bride to be on time!"

He retreated to a chair on the porch, lighting the last cigarette in the pack and trying to contain his anger.

The door to the bedroom finally opened. Ricardo got up from the chair and headed inside. He was dumbstruck at the sight of his daughter in a white lace gown. She looked radiant. Never before had he seen her look prettier. He choked with emotions and said, "You look nice, Joy." The doubts which assailed him waned.

As promised, he did not disclose to Joyanne that Annabelle had paid for the wedding. He beamed with pride as he escorted her down the narrow stairs to a waiting car.

Pangs of excitement engulfed Joyanne as the small, rustic church came into view. Its green steeple roof blended in with the panorama of waving coconut palms. The arched doorway was framed with palm leaves and red ixoras. The small crowd of friends, relatives, and churchgoers huddled together on the small landing as the car made its way along the long, earthen driveway. Ladies in brightly coloured hats, men in suits, girls in frilly dresses, and boys in bowties awaited her.

The parish priest, a thin man with white hair, hurried toward the car as it stopped alongside the door. Ricardo disembarked and greeted the glum-looking pastor.

"Good afternoon, Father. Something wrong?"

Father paused, trying to wipe away any signs of concern. "No. No. There's nothing wrong. It's just that the groom is a bit delayed. I'm sure he will be here soon."

The blood flushed from Ricardo's face as he shuffled back to the car.

"What's wrong?" Joyanne asked.

"Oh, nothing, dear. Um, Peter; well, Peter is late." Try as he might, he could not disguise the gloominess in his voice.

The blanched three-quarter moon hovered in the late evening sky. Bats and night insects replaced the birds and butterflies as the car rolled slowly out of the darkened driveway of the church. No words were spoken except for the driver of the car—an old friend of Ricardo, who mumbled, "Things does happen for the best."

When they arrived home, Joyanne rushed out of the car, ripping off the white, ornate veil. Ricardo walked sombrely behind; he knew there was nothing he could say or do to console her. An intense feeling of grief and shame consumed her. She threw herself on the bed, sobbing hysterically.

Peter never showed up.

The soft voice of Annabelle calling out to Joyanne snapped her out of her pensive mood.

"Could you fetch me my handbag? It's on the dressing table," Annabelle said.

While she fetched the bag, Annabelle used the time to rehash how she was going to reveal the truth to her. Joyanne returned a few minutes later with the black leather bag, and without hesitation, Annabelle reached for a pack of cigarettes from the handbag and struggled to light one amid the strong northeast trade winds. She took a long pull from the cigarette, exhaling slowly as she turned to look Joyanne in the eye.

"There is something I must tell you. It's one of those things that's best said without thinking about it." Turning her face away, Annabelle continued with an anxious slur in her voice. "I feel the time has come for you to know the truth."

"What is it?" Joyanne asked indifferently, as though anticipating what Annabelle was about to say.

"Joy ..." Annabelle paused to clear her throat. "I'm ... I'm not your aunt as you were brought up to believe. To put it bluntly, I'm your mo ... mother. I'm the woman who gave birth to you."

Annabelle felt a nervous twinge in her stomach as she braced herself for a response—good or bad—but there was none.

Joyanne's nonchalant expression prompted Annabelle to ask, "You knew? He told you?"

Joyanne was taken aback. She wanted to tell Annabelle about the letter her father had dictated to her but felt that

Annabelle was not strong enough to hear such shocking news.

Joyanne's mind wandered back to that fateful evening.

Ricardo sat in the hammock, which emitted a creaking sound as it swayed back and forth under the wooden house. His frail voice was regularly interrupted by a dry cough. He was a pathetic sight—a shadow of the man she once knew. The skin on his face stretched tightly over the raw skeleton of his face. He struggled to speak. "Has Annabelle responded to the letter?"

"Not yet, Papa," Joyanne replied. "I went to the pay phone in Rio Claro and called her, but a man answered and said, 'Wrong number.'"

Ricardo's voice grew more anxious. "Just in case I die before she gets here, I want you to deliver this letter. Keep it secret. Don't let anybody else read it," he said before erupting in a coughing spasm.

Joyanne could not contain her tears. She rushed to his side, saying, "Oh, Papa, please don't talk about dying."

Annabelle was curious at Joyanne's callous response to her startling disclosure that she was her real mother. She pressed the cigarette butt in the ashtray and turned to face Joyanne with a strict look on her face, startling her from her contemplation.

"You knew all along that I was your mother?"

Joyanne lingered for a while and then responded. "There is something important I have to tell you about that." She got up from the chair and hurried inside.

She returned moments later with a folded letter in her hand. Annabelle blotted the tears from her eyes and turned around to face the ocean. Her slouched frame, feeble voice, and teary eyes exposed her intense vulnerability. In a soft, rueful voice she rambled on, occasionally pausing to dry her eyes and blow her nose.

"I have made a good life for myself; I have more money than I would ever need. I've travelled to interesting places, met important people; but I realize now that those things don't bring about happiness. I would give up all of those things in exchange for the simple things in life—love, family. I want to spend the rest of my life right here with you. I don't know how much you've heard about me or what you were told. But you had a brother, you know. Well, half-brother. He was for my husband, Tom Johnson. Now, you are my only child." She paused to light another cigarette. Her voice was now stronger. "Whoever said life's a circle sure said a mouthful. I wanted so much to be a part of Bristol Village—your life and Ricardo's. But life grew difficult. My marriage—marriages—were, well, difficult. I started drinking, and I was always abroad. Guess the high life has its disadvantages and advantages, too.

"I may as well tell you that my sister—your stepmother, may God rest her soul—and I never got along. Neither did my own mother. I was my father's eyeball, and I guess there was jealousy. He always said how pretty I was and that I looked like his mother. My mother didn't like the fact that George—my pa—liked me more. They were hateful and spiteful toward me." She sighed and paused to light another cigarette.

"But things between us got even worse after Pa died. They blamed me for shaming and killing him. That's when you were born. One day, after Pa died, Ma sent me to Port-of-Spain with her stepsister. At first, I thought she wanted me to make something of myself, but afterward, I figured out that she wanted to get rid of me." She heaved a reproachful sigh and turned her head from side to side. "Is there more coffee in the kitchen?" she asked.

Joyanne went to the kitchen and returned with a steamy cup of Nescafé. She sat next to Annabelle and held her hand. "You should rest now," Joyanne said.

But Annabelle continued, "Things got even worse between us when I won the carnival queen title. It was as though I turned into someone they couldn't relate to. And your mother, she was jealous. I don't know why. After all, she got Ricardo, the only man I ever loved in my life. I remember how excited I was when I went home to visit them. Me, the queen; I was front-page news. The entire country knew about me." She snickered haughtily.

"You know, when I got there—home—my mother greeted me in a spiteful tone of voice. 'You come here to show off on us? Your father dead. Is me in charge now. Go back where you come from. You feel you better than your sister? Don't fool yourself. She happy and she minding your bastard child.'

"But what really hurt was when she said, 'And, oh, by the way, Ricardo say to tell you that he never liked you; it was your sister he really liked. He say he glad you leave and gone.'

"I was never sure whether Ricardo really did say those words or whether Ma was just being nasty. I didn't stop sending money to them."

She dragged on the cigarette and, with renewed vigour, lifted herself from the chair and sauntered toward the banister. Joyanne followed behind. Annabelle continued, "Joy, like my father used to say, I felt like a penny ice in the midday sun. I cried all the way back to Port-of-Spain." She stared at a helicopter heading to an oil rig and turned to Joyanne. "When I feel better, I'll arrange for us to ride in one of those." Joyanne snickered.

Annabelle retreated back her pensive state of mind and continued to unleash her deep, personal thoughts. "Joy, I'm devastated that I didn't get to meet Ricardo before he died. But, at least I have you. I can only pray that you will give me the opportunity to be your mother. To make up for ..." Her voice broke into a teary cadence.

She wiped her eyes, and her face lit up for the first time since her return to Bristol Village. "Wait a minute!" Annabelle gushed. "Your birthday is next week! Oh my gosh, we'll have a celebration right here—a small one."

Joyanne's callous face morphed into an affected smile. She remembered the gifts Annabelle had sent to her over the years, only it wasn't really her birthday. She took Annabelle gently by the arm and led her to the bedroom. Before getting into bed, Annabelle looked at Joyanne and asked, "What's that letter? Is it for me?"

"No, it's not for you. It's nothing," Joyanne said.

"But you said there was something important you had to tell me," Annabelle replied.

Joyanne paused for a moment, thinking of something to say, and then uttered, "Ah, oh yeah. We are planning a forty-day prayer meeting. Hope you can stay."

Annabelle looked at her curiously and climbed into bed. Just then, a shower of rain pounded against the galvanized roof. Annabelle threw her head against the pillow and retired to a deep slumber.

Joyanne opened the letter Ricardo had dictated to her and perused it once again:

Roland P. Joseph

Dear Annabelle,

I couldn't go to the grave without telling you that
our child, Joyanne, died. Rosey thought that you
would stop sending money if you knew. I was
against what she did, but things were hard, and
we needed money for the doctor ...

Chapter 4

•••

1945

News that the war had ended in victory for Britain and the Allies prompted an eruption of festivities on the island. The streets of the major towns exploded into a carnival-like atmosphere—natives intoxicated with revelry danced and pranced to the rhythm of calypso music which emanated from rusted, untuned steel drums. It was six long years since the natives celebrated carnival, and VE Day set free the pent-up spirit of bacchanal. The small agricultural town of Rio Claro was no different. Villagers took to the streets, chanting the punchline from an old calypso about the First World War—"Run yu run, Kaiser Williams, run yu run ..."

But George Castello stayed away from the celebrations. He said that there was little to celebrate, for the years ahead would be difficult ones, as the war had drained Britain and its commonwealth of resources. He anticipated that food and basic supplies would continue to be scarce and that the ration-card system would continue for a long time to come. He chastised the government for allowing shopkeepers to flourish at the expense of the depressed people. They extended credit on overpriced goods and illegally tampered with their scales to cheat on weight. Thirteen and fourteen ounces were a pound.

George exerted his energy and time on expanding his backyard garden, for not only would he be able to feed his family, there would be surplus produce which would fetch a good price at the market. He sweated in the hot midday sun, scraping the hard, sun-scorched earth with his bare hands and sowing seeds—pigeon pea, tomato, and corn. He utilized every square inch of land that was not already planted in cocoa and coffee, the sources of his main income.

He agonized over the extensive repairs he needed to do on the house before the approaching rainy season. He paused to survey the rotted laths of lumber, broken windows, rickety staircase, and leaking galvanized sheets. He didn't have a clue as to where the money would come from, as there were three children to feed, clothe, and send to school—and a disagreeable, greedy wife to contend with. But he was a strong-willed man, very proud and optimistic.

George Castello was a short man, about five feet four inches tall and of medium build. His ragged tan shirt stretched across broad shoulders and muscular arms; the left upper arm bore a blue tattoo. He wore loose-fitting khaki trousers, supported by a thick black belt. His trousers were tucked inside black rubber boots, and a dark brown stingy-brim fedora rested loosely on his head. His fair Spanish complexion reddened in the hot sun, emphasizing his wrinkled, round face of forty-four years. He atop his old black bicycle was a familiar sight between Bristol Village and Rio Claro. The villagers had nicknamed him Mano—for his exemplary skills in playing the mandolin, especially at Christmas time, when he brought to life the rural tradition among the Cocoa Panyol natives of paranging from house to house.

His favourite pastime—going to the cinema—started off as an escape of sorts from his nagging wife, but over time, the cinema grew into a Saturday night ritual. It mattered not what the movie was or whether he had seen it before. By 7.15 p.m. sharp, George's bicycle could be seen propped against the weathered façade of the cinema in Rio Claro. On dark-moon nights, he carried a torch in his back pocket to navigate his way back home through the pitch-black night.

He paused for a drink of water which he fetched himself from a steel drum located beneath the eaves of the roof. After gulping down two cans of water, he proceeded to sit on the bare earth with his back propped against a rough wooden stilt. As he removed his hat, without which he was rarely seen, his short greying hair added years to his appearance. He reached into his pocket for a cigarette, which he lit, then pushed his feet forward so his back could slouch against the post. He closed his eyes, pulled deeply on the cigarette, and retreated into his own nicotine haven—a temporary respite from the drudgery of life.

The land was inherent in George Castello. His father and grandfather survived off the land. His father and grandfather migrated to Trinidad from the mainland of Venezuela in the mid-1800s to work on the cocoa estate. George was born at the turn of the century in a barrack room on the estate where he spent his nurturing years. At age seventeen, the impatient yearning of youth propelled him to leave the estate in search of a better life. He hopped on the train with only the clothes on his back and the spirit of adventure in his head, not knowing what lay ahead.

George was intoxicated with excitement as he disembarked from the train station in Port-of-Spain. He craned his neck to absorb the vibrant ambiance of the city and felt as though he were in a different world—the flurry of the streets, large buildings, crowds of people, motor cars and buses amid horse-drawn carts and carriages. A sign posted in the window of a merchant house caught his attention. He paused to read what it said: "Hands Wanted—Able-Bodied Men". It might be the only type of job he could get—the only stipulation was physical strength, and he possessed quite a lot of that. George hardly ever went to school. The most he could do was write his name and read basic words. He and his younger brothers would leave the estate for school but never got there. After numerous complaints from the teacher, their father decided that he was wasting his time and kept them on the estate to do odd jobs.

George rolled up his sleeves as he approached the door of the merchant house, ripping the sign off the window on his way in. He approached the counter and in a stern affected voice demanded, "I want to see the boss!"

A short Chinese man decked in a merino vest emerged from behind the counter. "Who you? Wha you wan?" he asked.

"I want to see the owner," George replied.

The Chinese man responded, "Yuh look-in at the owner. Wha yuh wan?"

George handed him the sign he'd torn down.

The Chinese man lifted the latch of the counter and walked around George, making a thorough inspection of him. He cuffed him on his arm to test his stamina.

George flinched and retorted, "Whey the ass is this! Jes so!"

"Wha yuh name?" the man asked.

"George Castello, sir," he replied bravely.

"All ligh, Geo, tak them bag a lice from dey and pu them in the sto-loom," the owner said, pointing to the back of the store. When he returned, the Chinese man told him that he was hired.

The job was strenuous with long hours, but it provided lodging which compensated for the slave wages. After all, George had nowhere to rest his head. The lodging comprised a tiny room at the back of the store, with a small, dingy bed and a flat pillow leaned against a rusted headboard. The bed occupied the entire space except for a narrow L-shaped passage around it. An old cupboard with flaking green paint was attached to the wall above the bed. A narrow corridor which led to a craggy wooden structure at the back of the premises housed a crude latrine and adjoining bathroom without doors. But as far as George was concerned, this was his new home.

The weeks flew by, and George continued to work diligently, earning a small salary increase and the trust of Sam Lee, alias Chin, the proprietor of the dry goods store. In addition to his salary and free lodging, Sam now provided George with food and generous gifts of clothing. It was not very often that Sam got a worker as trustworthy as George. He had fired three workers in the past year alone for stealing.

But Sam's kindness toward George was not simply a reward for George's honesty; Sam had an ulterior motive. For now, he made George feel comfortable and at home.

Sam Lee was about twelve years old when he arrived in Trinidad with his father in the late 1800s, following the death of his mother. They came via Hong Kong under the voluntary free immigrants' condition, following the end to Chinese indentureship in 1866. Upon their arrival to the island, they were placed under the responsibility of a Chinese merchant house where Sam's father worked for a few years before establishing his own business. When Sam had reached the age of twenty-one, his father sent for a young Chinese girl from China to marry Sam. The union yielded two children in two years—the first a girl and the other a boy. But Sam's wife was incapable of adjusting to the new language and culture which was imposed on her and eventually begged Sam to allow her to return to China. He eventually gave in to her plea, and she left Trinidad with the younger child while the older child stayed with Sam.

Sam was overly protective of her and shielded her from the natives as much as possible. She attended the Catholic girls' convent in Port-of-Spain and went to church socials and private parties under the watchful eyes of Sam.

Named for the month of her birth, April was a petite girl with flawless complexion and long jet-black hair which matched her oriental black eyes. Though she was a bit self-conscious of her Chinese heritage in a society of predominately Negroes and East Indians that mocked her race with juvenile taunts—"Chinee, Chinee never die, flat nose and chinkee eye!"—she was proud that her race was reputed for academic brilliance and acute business sense and would retort in a fiery tone, "Go get an education, you illiterate fools." Her detractors soon discovered that she was not to be trifled with. In spite of that, she seized every opportunity to socialize and mingle with the cultured echelons on the island.

The very first day she laid eyes on George, a strange tingling feeling engulfed her. She found herself drifting off into spasms of imagined romantic encounters with

George. She would lay awake at nights, concocting erotic thoughts about George and her. But when reality hit, she lay supine, staring at the ceiling with harrowing thoughts. Did he feel the same? After all, he treated her like a child with his silly questions: "You want me to bring ice cream for you?"; "You write your letter to Santa Claus yet?" And too, her daddy would never approve of George—he was the hired help with little schooling. She would press her face against the pillow and sob herself to sleep.

Sam, on the other hand, cared little for class and education—he favoured honesty and true love above everything. He wanted someone who would respect her, worship her, and not pursue her just for her wealth.

Though he did not make it known to anyone, not even April, Sam was concocting plans of his own. He wanted April to find an ideal husband, who, along with her, would take care of the business, and he in turn would travel to China to visit his wife and son. He believed that he had found that man in George.

It was a stormy August night. The rain pounded on the galvanized roof and against the windowpane, prompting George to pull the blanket over his head and drift off to sleep. Between sleep and wakefulness, he heard a faint knocking on the door. He turned to face the door and listened attentively for a few moments but heard nothing. He dismissed the knocking to some disturbance caused by the wind, but as he was about to shut his eyes, the knocking resumed.

George jumped off the bed and cautiously opened the door. His heart flipped at the sight of April decked in a gauzy nightgown which barely covered her firm breasts. She stood statuesque, leering at him through lustful eyes. George began to tremble; a part of him wanted to take her in his arms, and another was scared to death. *What if Sam found out? He would kill me for sure!* But before George could utter a word, April moved his arm from the doorway and eased her tender body beneath the blanket of George's bed. These rendezvous continued over the weeks that followed. Though Sam acted as though he didn't suspect a thing, somewhere in his mind, George harboured a notion that Sam knew about the sordid relationship between him and April. He felt like a traitor—after all, Sam was like a father to him. A deep-seated feeling of guilt and shame gnawed at him. The thought of running away did cross his mind. For now, he knew he had to end the affair with April, but he was hopelessly in love.

He began spending more and more time away from home. On evenings and off days, George went to the newly established cinemas to view silent picture sequences or live shows consisting of singers, dancers, and magicians or to the night clubs for beers and a friendly game of cards. It was difficult to make friends in the city, and Sam had often cautioned him to be particularly careful of the type of persons he befriended. "Friends does carry you, but they doh bring you back," his own father used tell him and his siblings. So, most times, he was alone.

Over the months, he made a few casual friends—the guys he met regularly at the clubs, the drivers and loaders on the goods trucks, and the coconut vendor who parked his Bedford just outside the club he frequented. On his way home, George often stopped for a drink of coconut water. He believed that coconut water purged his body of the excessive alcohol he consumed. George and the coconut vendor became casual friends; they conversed for hours on end on subjects ranging from politics to religion.

The coconut vendor, Sonny Samsundar, was a stout, dark man with bulging muscles. He had a big square face with large jowls and thin lips framed by a mass of black moustache. The shadows on his face, cast by the flambeaux on the hood of the truck, darkened his deep-set eyes and bushy eyebrows, giving him a somewhat creepy look, like the shadowy figures in the horror films. But, he was a rugged man, a man whose company George enjoyed when no one else lingered to talk. Besides, he was pleasant and carried on engaging conversations.

But his daughter's annoying grin repulsed George. Sonny told him that he named her Rosey because of her fat, rosy cheeks. She was a chubby girl, probably in her late teens or early twenties with square hips and a fat, round face with a three-tier chin and large, round eyes. A dingy white ribbon, which dangled loosely from the crown of her head to her shoulder, held her long, coarse hair in a ponytail. She wore a blue flowered dress with ripped pockets and missing buttons and sat on a small stool among the coconuts in the wooden tray of the truck. With her bare feet, she trotted around assisting her father to collect the monies from the sale of the coconuts. She had no recollection of her mother, and her father rarely spoke about her. Sonny was a doting father. He smothered her with love and everything she needed, except for satisfying her girlish needs—combing her hair with fancy ribbons, dressing her in frilly dresses, and keeping her tidy.

George loathed the silly grin on her face which greeted him when he approached the truck. He was even more enraged by Sonny's comments: "George, Rosey like you a lot. You doh see how she face does light up when you come by? She will make you a good wife."

George, seething with rage, would pelt the coconut shell into the tray of the truck and scamper away. A malicious grim would emerge on Sonny's face.

Sonny was married to a young mixed-race woman named Louisa, whom he had met in Port-of-Spain when he assisted his now-deceased uncle with selling coconuts in the city. Louisa worked at a nearby nightclub as a waitress, and when Sonny proposed to her, his uncle was dead set against the marriage. He warned Sonny that she was a prostitute and that she was taking advantage of his young, naive mind. Sonny flew into a fit of rage and accused his uncle of jealousy. A month later, they were married, and Louisa bore Sonny two girls—Catherine and Gertrude. Life in the small, sleepy village of Mayaro proved too sedate for Louisa, who was used to the fast-paced life of the big city, and she had grown tired of Sonny. She returned to Port-of-Spain with their two daughters, against Sonny's pleas to leave the children with him.

A year after she left home, Sonny became intimate with a woman he had met at a nightclub. He knew little about her except that her name was Indra and that she came from the eastern town of Sangre Grande. She was a petite woman of East Indian descent with long black hair and large, dark eyes. A few months later, she became pregnant with Rosey and lived with Sonny during the pregnancy, but after Rosey was born, she began staying away from home for long periods. When Sonny thought she was gone for good, she would appear without any explanation. While she was gone, Sonny arranged for his sister, who lived a half mile away, to take care of Rosey when he was out selling coconuts. When Rosey turned two, Indra left for good.

The skies over the city were suffused in a lurid red glow as the flurry of the city waned into a sedentary mass. George locked the door of the shop and returned to the storeroom to supervise the men who were stacking bags of sugar in one corner. A loud sigh emanated from one of the men as he rested the final bag of sugar on top the pile. He asked George for a towel and proceeded to wipe the sweat from his face and naked chest. George sat on stack of bags, waiting to close the storeroom when they were through. The man threw the towel for George to catch and politely asked for a glass of water. George went into the shop and returned with a large pitcher of cold water and an enamel cup. The man gulped down three cups, thanking George as he returned the pitcher and cup.

"It's Friday. Where you off to tonight?" the man asked.

"No plans yet," George said.

"Well, I will be at the club tonight. There's a big gambling game on if you feel like it. Maybe you could meet me there," he said.

"I'll think about it," George replied.

George had spotted the man at the club before, and their eyes might have met, but they never exchanged words. He was a tall, dark man with strong, well-defined muscles, broad chest, and a six-pack stomach. There were at least five visible scars on his chest and back, the largest one running diagonally from his left ribcage to his right collarbone. His long, thin face bore at least four scars—a curved one over his right eye which divided his eyebrow, one partially hidden across his bushy chin, another across his left cheek, and a deep, short one just above his slim, straight nose. A scanty growth of hair lined his thick lips, and stumpy sideburns flowed down to meet his boney jawline. He was, however, a strong, handsome man perhaps in his late twenties.

Bored out of his mind, George went to the club to meet the man, and over time, they developed a casual friendship. Through regular association, George gleaned a lot about him—that his name was Sticks and that he had a sinister past. But one night, George saw a side of Sticks he could not have imagined existed. Beneath the gruff and callous exterior was a sensitive, emotional man. It was a slow night at the club, and Sticks was unusually pensive. George didn't want to intrude, so he left Sticks at the table and went to the bar and ordered a beer. The waitress came up to him and playfully ran her fingers through George's hair. He bought her a beer, and they started talking.

"You come here often with your friend over there," she said, gesturing at Sticks with her eyes.

"Well, he's not really my friend. We gamble sometimes. That's all," George replied.

"So, you don't know …" she said with reluctance.

"Know what?" George asked curiously.

"Just that I find you two an odd pair. You look like a decent boy," she replied.

"Well, we gamble together, that's all. I don't know much about him," George said.

"Well, it's just that …" she began.

"What are you trying to tell me?" George asked.

"It not important, and you say he's not your friend," she replied.

She placed the empty bottle on the counter and was about to walk away when George folded a five-dollar bill and placed it in her cleavage.

She smiled and said, "Let's go in the back."

George glanced at Sticks and saw that he had rested his head on the table.

She invited George to sit on the bed while she changed her blouse.

"Why do you want to know about Sticks?" she asked.

"Well, I gamble with him, and at times we drink together, but I don't really know much about him," George replied.

"Lucky for you he's your friend," she said.

"What do you mean?" George asked with concern.

"Better a friend than an enemy," she said.

"Are you playing a game with me?" George retorted.

"For another five ..." she said.

"Sorry," George said and got up from the bed.

"I'm not trying to scam you. Just that I need money for my daughter," she replied.

"Okay, but tell me about Sticks, and I'll give you the money," George insisted.

"But promise you won't tell him what I told you," she said.

"Promise," George said.

"He has a reputation for being a 'bad john'. He's a hired hit man. Businessmen pay him to beat up guys who wrong them. I've heard even kill," she said.

"My God," George muttered. "So what's wrong with him tonight? I've never seen him like that."

George retrieved his wallet and gave her a ten. He lit a cigarette and listened to her discourse about Sticks. His given name, Nathaniel Ransome, was known only to a few people. Everyone else knew him as Sticks, a name he had earned from playing "stick fight" throughout the island—he was reputed to be the best stick fighter in all of Trinidad. He was a chronic gambler and sore loser. He was raised on the streets of Port-of-Spain, as his mother was a nightclub woman; he never knew his father. He met his common-law wife, Paulette, at a nightclub on George Street in Port-of-Spain, where she worked as a waitress and was hired out as a prostitute to wealthy men and sailors by the proprietor for large sums of money. But

Sticks put an end to all of that when he took her home, though at times she would say to him that she was better off in that life than she was with him. He was insanely jealous of her past relationships with the men she was paid to sleep with, and often beat her until her eyes were swollen. She was a nice-looking woman—milky white skin, round face with piercing grey eyes. Her mother was a waitress at the same nightclub, and word around town was that Paulette's father was a Norwegian sea captain.

She bore Sticks two beautiful children—a boy and a girl. It had been a year since Paulette disappeared with the children, and Sticks's search for them was futile. Paulette had left Sticks countless times before but always returned; the longest she had ever stayed away was five days. So on that fateful night when he went home drunk, hurling obscenities at her—calling her whore and prostitute—he did not know that it was the last time he would abuse her. When he got up the next morning, nursing a terrible hangover—vomiting his guts out and calling out for her to rub his head—he realized that she was gone. After a week, he grew frantic and searched every possible place for her but came up empty-handed. At times, especially when he was alone, he sat for long hours, thinking of her and his two children. He swore that he would be a better husband and father if they ever returned. On their beds in the tiny apartment were unopened presents which he'd bought, anticipating their return.

When the waitress was through, George was shocked and anxious. But she told him, "From what I know about him, he takes care of his friends. He must really like you."

"Yeah, he told me I was the brother he never had, and I guess I feel safe with him around," George said. "And if he could become so sad for Paulette and his children,

I guess he must have good in him." But deep inside, the news made him uneasy and scared. He wished he had never met Sticks.

She unbuttoned George's shirt and eased herself into the bed.

It was a bleak Saturday night following a day of incessant rain, and piles of debris were deposited on the streets of the city by floodwaters. The streets were like mirrors, reflecting the lights of the streetlamp, when the outline of two figures—one conspicuously shorter than the other and both decked in dark lumber jackets—hurried up Henry Street and turned onto a side street when they approached the corner. The figures were those of George and Sticks paying their routine Saturday night visit to the club.

Loud noises and laughter emanated from the club which was situated in the upstairs of a row of two-storey wooden buildings with façades of unpainted wood and large windows framed by wooden louvres. In bold lettering, Tropical Haven Nightclub straddled the width of the gallery. Both men leaped up the narrow stairway to a landing where two strapping men moved aside and allowed them entrance to the club. A quarrelsome atmosphere greeted them as they entered the room—men sat around tables, engrossed in deep concentration, plotting their next play of cards. Sultrily attired women stood over the tables, some with their hands placed loosely around the shoulders of the men while others served drinks. The walls of the dimly lit room were plastered with pictures of bare-breasted women. Behind the bar hung a huge, framed black-and-white picture of Greta Garbo.

George and Sticks pulled two chairs around a small table and sat opposite each other. Sticks shuffled a pack of cards, which inveigled two men who were leaning against the window to join in the game. One of them, a tall, strong man with short hair, reached into his wallet and placed two crisp twenty-dollar bills on the table. The other followed suit. George glanced at Sticks as if to silently solicit his opinion. Sticks reached into his wallet and matched the sum of money. George was left with no other choice; he too matched the sum. They proceeded to play with deep concentration.

Two hours passed by, and the stakes were in Sticks's favour. He sprang from the chair and declared, "Gentlemen, I think we better call it a night!" He stuffed the winnings into his coat pocket and gestured George to the door.

The tall, strapping man flew up in a rage with fire in his eyes. He shouted at Sticks and George, "The game isn't over yet!"

He hurried toward them and grabbed Sticks by the back of the collar. Sticks turned around and fired a cuff to the man's face. George darted down the stairs. The man retaliated; he fired a cuff to Sticks's face with all his might. Sticks ducked and responded with a furious left which connected with the man's stomach. Writhing in pain, he fired a kick at Sticks, who rolled down the steep stairs and landed on his back at the foot of the stairs.

George's eyes reddened with fright when he saw the man pull out a knife from his waistband, brandishing it about and proceeding toward Sticks. Sticks struggled to get up. All eyes were riveted on the commotion. Men and women abandoned what they were doing to secure a vantage point to view the fracas. George's heart pounded violently. The landings of the buildings were packed to capacity, and a crowd had gathered in the street. Sonny, the coconut vendor, abandoned his truck and joined the crowd. George, fearful that the man would murder Sticks, spontaneously jumped in and kicked the knife from the man's hand. Sticks caught the knife and pushed it into the man. The altercation was over in the wink of an eye. The man lay motionless in a pool of blood. A nauseous ripple raced through George's trembling body.

George and Sticks stood transfixed over the man's body. The ominous silence which followed was interrupted by the approaching sound of a police siren. Sticks ran off and disappeared in the darkness. George froze in shock. As the police siren grew louder and louder, the crowd scampered away. Sonny, seeing what was happening, ran toward George, grabbed him by the waist, and pulled him to the truck. He lifted him into the tray and threw a tarpaulin over him.

The doors of the police vehicle opened, and three policemen rushed out with guns in their hands. One hurried to the man who had been stabbed, feeling for a pulse.

"He's dead!" he shouted to the other officers who were proceeding toward the coconut vendor.

Chapter 5

· ·

The crowing of cocks trumpeting the breaking of dawn greeted Sonny as he approached the Manzanilla Road bound for Mayaro. The copious stretch of coconut palms was still a mass of dark silhouettes against the light of the full moon. The occasional headlights of passing vehicles were the only moving objects in the peaceful aurora of Sunday. The two-hour drive from Port-of-Spain and the drama of the previous night had left him drained of energy. He longed for his comfortable bed and a cup of strong Creole coffee but fought to keep awake behind the wheel of the old Bedford.

The embryonic light of the rising sun gained prominence over the blanched moon as Sonny Samsoondar drove his dilapidated truck into the driveway of bare earth etched with swaths of new and old type imprints. He alighted from the vehicle, walked to the tray of the truck, and pulled the tarpaulin aside.

"Wake up, boy. We reach home!" he called out to George.

George turned his sleepy eyes to face Sonny and gazed at him, disoriented. He rubbed his eyes with his both hands and let out a loud yawn. "Where we at?" he asked curiously.

"Get out the truck; there's a warm bed waiting for you inside," Sonny replied.

George eased himself languidly from the truck and lifted his hands high in the air, stretching his stiff body while he again yawned, this time with his entire face.

It was a squalid house supported by short wooden pillars, with a rusty galvanized roof. The doors and windows were of weathered wood screened with gauzy red curtains. Two fowl coops were propped against a dilapidated fence, incapable of keeping anything in or out. Over to the left, a makeshift spout from the guttering flowed into a steel barrel filled with murky water. Standing side by side at the rear of the property were a roofless bathroom and an old latrine with gaping holes. Yard fowls fluttered about the untidy backyard which overflowed into the sandy coconut palm shore of the tempestuous Mayaro beach.

George followed Sonny into the small gallery, lifting a crocus-bag hammock to gain access through the narrow front door. On entering the choked living room, he removed a stack of newspapers from a dingy chair located at one corner of the room.

"Sit here. I will be back just now," Sonny said with urgency as he hurried out the back door and into the latrine.

George retrieved a newspaper and pretended to read; he felt ill at ease in a strange place so far away from home. Besides, Sonny was just a mere acquaintance. Why did he go that length to protect him? He was curious.

Sonny returned and proceeded to pour water from a bucket into a dented kettle which he placed on a coal pot atop a rickety stand. He shouted to George, "Coffee will be ready in a short while. And, oh, the latrine is in the back, through that door if you want to use it."

"No, thanks!" George replied. His thoughts drifted to Port-of-Spain as he recounted the night's surreal events.

He lay on his back in the tray of Sonny's truck, shivering with intense fear as the deep, unsympathetic voice of the policeman interrogated Sonny.

"You were here; you must have seen the incident! Either you speak up right now, or we will take you down to the station and book you as a suspect. Do you or don't you know who the other man is? We were told that he was seen conversing with you on many occasions!"

Sonny began to stutter, "Officer, I is not really a friend of the boy. He often buy coconuts from me ..."

"What's his name?" the policeman demanded.

"I think they does call him George, sir. I don't know his last name, sir," Sonny replied in a frightened tone.

"Which direction did he go, or is he hiding in your truck?" the policeman asked.

Sonny's heart pounded violently against his chest as the policeman proceeded to lift the tarpaulin. Lucky for George, the policeman's attention was diverted to a turmoil which erupted in front of the club. He left Sonny and ran toward the club.

Another police car pulled up, its siren sounding menacing. The rotating blue light blazed through the darkness as four policemen scurried from the vehicle with their weapons in their hands. The policeman who had been interrogating Sonny shouted to the other officers, "We have captured one of the suspects; the other is somewhere around here. His name is George. We have a description of him."

A crowd gathered around the police vehicle and gawked at Sticks, who was seated in the back seat with his hands behind his back, and his face, which bore the nonchalant look of a seasoned criminal, stared straight ahead. All the policemen were engaged in conversation, probably planning a strategy to search for George. Oblivious to them, Sonny jumped in the truck and drove off into the darkness.

The voice of Sonny as he re-entered the living room with two smoking cups startled George from his thoughts. He handed a cup to George before sinking himself into a chair facing him. George barely sipped from the cup before resting it on the table.

"I not hungry. I can't eat anything," George said in a tone of self-pity.

"You must put something in your stomach, man. You have to maintain your strength!" Sonny replied. But George was not listening to Sonny; his mind had again drifted off to Port-of-Spain. But the loud slamming of a door snapped him out of his reflection. He looked around to see the disgusting sight of Rosey wrapped in a towel. Her broad face morphed into the annoying grin which aggravated him. She stared at him, giggling as she headed for the bedroom. A short while later, Rosey came out of the bedroom in a blue flowered dress, her hair bundled into a roll, secured by a blue ribbon. She filled the room with a cheap fragrance, flirting and blushing shamelessly as she retrieved the coffee cups from the table.

Sonny called out to her, "I want you to return your aunt's bowl right away!"

As Rosey disappeared through the front door, Sonny declared, "We need to talk!"

George listened attentively to what Sonny had to say; he knew that he had found himself in an awkward situation—between the devil and the deep blue sea. But he was certainly unprepared for the obnoxious proposal which Sonny made. It took him by surprise.

Marry Rosey? Did he hear right?

He flew from the chair in a rage, knocking it over as he rushed out of the house, hurling obscenities at Sonny. His eyes were dark with affront; he was intimidated and insulted. He stopped a taxi en route to Rio Claro, from where he would catch the train back to Port-of-Spain. Sam would find a solution, he consoled himself. Anything but this, he swore.

Dusk had already fallen over the city of Port-of-Spain when George alighted from the train. He tried to appear as inconspicuous as possible with his head buried in a straw hat and an oversized jacket flung over his shoulders. He walked along Marine Square with his head bent. A moment of excitement confronted him as he heard the sound of a siren approaching from behind. He felt like running as fast as he could. Spasms of anxiety raced through his body as the sound got closer and closer.

George started to pray, "Heavenly Father, please have mercy on me." Then he let out a long sigh of relief. He felt as though a weight was lifted from his shoulder as the police vehicle passed him by. *Thank you, Father! Father, thank you! Oh, thank you, Father!* he repeated in his mind as he hurried toward Sam's shop.

The door of the shop was bolted tight; the weathered Coca-Cola sign was conspicuous against the weathered board. He knocked, but there was no reply. He pounded harder, calling out to Sam in a subdued tone, "Sam! Sam! Please open the door; this is George."

There was no reply.

As he stood in front of the shop, looking over his shoulder, he could hear the faint sound of the police siren approaching. In desperation, he began pounding vigorously on the door and in a loud, anxious tone cried, "Please, Sam, open the door! They are coming to get me! Oh, please, Sam!" His voice faded into a frantic whisper.

The siren sounded as if it was mere seconds away as he stood propped against the door, praying in his mind. It was the first time in his life that he recalled ever being so frightened. With mere seconds to spare, the trapdoor to the shop was opened. George threw himself inside, landing on his chest. As Sam slammed the door, the police vehicle pulled up in front of the shop.

"Open this door immediately or else we'll break it down!" the policeman commanded.

Sam grabbed an old newspaper and, with a callous look on his face, pulled the door open. Without hesitation, four policemen bolted inside the shop.

"Where is he? Where is he?" an officer demanded as the others proceeded to search the premises.

"Where who?" replied Sam.

"Don't play smart with us!" the policeman retorted.

"Look, fellas, if yuh lookin for Geo, he no here. After the figh at the clab, he no come bac here, search all yuh like, yuh no fine nothing," Sam said nonchalantly.

The search came up futile; George was nowhere to be found.

Before leaving, they issued a stern warning to Sam. "It's not over yet; we'll continue to monitor you like a hawk. If we find the slightest evidence that you were protecting him, we'll slap an accomplice to murder charge on you! If you hear anything, we mean anything at all, no matter how insignificant it may appear, you'd better report it to us immediately!" one of the officers shouted.

Sam mumbled a few words in Chinese after they left. The place was a mess—overturned furniture, goods, and household items strewn all over the floor.

Sam headed for George's bedroom and pushed the bed aside. He lifted an old Chinese mat and pulled a lever. He grabbed George by the hand and pulled him from the underground cellar. "Geo, beside me, yuh is the only person who know bout this tlap door," Sam said.

Before Sam could say another word, George pleaded, "Please help me out of this mess; tell me what to do! I'll do anything you say."

Sam nodded. "The police lookin for yuh; there is a wallant for yuh arrest; this is the fifth time they come here; yuh taking a big risk being here. Do yuh wan go jail? If yuh guilly or not they go charge yuh for murder and throw yuh in jail till the case come up in cour; this could be years. Why yuh come back here?" Sam said.

George rehashed the events of the previous day to Sam, who listened attentively.

Sonny had told him, "I sure by now the police have a warrant for your arrest. Sticks was probably tortured into telling them about you. You safe for now, but be careful. I will do all in my power to make you safe. I have a proposal to make you; I want you to think about it. You don't have to reply now. In fact, you could think on it for a couple of days."

George cleared his throat before disclosing the grim news to Sam. He still felt the anger gripping him inside at the obnoxious proposal Sonny had made: "This is the deal; you can't go back to Port-of-Spain. In fact, you can't go nowhere where you could be recognized. I have a parcel of land in a small village not very far from here—Bristol Village. It ideal for agriculture, and it not so out of the way, but no one would find you there. It have a small house on the land which is liveable. One other thing—you have to marry Rosey. She go make you a good wife, and both of you could start a new life."

Sam saw the rage on George's reddened face rise at the thought of marrying Rosey. But Sam told him, "Is either that or yuh go to jail! I will arrange for yuh to go back to Ma-lie-yo tonigh."

George was daunted.

There was a noticeable absence of frills, fancy, and happy emotions usually associated with a wedding. The small crowd of no more than a dozen people was attired in ordinary, everyday clothing. The bride wore a shiny blue dress, which fell into a frill just below her knees. A broad white hat fringed with a wide blue ribbon and decorated with white flowers emphasized her broad, flat face. George wore a pair of brown trousers and a plain white shirt open at the neck. They stood apart on the altar like stark strangers as George mumbled his vows in a remorseful tone. His reluctance was easily detectable as he callously slipped the ring—which he had only now seen for the first time—on Rosey's finger without even looking at her. His face was bent down throughout the ceremony. His thoughts were rife with visions of April's appealing face. He did, however, manage to hold back the tears.

Chapter 6

∙∙

George awoke from a shallow slumber just in time to hear Rosey bellowing his name in her high-pitched voice, "George! George! Yuh best light the coal pot if you want to eat dinner this evening!"

He lifted himself from the hammock and stared up at the sun in the blue, cloudless sky to gauge the time of day. It was midafternoon, and George anticipated the arrival of the children from school anytime soon. There were chores to do—the water barrel needed refilling and the yard cleared of fallen leaves from the large immortelle trees which framed the property.

Besides cooking, Rosey did very few household chores and delegated most of the work to the children, while she lay in the hammock on the porch, either daydreaming or gossiping with a neighbour. George detested gossiping but avoided any confrontation with Rosey and left her to do as she pleased. As a child, he had often heard his mother say, "Silence is golden." His mother was a dedicated woman, George recollected, and he often regretted his decision to run away from home. He should have followed his father's advice and stayed in school. His father was a poor man who made many sacrifices to provide for his family. George often recalled his father's favourite quotation: Time is wasted on youth.

As far as Rosey was concerned, her father, Sonny, did George an enormous favour. He could have been rotting in jail all this time. He had to earn his keep, after all. The house and property—even the shirt on George's back—belonged to her, and she spared no opportunity in reminding him of this. George tried his best to avoid any fights with her and instead focused his time and energy on his children, whom he loved dearly.

Sonny had promised to transfer the deed of the property to George upon his marriage to Rosey. But George soon realized that Sonny was not eager to put the property in his name, perhaps fearful that he would abandon or mistreat Rosey. The legal document was in draft when news of Sonny's death reached George. He rushed over to the lawyer only to learn that Sonny had not signed the document.

It was a rainy Friday evening when Sonny had driven his truck to the city for the last time. He had just finished lighting the flambeau when a tight pain enveloped his chest. Sonny immediately dismissed it to a gas pain, as he had missed lunch on that fateful day. But as he lifted his hand to cut a coconut, he was crippled by an intense chest pain and collapsed on the sidewalk, never to regain consciousness.

A small funeral service was held at the church where George and Rosey had exchanged marital vows. George's absence from the funeral drew speculations from the small crowd which had come to pay final respect to the man they knew as Coconut Man. The only tears came from Rosey at the graveside, which subsided with the closing of the grave. Rosey seemed more concerned with the attention she received from friends and well-wishers than with grief. She was conspicuously attired in a black lace dress and broad white hat. The signal-red lipstick and rouge could be seen from a mile away.

Rosey masked a sombre look when she noticed the two elegantly dressed women, whom she had earlier spotted in the church, coming her way. She wondered who they were and deliberately turned her head in the other direction as they approached her.

The elder of the two greeted her. "We are so sorry, Rosey, but we should be consoled by the fact that our father was a good soul."

Rosey's heart skipped a beat at the words "our father was a good soul." It didn't take long for her to figure out who they were, but she continued with the pretence. With a feigned puzzled look on her face, she responded in a soft tearful voice, "Thanks, but I doh know how I'd survive his loss."

The woman continued in her refined accent, "Oh, Rosey, I can tell that you don't know us. I'm Catherine, and this is my younger sister, Gertrude. Sonny was our father too. Don't you remember?"

Rosey acted surprised. "Yes! I remember now. When I was little, you all came to Mayaro."

Both Catherine and Gertrude were exquisitely attired in dark suits. Catherine wore a black fascinator and a net covering half her face while Gertrude had a black mantilla draped over her head. They drew stares from the crowd.

One woman wondered aloud, "They are probably movie stars."

All eyes turned in their direction as they departed in a chauffeur-driven car, kissing Rosey on the cheek and promising to visit her soon.

Children playfully prancing along the main road disturbed the tranquillity of the hamlet, the sun casting elongated shadows behind them as they ran crisscross on the street. Upon reaching the muddy entrance to the Castellos' house, three of the children departed from the group and raced toward the wooden shed, which cantilevered from the side of the house. The girls were attired in navy-blue overalls and dingy white shirts, and the boy wore a light blue shirt, partially tucked inside a pair of short khaki pants, with dark socks rolled down his boney ankles.

As the eldest of the three headed for the shed, she shouted, "Pa! Pa!" and leaped into the waiting arms of George, who planted a big kiss on her forehead and lifted her high in the air. The other girl awaited her turn, while the boy ran over to the cattle shed to pet the young calf which he had named Katie. He avoided his father, who would have surely noticed his ripped shirt and bruised face. He was scolded many times before for fighting in school.

As George gently lowered Annabelle, he proceeded to lift Rosabelle for her kiss. Annabelle ran to the cattle shed to join Danny, with her long, wavy hair blowing in the wind as the ribbon, which held it in a ponytail, became undone. As she cleared strands of hair from her eyes and tucked them behind her ears, her pretty face with strong Spanish features from her father was revealed. Physically, she looked like a young teenager, but her demeanour was still that of a child. Unlike Annabelle, Rosabelle adopted her mother's broad features and dark complexion. Danny possessed no distinct features for either of his parents, but hints of George were evident on his boyish face.

The presence of the children brought about a visible transposition in George's face, from gloomy to cheerful, while Rosey sat in the hammock unperturbed. George showed more affection for the eldest child, perhaps subconsciously—not that he did not express overt love for the other two, but the birth of his first child was his deliverance from a miserable, almost suicidal life.

Annabelle, as he had named her, was born some nine or ten years after George's coerced marriage. George could not muster up the urge to sleep with his wife. He despised her even more when he realized that Sonny had not fulfiled his end of the bargain to transfer the deed of the property to him. The marriage was consummated a few years after they were married. George slept in a small room downstairs while Rosey slept in bedroom upstairs of the house, and he purposely came home late at night or in the wee hours of the morning. The first intimate encounter with Rosey occurred one night when he had come home intoxicated. He tried in vain to drown his frustrations with rum, but the more he drank, the gloomier he became. In this mood, he would fantasize about April and the life they could have had. Thoughts of suicide crossed his mind many times, but he knew he could not build up the courage to take his own life. When he reached home, he threw himself in the bed of the thatched room, pining away over April until he fell asleep. When he awoke the next morning he was appalled to find Rosey asleep next to him. He had no recollection of what had transpired the night before. Over the years, these intimacies were sporadic and occurred only when George was intoxicated. His spirit was lifted with the birth of Annabelle, and a year later came another girl, Rosabelle, followed by a boy two years later, whom he called Danny.

It was the end of the school term and the last day of school until the new term in early January. Annabelle did not know it as yet, but it was the end of her schooldays. She had finished primary school, and George could not afford to send her to college. Like most rural girls, she would learn the art of homemaking in preparation for married life and the craft of dressmaking, which she would acquire from the village seamstress who lived a few houses down the street. George yearned for a better life for Annabelle and had already made plans for her. It was only a matter of time before he revealed his plans to Annabelle.

George was a customer at a small pharmacy in Rio Claro where he bought his medical supplies. He developed a friendship with the owner, Rafeek Baksh, who extended credit to him in times of emergency or when his crop did not yield as well as expected. Mr Baksh was a tall man of medium build and greying hair. He, along with his wife and eldest son, came to Rio Claro from a small town in the late 1930s to open a pharmacy in the growing rural town. Their other two sons were born in Rio Claro.

His wife, Sally, a talkative woman, assisted Mr Baksh with the business, and like her husband, she had befriended George, whom they admired for his hard work and simple values. They engaged George in prolonged conversations whenever he visited the shop and gave Annabelle, who often accompanied George to Rio Claro, sweets from the store.

Mr Baksh often said to George that Annabelle would someday make a good daughter-in-law for him and his wife. Her good looks would produce good-looking grandchildren, he jested to George. His eldest son, Zaid Baksh, was in his mid-twenties; he was thin, tall, and looked exactly like his father, except for his fair complexion, which he inherited from his mother. He studied accountancy in the urban town of San Fernando, where he stayed with his aunt and uncle, returning home by train on weekends. He was an extremely shy youth who was still embarrassed to speak with girls. Whenever he was at home when George visited the shop with Annabelle, his father summoned him to chat with her, but both of them just stared at each other and giggled.

One afternoon, George went to the pharmacy to acquire some aspirin for Annabelle, who had developed a cold and mild fever the night before. While being attended to by Sally, Mr Baksh came up to him and, in a serious tone, said that he wanted to speak with him in his office.

George became concerned, as Mr Baksh had never spoken to him in such a serious manner before. He at once assumed that it concerning his long-overdue bill. He knocked on the door of the small office with boxes scattered about.

"Come in," Mr Baksh replied. "Have a seat, please."

George looked at him with a look of concern on his face, and before Mr Baksh could utter a word, George said, "I know this is concerning my long-outstanding bill ..."

Mr Baksh smiled and said, "This has nothing to do with your bill. You have all the time you need to settle that."

George's curiosity was aroused.

"This is about my son, Zaid. He recently graduated from school and did well and will be proceeding to England for approximately one year to complete his studies. I have made him a full partner in the business, which I plan on expanding. Anyhow, let me cut a long story short."

George was now filled with anxiety.

Mr Baksh continued, "I would be very honoured if Annabelle would be my daughter-in-law when Zaid returns from England."

George was taken by surprise. A twinge of excitement trickled through him and rendered him speechless.

Mr Baksh continued, "I had nothing to do with this; it is strictly Zaid's idea. He truly loves Annabelle, you know."

Mr Baksh leaned back in his chair, awaiting a response from George.

But George was too overwhelmed with happiness to speak right away. He cleared his throat and, with an anxious slur in his voice, said, "I feel very happy that you think so highly of me and my family. I'll talk it over with Annabelle and give you a reply very soon. But as far as I am concerned, the answer is yes."

George was too elated to pursue any other business in Rio Claro. Rosey wanted some thread and a zipper to take to the seamstress, but that would have to wait. He jumped on his bicycle and headed for home.

His heart soared.

Chapter 7

· ·

A mild drizzle amid the breaking dawn provided a dulcet ambiance conducive to prolonged sleep. But Annabelle was too filled with anxiety to fall back to sleep. For the past hour or so, she lay on her back, listening to the gentle trickling of the rain on the roof and George's axe chopping firewood. It was Saturday morning, and unbeknownst to anyone, Annabelle had acquired a new habit of awaking at this hour to listen for another sound, but she was cautious not to be noticed, especially by Rosabelle, who slept next to her on the bed.

Her heart leaped at the sound she had long waited to hear. She cautiously crept out of bed and proceeded to open the window, trying hard to keep the creaking sound as low as possible. She frequently looked over her shoulder at Rosabelle and for Rosey, who would enter the bedroom to wake the girls on her way to the kitchen. She also had to be cautious that George didn't see her from the work shed.

A light, feathery feeling filled her stomach as the screeching sound became louder and louder. She cautiously pulled the curtain aside to view the narrow track leading to the work shed. The loud screech of the bicycle's brake signalled its arrival. She took a final glance over her shoulder and stood statuesque behind the curtain with her eyes glued at the muddy track.

Overpowered by emotion, she sucked her watery lips with her tongue. An electrifying discharge flowed through her body, and goose bumps emerged on her arms and legs as she stood swooning at Ricardo Simon pushing his bicycle along the track. Her friends at school often spoke of something called love, but in a taboo sort of way. Was this love? She had never felt like this before. Satisfied that she had seen Ricardo, she cautiously pulled the window shut and eased herself back into bed.

Annabelle pretended to wake from a deep sleep, yawning loudly and wiping sleep from her eyes, when Rosey entered the room soon after with her morning mantra: "Girls, time to rise and shine. I could use some help in the kitchen."

Rosey noticed the faraway look in Annabelle's eyes. She had to repeat instructions several times before Annabelle responded.

"Something the matter?" Rosey asked.

There was no reply. There was a visible distant look in Annabelle's eyes.

Maybe it was women's intuition or mere experience, but Rosey was almost certain that the look on Annabelle's face had to do with a boy. Zaid Baksh, she concluded, as George overflowed with excitement when he disclosed the news to the family the day before.

He had a big smile on his red face as he hurried up the track. The bicycle fell to the ground when he attempted to lean it against the post, but he did not bother to pick it up. He continued up the stairs with added haste.

"Annabelle! Annabelle," he called, excited.

Everyone ran out to hear his eager news.

"I have great news. Mr Baksh asked for Annabelle's hand for his son, Zaid!" he exclaimed, pausing to catch his breath.

Rosabelle walked away with a look of envy in her eyes.

Rosey mumbled half-heartedly, "That's good."

Annabelle's reaction was obscure.

Rosey noticed the blush on Annabelle's face when she asked her to take some bread and coffee over to Mr Simon but again assumed that she was preoccupied with thoughts of Zaid Baksh. On her way to the work shed, she passed George. He was heading for the kitchen. He paused to pat her on the head, causing her to flinch. He ascribed her reaction to being embarrassed by her pa treating her like a little child in front of company.

Annabelle was nervous at the thought of being alone with Ricardo. She paused to fix her hair as she approached the shed. A twinge of anxiety caused her to twitch as she approached Ricardo, whose head was bent down as he playfully moved an object around in a circular motion with his feet. A loud sound startled him. He looked up to see Annabelle standing over a mess of spilled bread and coffee. Her face drooped with embarrassment as he held her hand to help her up.

"It's all right, little one. It was an accident. Besides, I had a bite to eat at home," Ricardo said.

Before he could say another word, she darted off and scurried up the rickety stairs and into her bed. She was weeping profusely when George entered the room.

"It's all right. Accidents happen," George said in a comforting tone.

But Annabelle did not hear a word he said. She was infuriated at Ricardo for treating her like a child. She tried her best to attract his attention. She combed her hair in mature styles; pulled her dress above her knees when he passed by; blushed shamelessly and protruded her chest so he could notice her developing breasts. But all he could say to her was "little one"! She was devastated.

Annabelle's affection for Ricardo was conceived a few months before. His mother, Besey Simon—known to the villagers as Miss Simon—was the village seamstress who was teaching Annabelle to sew, but Annabelle was more interested in flirting with Ricardo than she was in sewing.

Besey Simon watched over Annabelle and her siblings when Rosey and George were away, and as a favour to Miss Simon, Ricardo was recruited by George on a seasonal basis to assist with the reaping of the crops and odd jobs around the house, for which he was paid small wages.

Miss Simon was the first neighbour of George and Rosey when they moved to Bristol Village. She had moved to the village with two small children, Ricardo and Elsie, a year or two before. Elsie had since migrated to England with Miss Simon's sister. Except for her children, Miss Simon never spoke of anything or anyone from her past. She was an extremely compassionate woman and had earned the love and respect of everyone in the village. She made a living by sewing and doing domestic chores for a few families in Rio Claro.

Ricardo Simon was perhaps ten or even twelve years older than Annabelle. He was a man of simple means—a loner who was rarely seen in the company of anyone. He was of medium height and build with muscular arms and legs. Soft red hair sprouted along his elongated light brown face, and a mass of tight curls streaked with gold carelessly dangled above his unique light brown eyes. His spare time was spent tending to his kitchen and provision garden, which earned him extra money at market. He also reared chickens, which provided the festive stew and breakfast eggs.

Ricardo's prized possession was a bicycle that had been given to him by the former pastor of the Bristol Village church, for his assistance in maintaining the church building. He hardly ever went to church except on special occasions like Christmas and Easter, but he was considered a valuable part of the congregation. His mother served as an elder and rarely missed a Sunday morning service.

The Christmas morning service was a few weeks away, and Annabelle was bursting with excitement. She badly wanted the dress and matching hat that was on display in the store show window in Rio Claro, but George had no money to spare. The incessant rain over the past week had delayed the drying of the cocoa, and George was counting on the sale of this crop for the Christmas goodies. Annabelle was adamant that it was time Ricardo saw the woman in her, for she knew that he went to church every Christmas morning. She must contrive a way to get that new outfit. The thought assailed her mind.

For the next few days, she thought of various schemes that would get her the dress, but they were all hopelessly farfetched. But something was bound to happen that would work in her favour. She would get the dress, she concluded.

It was a lazy Saturday afternoon when Rosey moved around the kitchen, gathering the ingredients to bake a cake for the Sunday school Christmas treat, which was to be held later that afternoon. She proceeded to place the butter and sugar in the mixing bowl for Annabelle to stir, but to her dismay, the cupboard was out of baking powder. George had already left for Rio Claro, so Rosey sent for Ricardo to run the errand for her, but he too was not at home. In desperation, Rosey decided to send Annabelle to Rio Claro to fetch baking powder, but not before issuing a stern warning to her.

"You are to go to the shop to fetch the item! Do not wander about! Get right back home, or else I'll cut your ass," Rosey said sternly.

Annabelle felt a sense of freedom and adventure as she alighted from the car in Rio Claro. It was the first time she was so far away from home all by herself. Although she had been to Rio Claro on many occasions with her father, being alone made the town appear new and exciting.

The rural southeastern town, which served as the administrative and business centre for the pockets of hamlets along its periphery, including Bristol Village, sprang up around the train station that had rolled into the agricultural town in 1914, following much protest from the cocoa farmers there, regarding restricted means of transportation for their produce. The colonial government eventually responded and extended a leg of the train line into Rio Claro. The population, which was concentrated farther west, shifted toward the train station. The main business houses—mainly a Chinese shop, two clothing stores, and a few rum shops—were located in the vicinity of the small roundabout, which stood at the junction of two main roads from which tentacles of secondary roads and tracks emanated. Over to the south of the roundabout, a section of squalid, dilapidated sheds served as the town's marketplace. Itinerant vendors along the pavements coloured the landscape with clothing, household wares, and foodstuff.

Annabelle crossed the street to ensure that her dream outfit—a light green dress trimmed with white lace edging and matching wide-brimmed hat with white roses—was still in the show window. She was relieved when she saw that the ensemble was still on the mannequin and stood daydreaming of herself in the outfit with Ricardo drooling over her.

For a while, she had forgotten her mother's strict warnings. Rosey expected her home within the hour, but she felt as free as a newly escaped bird. She had already exhausted half an hour of her allotted time when she eventually reached the Chinese shop—a flat wooden building level with the road with two large doors that straddled the entire façade. In one corner, bees fluttered around a stack of sugar bags, and straight ahead, a countertop with an old scale and a block of cheese wrapped in cheesecloth separated the customers from the shopkeeper and shelves of goods. An enclosed space to the left served as a makeshift rum shop with tables and chairs.

Annabelle handed the note with George Castello's name to the short Chinese man, Henry, as he was called by the villagers. His wife, a tall, strapping, dark-skinned woman, did not hesitate to manhandle him in public, much to the amusement of the customers. He was forced into marriage by her brothers when she became pregnant. Nine months later when the child was born, no hint of Chinese features was evident in the dark-skinned baby boy.

"Are you charging this to George's account?" Henry asked.

"Yes," replied Annabelle.

"I cyar extend no more cledit. George no pay for two mon," Henry said.

"But my father pay you last week," Annabelle insisted.

"Wait wan min-nate. Wha count you talk bout?" Henry asked.

"How many accounts my father have?" Annabelle enquired.

"Nev mine," Henry replied and turned around to fetch some wrapping paper. Annabelle made sure that his back was turned and proceeded to peruse the credit book which lay open on the counter. She was most surprised and shocked at the discovery. George Castello maintained two credit accounts for two separate households. Annabelle took a mental note of the address of the other account.

It was the first time that Annabelle had gone to purchase groceries on her own; she had accompanied George only on a few occasions, so Henry did not recognize her. In fact, Henry mistook her for one of the other girls who came regularly to purchase goods on George's other account.

The sedate ambiance of the afternoon appeared somewhat ominous through Annabelle's curious mind. The address listed as three-quarter-mile mark, Guayaguayare Road, Rio Claro, occupied her thoughts; she felt compelled to investigate this, so she cast aside Rosey's warning and proceeded to the address.

The stinging afternoon sun cast a dark shadow to her left as Annabelle strolled along Guayaguayare Road. She had walked for more than fifteen minutes when she began to harbour second thoughts. She felt afraid and guilty for invading her pa's privacy, and Rosey would murder her for sure when she got home. But she had already walked all this way and curiosity got the better of her, so she continued on her mission half-heartedly.

She froze in shock when she spotted George's bicycle leaning against a mango tree at the side of a small wooden house. She almost passed the house, but the playful sound of children caused her to look. She stared at the bicycle in disbelief; it was unmistakably George's bicycle—the flaking paint, the rusted bell, and the ripped seat.

She turned around, forcing her tired feet into agility. She must get out of there as fast as she could, before George spotted her. The vision of two children playing hide-and-seek in the yard haunted her. Could they be her brother and sister? Rosey would kill him if she found out.

She hurried out of the neighbourhood. The sound of an approaching bike caused her heart to flutter from her chest to her throat. The sound grew louder and louder. She kept her eyes focused straight ahead and continued to walk.

Chapter 8

∙∙

Annabelle placed the final button on her yellow satin dress as Miss Simon looked over her shoulder, monitoring her skill.

"That's very good, Annabelle. No one will know that's an old dress. It looks brand new," Miss Simon declared with a sense of pride.

It was the final sewing class until the end of the Christmas season. Although Annabelle felt pleased at the remarkable transformation of the old dress, traces of disappointment were visible on her face. Ricardo was not around; she felt like asking Miss Simon for him, but the question might provoke curiosity. She could not take the chance.

The small group of girls sat in the gallery of Miss Simon's house, sipping soft drinks from enamel cups in celebration of the end of the term and the upcoming Christmas season. Annabelle sat on the stairs, staring at the lonely road and praying for Ricardo to return home. Sally, one of the students and Annabelle's friend, eased herself next to her, startling her out of her contemplation.

"Will you be wearing that dress to the party tonight?" Sally asked.

"It's the only pretty dress I own. Of course I'll be wearing it," Annabelle replied. "What will you be wearing?"

"Oh, I'm not sure I'll be attending," Sally replied.

"Not attending? Why not?" Annabelle exclaimed.

Sally hesitated before saying, "My mother and father fight again last night, and Daddy say I can't attend. He just want to spite my mother."

"Spite your mother? But it's you he spiting," Annabelle replied.

"Well, he think he's hurting my mother," Sally said.

"Maybe if my pa ask him, he might change his mind. He has a great deal of respect for Pa," Annabelle declared.

"I don't know," Sally replied.

"What's the matter?" Annabelle enquired. "Don't you want to come to the dance?"

"I have nothing to wear," Sally replied.

"We can fix up one of my old dresses. You're older than me, but we're about the same size," Annabelle suggested. "What are best friends for?"

Sally continued with enthusiasm in her tone, "But I don't have a boyfriend to bring. I'd feel stupid."

"You don't need a boyfriend, silly girl. There'll be lots of boys at the dance, and say what, you are a very pretty girl and very mature. You could have any boy you want," Annabelle said.

Sally grinned and replied, "You bringing anyone to the dance?"

The excitement on Annabelle's face faded. She paused for a moment and then replied, "My father invited Zaid Baksh to escort me to the dance."

"You don't sound very excited. Don't you like him? He's smart and rich. I wish I was in your shoes," Sally declared.

"Well, you can have him if you like," Annabelle replied.

"You're being silly now," Sally said.

"Oh, am I? Well, let me tell you the God truth 'bout that," Annabelle insisted. "I don't like him; I have to go out with him to please my pa. He has dreams of me marrying that rich boy someday soon."

"But he'll give you everything you'll ever need. You'd never be poor again, and your children would never go hungry," Sally replied.

"Enough of this nonsense; we have work to do. You coming to the dance if you have to sneak out the window. Let's go get you something to wear. You'd look pretty in my blue dress; we'll add some frills to it," Annabelle insisted.

They were about to lift themselves from the stairs when Annabelle fell back blushing shamelessly.

"What's wrong, Annabelle?" Sally asked.

There was no reply. Sally's eyes followed Annabelle's stare and saw that she was looking at Ricardo and drooling. Sally was confused.

"Hello, girls," Ricardo said.

"Hello, Ricardo," Sally replied.

"Oh, Sally, you look nice. How's your sewing coming along?" Ricardo asked.

"Okay, I guess," Sally replied. "You coming to the dance tonight?"

"Oh, I'm not sure as yet; I have an errand to run. If I have time I will be there," Ricardo said.

Annabelle sat stewing with anger as Ricardo ignored her, and she detested Sally for being forward with him.

He turned to Annabelle. "Oh, hello. I have something for you," Ricardo said.

Annabelle's face lit up.

Ricardo pushed his hand in his pocket while she sat brimming with anxiety.

He pulled his hand from his pocket and handed her some sweets. "These are for you," Ricardo said.

She was too angry and disappointed to respond. She pelted the sweets on the ground and ran off.

Sally and Ricardo looked on with shock as she ran up the street.

George sat in the shed behind the house, staring up at the cloudy sky. He said a silent prayer for a few days of sun to dry his cocoa, which was piled in the sweat baskets in the corner of the shed. The buying agent—Henry, the Chinese shopkeeper in Rio Claro—had given George a few days to have the produce delivered to him. He had already collected a sufficient supply from other farmers to dispatch to the export house in Port-of-Spain.

Christmas was just weeks away, and George desperately needed money to buy lumber and paint to spruce up the house, gifts for the children, and rum for his friends. Rosey needed money for the ham and cake, curtains, and new tablecloth. George wanted to surprise Annabelle with the dress she saw in the store window and had already asked the storekeeper to hold the outfit for him. Annabelle had earned it, he thought; she kept his secret safe, and besides, she needed to look pretty for Zaid Baksh.

His mind drifted back to the fateful evening when he encountered Annabelle snooping.

He could detect feelings of embarrassment and anxiety in Annabelle when he approached her on his bicycle. He pulled up alongside her with a stern look in his eyes, though deep inside, he was mortified.

"What are you doing here?" George asked.

Annabelle did not reply.

"It's not what you think; I can explain," George said.

Her face became flushed with embarrassment.

He placed her on the bicycle and pedalled to Rio Claro. Not a single word was uttered between them. When they reached to Rio Claro, he put her in a car headed for Bristol Village, and he rode the bicycle home.

For the next few days, both George and Annabelle avoided each other until she broke the silence by assuring him that his secret was safe with her. But he knew all along that his Belle would never betray him.

The rain subsided. The sky was suffused in hues of pink and purple as bats and night creatures emerged. The street was lively with silhouettes of men and women leading goats and cattle home. Fowls were ascending trees and coops, and the lights from lamps and candles flickered through crevices and open windows.

It was against this ambiance that Bristol Village prepared for its annual Christmas dance. The hearts of the young and the young at heart were filled with eagerness, for it was the biggest and most anticipated social event in the village. For the women, it was an occasion to wear their best clothes and catch up on the village gossip and also an opportunity to show off their cooking skills, each one trying to outdo the other. On this one night, the men had the blessings of their wives to consume all the alcohol they could and make a spectacle of themselves. The younger folks looked forward to dancing the night away with their love interests.

George sat in the work shed, illuminated by a single flickering candle, practicing a tune on his mandolin for the dance, while he said a silent prayer for the sun to last for a few more days.

Annabelle sat in front of the mirror in the bedroom, combing her hair. Rosabelle lay on the bed, staring at her with envy, childishly wishing that Annabelle's hair would drop off her head. She was insanely jealous of Annabelle's beauty and the attention George showered on her. She wished that she was going to the dance too, but George said that she was too young.

It was Annabelle's first time to the dance. She had come of age, George insisted to Rosey, and besides, she was almost engaged to Zaid Baksh. Both George and Mr Baksh felt that Zaid and Annabelle should get to know each other before plans of the wedding were announced. But Annabelle had her own plan. She was insistent that Ricardo saw the woman in her, and tonight provided the perfect opportunity.

The shed of the wooden church was gaily decorated with festoons of brightly coloured streamers, which fluttered in the cool breeze. The flickering lights of lanterns wrapped in coloured paper lined the muddy track and conspired with the light of the full moon to incite a romantic ambiance.

A cacophony of croaking frogs and night creatures echoed through the silent night amid the emerging strains of the three-piece band—an elderly man seated behind the church organ; a teenage boy with a guitar strapped over his shoulder; and a man sucking on a mouth organ—calibrating and recalibrating the harmony. Although the tune they were playing was unfamiliar and discordant, it penetrated the hamlet with a magical ecstasy.

Soft sprinkles of rain prompted Annabelle to turn around to fetch her umbrella. She would have otherwise enjoyed a walk in the rain, but tonight was special; she did not want to risk ruining her dress and precocious make-up. The sweet sound of George's mandolin rang through as she hurried back home for the umbrella. Rosey was already in bed; she never attended the village socials, as she thought herself to be unsociable.

As Annabelle hurried up the street with the open umbrella, she observed the dark outline of Ricardo scurrying ahead of her, smartly attired in a pair of dark trousers and light long-sleeved shirt. She trotted behind, maintaining a safe distance so as not to be seen. To her surprise, he passed the church and continued up the street with haste. She was extremely curious. After all, he did say he had an errand to run and wasn't sure if he could attend the dance.

She arrived at the church with thoughts of Ricardo weighing heavily on her mind. Her cold responses to her friends' warm greetings did not go unnoticed. She sat on a chair with a faraway look on her face, as the band played "O Christmas Tree, O Christmas Tree".

What could Ricardo be up to? Could it be a girl? she thought painfully. The sound of a friend calling out her name snapped her out of her pensive mood.

"Annabelle! Annabelle! Could you assist us with the tablecloths?"

She jumped off the chair, trying to conceal the worried look on her face.

She was too preoccupied with thoughts of Ricardo to notice the arrival of Zaid Baksh as he alighted from his father's car. He was dressed in a navy-blue suit and white shirt, and in his right hand he carried a bottle of rum while his left hand delicately clutched a corsage of white roses. He handed the rum to the barman and approached Annabelle from behind. He startled her when he touched her on the shoulder to present her with the corsage. Without notice, he kissed her on the cheek.

She flinched and rebuked him. "Not in front of people," she retorted.

"Well, can we dance then?" he asked.

She twisted her face into a frown. "I can't right now; I have to assist with the food. One of the other girls would love to dance with you," she said and turned her back and walked away.

Zaid was perplexed and disappointed. He pulled out a chair and sat down.

Annabelle frantically glanced through the crowd for Sally, but she was nowhere in sight. She beckoned another girl and sent her over to Zaid. He was peeved; he was a clumsy dancer, and Annabelle had promised that she'd teach him to dance at the party. He dismissed the girl and went outside, seething with anger.

George arrived strumming a lively Castilian rhythm on his mandolin, rousing the men and women and girls and boys to pair off and rush over to the dance floor. While the couples were dancing the parang, some of the women held on to their dresses and emulated Spanish flamenco dancers, moving and twirling across the floor. From the corner of his eyes, George noticed Annabelle sitting all by herself with a gloomy look on her face. He glanced around the shed for Zaid, but he was nowhere to be found.

Oh, poor thing. She's probably disappointed that Zaid didn't come, he foolishly thought.

Zaid had earlier departed in disgust.

Annabelle was oblivious to the cheerful mood around her. She felt defeated by her own game. She had ensured that she was the best-dressed girl at the dance, and she was, but it was all in vain. Ricardo wasn't there to notice her.

The yellow satin dress trimmed with bunches of white roses enhanced her Spanish complexion. The bright red lipstick and rouge, which she stole from Rosey, added years to her appearance, and so too did the dark eyeliner and the mole on her cheek. The dress stretched tightly across her small breasts, which she intently thrust forward. Her hair, which was bundled in a roll above her head with curls cascading down the side, framed her pretty face. She looked like the carnival queens on the front page of the newspaper whom she emulated with Rosey's clothing and make-up.

As she sat impulsively tapping her feet to the rhythm, she noticed the dark outline of two figures—a man and a woman—making their way down the deserted street, holding hands. Annabelle twitched when she recognized that it was Ricardo, but she wondered who the woman was. Annabelle sat statuesque in the chair as they approached; she almost lost her balance when she noticed that the girl was Sally. Rage emerged in her tearful eyes.

"That ungrateful bitch! That back-stabber! After all I did for her!" she said to herself. Her hands formed into a fist, and she gnashed her teeth with hate as they approached the shed. Annabelle looked away pretending not to notice them.

Sally walked up to her. "Hello, Belle. I finally got permission to come to the party, thanks to you."

Sally, anticipating an enthusiastic response from her, had a broad smile on her face, but Annabelle's curt reaction took her by surprise.

"Oh, is something the matter? Where's Zaid?" Sally asked.

Annabelle made a tremendous effort to contain her anger, and then suddenly, a malicious thought struck her. *It's my game. Sally can't beat me; she's even wearing my dress! Ricardo is going to be mine tonight! Sally doesn't have what it takes!*

With verve and élan in her stride and a determination to win, Annabelle sprang from the chair, preening her hair and dress. George was playing his final tune when she proceeded to the centre of the dance floor and started dancing. She lifted her dress up to her knees and moved her nimble feet in perfect time to the Castilian rhythm. The crowd receded, forming a circle around her and clapping their hands to spur her on. She twirled and twisted, moving around the small dance floor with a conceited smile on her face. George fuelled her spirit by playing the mandolin more sweetly, gradually increasing the rhythm. She glanced at Ricardo, who drifted in and out of sight as she moved faster and faster around the dance floor, kicking off her shoes. She was gratified to see the lust in Ricardo's light eyes as he caressed her from head to toe. She knew she had won. Ricardo would have no other choice but to see her as a woman. Whether or not it was woman's intuition, female instinct, or if she had heard it said before, in her precocious mind, she knew she must not give herself away. She must let him drool over her.

She glanced at Ricardo one final time. He continued to stare at her with lust in his eyes. She winked at him in a suggestive manner. She felt like a queen as she took George's arm and strolled home under the stars.

Chapter 9

· ·

George sat under the house, staring at Annabelle perched on the tray of the cocoa house, merrily dancing the cocoa, spreading out the beans to dry in the sun. He stared up at the cloudless sky and offered a word of prayer.

"Our Father which art in heaven," he began, pausing at the end of each line to search deep into his memory for the next line. "He leadeth me besides still waters." He questioned himself, "Is that the correct line?" He continued, "Anyway ... the Lord know I am thankful for the sun."

He turned to look at Annabelle. His thin lips twisted into an introspective smile.

Oh, how she's grown—no longer a child, he thought. *I'm so glad she'll be married to someone capable of providing a better life for her.*

Then he felt sad at the thought of losing her.

Lord, please bless her and all my children, he continued to pray silently.

Annabelle's eyes lit up with excitement as she glanced at the figure of Ricardo walking up the street. George noticed the blush on her face, but from where he sat, he could not see Ricardo. She turned her back as Ricardo approached the track leading to the house, and she lifted her dress above her knees, dancing with more vigour.

George noticed the conspicuous blush on her face as Ricardo approached, but he shrugged off his suspicion. He consoled himself with the notion that he was making a mountain out of a molehill. In any event, he had already planned on telling Mr Baksh that Annabelle and his son ought to be engaged or even married before Zaid left for England.

George had earlier sent for Ricardo to assist with the cleaning up of the sweat baskets and the waste from the cocoa. Ricardo's mind was filled with thoughts of Annabelle from the night before but he dared not look at her or give any hint that he had developed feelings for her. He had great respect for George, whom he considered a father.

But Annabelle had already decided that she wanted Ricardo. In her own naive way, she had hinted to him that she was in love with him and waited on him to make the next move. She was new to the game of love but certainly not a novice at drawing attention to herself. As a child, she recalled running away from home and sleeping under a tree for the entire night. Rosey had taken her doll from her to give to Rosabelle who insisted she must have Annabelle's doll, as it was prettier than hers. When she was found the next day by George and a party of villagers, she used her girlish charms to elicit sympathy from the group. For weeks on end, villagers gossiped about Rosey's wickedness toward Annabelle.

Sally came over to return Annabelle's dress, which she had worn to the dance. Annabelle fixed a deceitful smile on her face.

"Hello, Sally, so glad to see you. Let's go downstairs where we'll be alone," Annabelle suggested and led Sally down the stairs.

"Thank you again; I had a great time at the dance," Sally gushed.

"And you were concerned about not pairing off with a boy," Annabelle teased.

Sally blushed. "Oh, stop that. We weren't really a couple. He probably felt sorry for me," Sally replied.

Annabelle carefully hashed out her response, and with a snide look on her face, she said, "I believe Ricardo likes you; I saw it in his eyes. The question is, do you love him?"

Sally blushed and asked, "Do you really think he likes me?"

"There's one way to find out," Annabelle replied.

Sally grew uncomfortable with Annabelle's intimate comments.

"I have to go now; Ma's expecting me," Sally said and ran off.

Annabelle smiled maliciously.

She had planned on using Sally in a game she had concocted. She would lead Sally to believe that Ricardo loved her and would tell Ricardo that Sally was the girl for him. In her twisted mind, she wanted to torment Ricardo into confessing his love for her.

Annabelle had subtly harboured ill feelings for Sally, who many said was prettier than she. When Annabelle was twelve, she fell head over heels for a boy in Sunday school. He, however, ignored her advances and pushed her to the ground, telling her that he liked Sally, who was the prettiest girl in the village. Annabelle ran home crying.

Traits of French ancestry were evident in Sally Francois's cat-green eyes, which she had inherited from her father. Her full lips and coarse, dark hair were her mother's. She was an extremely attractive young woman, older than Annabelle and physically more developed, but she was still naive about many things, such as love. She was oblivious to life and its deceptions; through her innocent eyes, everything seemed as it appeared.

Annabelle grew more and more insecure about ever marrying Ricardo—the odds were against her. She knew that George would never approve of him and that plans for her to marry Zaid Baksh were already made. And there was another obstacle in her way—she overheard George joshing to Ricardo that word around the village was that Miss Simon and Sally's father were in favour of a union of their children, Ricardo and Sally, who were about the same ages.

"She's the perfect girl for you," George jested to Ricardo.

Annabelle lay in bed, rankled with doubts and insecurities. She felt defeated but was dead set on making Ricardo hers. She had to. She was desperately in love with him.

Chapter 10

· ·

George Castello grinned mockingly at the drizzle of rain as though to assert victory over nature. He had just thrown a large tarpaulin over the bags of cocoa, which he loaded in the tray of the truck bound for the buyer in Rio Claro. As far as George was concerned, it could now rain for eternity, as the rain had subsided long enough for him to dry his cocoa beans, which would earn him the money he needed for Christmas.

Annabelle beamed with excitement as the truck departed. Her mind overflowed with visions of her decked in the dream outfit with Ricardo drooling over her. She was certain that George would buy her the outfit, with him knowing how much she wanted it and his tendency to spend money freely. And too, she deserved it; she kept his secret from Rosey. Besides, anyone could get anything from George once he had money in his pocket. He lived for the moment, rarely sparing a thought on tomorrow. His philosophy, that money was made for spending, was the source of most of the fights he had with Rosey.

The seasonal apple vendors occupied every space they could find along the main streets of Rio Claro. The rain poured as George delivered the final bag of his produce with a look of triumph on his wet face. He tucked the balance of money into his pocket after Henry had deducted the amount he owed on his two credit accounts. George gathered his friends around the counter and bought all the rum they could drink. Some of them had already flocked to the bar when they spotted George unloading his cocoa.

George sat on a barstool with his back toward the road, carping to his friends about the unfair prices which farmers were paid for their produce, while the agents and exporters were richly rewarded for doing almost nothing. He proceeded to refill his glass when he froze with surprise. He searched deep into his memory. "My God, that voice, that menacing tone of voice. I've heard it before! But it can't be!" he mumbled to himself.

He ignored the voice and continued his conversation, but his uneasy demeanour was all too obvious. Maybe it was nothing, he consoled himself. But as he was about to lift the glass from the counter, a powerful hand grasped his shoulder. His heart flipped as a loud, cantankerous laughter accompanied the grasp. George stood statuesque as the laugh waned into a whisper.

"Georgie boy, ain't you glad to see an old friend?" The notorious stranger erupted into a spasm of mocking laughter at his own question.

By now, everyone in the room was curious.

In his coarse voice, the stranger continued, "Well, Georgie boy, ain't you going to offer your old friend a drink for old times' sake?"

The stranger snatched a glass from off the table, wiped the rim clean with his shirt tail, and invited himself to a drink. After emptying the bottle in his glass, he pounded the bottle on the counter to attract the attention of the shopkeeper. He erupted in stitches of laughter when Henry arrived. Looking at George with a malicious grin on his face, he poked fun at the Chinese shopkeeper. "Sam, bling a bottle of lum here," he jested, turning to George, who had not yet looked him in the eyes.

"Remember the good old days, Georgie boy? We have so much to talk about." His voice grew sentimental. "Georgie, where's your manners? Ain't you going to introduce me to your friends?"

George did not reply. He wished that the man would go away.

"Anyway, guys, I'm Georgie's old friend Nathaniel, but my friends call me Sticks," he said.

The men stared at him curiously.

He placed the glass to his thick lips and, with one gulp, emptied the contents of the glass and slammed it on the counter. He took George by the arm and led him to the far corner of the bar.

They occupied a small table in the extreme corner of the bar. A pathetic look was evident in Sticks's dark eyes, almost like a child begging for attention. His voice grew soft.

"You are probably wondering why I'm here; well, I'll tell you. I desperately need your help," Sticks said.

As he spoke, George bent his head to avoid eye contact.

"You owe me big, you know!" Sticks exclaimed. "I took the rap for the murder. I confessed to doing it alone, letting you off the hook. Have you ever wondered about the police not searching for you? I thought I had nothing to live for. My wife and children had left me—I wanted to die. The charge was, however, reduced to manslaughter.

I was released a few years ago. I went to visit Sam and April."

George's eyes collided with Sticks at the mention of the name April.

"But that is water under the bridge. I will not torture you with 'should have been', but one thing I'm tempted to say and, what the heck, I'll say it anyway. April never forgot you. She has ..." Sticks stopped when he saw the pain in George's eyes.

"Anyhow, are you married?" Sticks asked.

"Yes," George replied, trying to force a smile. His mind wandered back to the easy-going days in Port-of-Spain when he was young and free. Looking back, he realized that Sticks was a good friend to him. He was satisfied though that he did not kill anyone. It was Sticks's knife that penetrated the man's chest.

A reflective moment of silence ensued before Sticks blurted, "George, I desperately need your help." He paused and looked at George to observe his reaction.

George stared at him and braced himself for the worst.

"I need to find Paulette and the children real bad," Sticks blurted.

George felt relieved. He thought the favour might be more wretched than that.

"I'll do anything I can," George replied in a less tense tone.

Sticks continued, "I was told that Paulette was seen in Rio Claro on a few occasions; I believe that she lives around here."

"I don't know if I'll recognize her now. I vaguely recall what she looked like, but I will keep my eyes open," George replied.

"That's not all. I need a place to stay for a few days. It's the only chance I'll have to find my family," Sticks said. He paused to swallow his spit. "Please, you have to help me. I'm sure you have a shed or somewhere I can sleep in. I'm not looking for anything fancy."

George found himself in a dilemma; he felt as though he owed Sticks a favour, but Rosey would be opposed to a stranger staying in the house.

He, however, told Sticks that there was a small room in the downstairs of his house where he could stay for a few days. He said that he would go on ahead and talk it over with Rosey. He'd tell her that he hired Sticks to help till the soil to expand the garden. He gave Sticks directions to his home and warned him that there was to be no talk about their young days in Port-of-Spain, especially about April.

Sticks smiled mockingly as George rode his bicycle home.

The dark rain clouds which hovered over Bristol Village brought a premature end to the day, rousing villagers to prepare for an imminent downpour. They secured their goats and cattle in pens, gathered the wash from the clothes line, and shut the doors and windows. Rosey lay in the hammock in sweet repose while Miss Simon assisted Annabelle with the sewing of the Christmas curtains on a noisy Singer sewing machine. George was downstairs preparing the dilapidated room for his visitor, assisted by Rosabelle and Danny.

Convincing Rosey to allow Sticks to stay for a few days was not as difficult a task as George had anticipated. After all, the journey from Rio Claro provided sufficient time for him to concoct a convincing scheme. The money from the sale of the crop, the new curtains, and the scrumptious black pudding assisted him tremendously.

When he arrived home, he rushed into the kitchen where Rosey sat instructing Annabelle, who was bathed in flour, in the method of baking bread, while she sat sipping a cup of coffee with Rosabelle, whose face mirrored disgust, fanning her with a newspaper.

George was immediately interrupted by Rosey as he opened his mouth to speak.

"George, I send Danny to collect some bread pans from the neighbour two hours ago, and up to now, he not returned. You training that boy for trouble!" she lamented.

George replied as he always had. "Danny is a boy child. I don't intend on bringing him up like a sissy. He probably playing with the other boys."

Rosey snapped, "When he get he ass in trouble, I hope that you can deal with it on your own!"

Rosey forgot about Danny as George presented her with the black pudding. Water spouted from her mouth as she grabbed the pudding. She wiped the dribble on the sleeve of her dingy dress. "This would go down good with this coffee," she said.

George handed her the money, which she pushed in her bosom. He was satisfied that this was the ideal time to tell her about Sticks.

"Do you recall me saying that I wanted to expand the cocoa field?" George said.

There was no response, as her mouth was filled with food.

George continued, "Well, I found someone; an old acquaintance of mine who is capable of the task. It took some convincing but he finally agreed. All it would cost me is a few dollars and a place for him to rest his head for a few days."

Rosey swallowed the contents of her mouth, placing her hand on her chest for leverage. "What you need from me?" she asked.

"Well, I need your consent for the man to stay in the room downstairs," George replied.

She pondered for a while and said, "Once is only for a few days and he don't get in my way."

George was relieved.

Two dark silhouettes—Miss Simon and Sticks—hurriedly crossed each other's paths in opposite directions along the track of George's home. As Miss Simon neared the road, a torrential downpour of rain caught her. Sticks narrowly escaped the downpour as he arrived in the nick of time. He stood in the downstairs of the house, staring at the figure of Miss Simon as she was battered by the rain while hustling to her home. It was not like Sticks to easily feel compassion for anyone, but his heart went soft for Miss Simon.

Later that night, George was awakened by a loud sound coming from the work shed. He got up wiping sleep from his eyes and headed for the shed. It was dark; the cocks were yet to commence their morning prelude. To his surprise, he found Sticks preparing firewood. George took a seat on a nearby log, startling Sticks.

"What are you doing up this early?" George asked.

"Just couldn't sleep," Sticks replied. "I'm desperate to find my family. I don't need nothing from them. I just want to say how sorry I am …" His voice broke into a teary lilt. "I just want to hold my children in my arms and say I'm sorry."

Memories of the night at the club with Sticks's head resting on the table, pining for his wife and children, occupied George's mind. It was the first time he saw the sentimental side of Sticks. Like he did on that fateful night,

George walked away and left Sticks to grieve. He wasn't quite sure how to react or what to say to a sinister man with a bizarre soft side.

The morning light peered through a thick blanket of rain clouds as Sticks quietly worked in the garden, sowing seeds. The silence was broken by the sound of Ricardo's bicycle, which provoked a riot of barking dogs. The creaking of the window had awoken Annabelle, but she pretended to be asleep as she cautiously observed Rosabelle looking through the window. Rosabelle twitched when she felt Annabelle standing behind her.

"I'm looking at that man and wondering if he can be trusted," Rosabelle said.

"No, you wasn't. I'm not stupid. You were looking at Ricardo!" Annabelle blared.

"So what concern is that of yours?" Rosabelle retorted.

"I will tell Pa, that's what I'll do!" Annabelle shouted.

"You think that I stupid. I saw you all those mornings opening the window to stare at Ricardo," Rosabelle replied.

"You ugly duckling!" Annabelle blurted. "Ricardo would never like you!"

Rosabelle went off in a tirade. "You tried your best to attract him, but he doesn't want you; he is in love with Sally, you fool! I'll tell him all about you and Zaid!"

Annabelle could not contain her anger any longer. The names Sally and Zaid incited a demon in her. She rushed up to Rosabelle and slapped her in the face with all her might.

Rosabelle responded by kicking her in the stomach.

Annabelle's loud scream attracted the attention of George, who rushed into the room and parted the fight. Both girls remained silent when questioned.

Ricardo was taken by surprise when he encountered Sticks pruning the plants, as that was his job. Sticks's back was facing him when he approached and rested his work bag in the shed. He sat idly tapping his feet while he waited on George.

An eerie feeling overcame Sticks when he turned around and saw Ricardo.

"Oh, I'm sorry. I did not realize that someone else was here," Sticks said apologetically.

Ricardo felt ill at ease as Sticks gawked at him. His dark, sinister eyes and rugged looks scared Ricardo.

"Is something the matter?" Ricardo asked.

There was no response. Sticks continued to stare him in the face.

Ricardo repeated, "Mister, is something the matter?"

"Oh no, it's just that you remind me of someone I knew a long time ago," Sticks replied.

Just then, George arrived in the shed. "Oh, I see you two have already met," George said, "but allow me to formally introduce you. Ricardo, this is an old friend of mine. He is known as Sticks. He is here to assist with the clearing of the land to extend the cocoa field."

Ricardo nodded.

"And, Sticks, this is Ricardo. He's like a son to me. He helps out around the house," George said.

When Ricardo was a safe distance away, Sticks confessed to George, "In desperation to find my family, I was convinced that Ricardo was my son."

"You have to stop this. If you don't, you will think that every young man you meet is your son. If your family is around here, we'll find them," George chided.

Sticks was distracted by Miss Simon's voice calling out to Annabelle. He looked toward the track and saw that her face was draped in a large towel to shield her from the frigid atmosphere. She had contracted the flu from the soaking she got the evening before.

Sticks enquired from George, "Is that the woman who passed me on the track last evening?"

"Yes," replied George, "she's a very good friend of the family. She teaches my daughter to sew, and she's Ricardo's mother."

"She look like a very pleasant woman," Sticks said.

"Oh yes, she is," George replied.

Sticks's curiosity was aroused. "What's her name?" he asked.

"She's known as Miss Simon to everyone," George replied. "Why you so interested in Miss Simon? I'll kill you first before I allow you to befriend her. She is a decent woman," George said angrily.

Sticks continued to stare at her with a curious look in his eye. He craned his neck to have a closer look at her as she proceeded up the stairs. He could not see her veiled face, but her light-coloured eyes triggered a feeling of old familiarity. Sticks, however, dismissed the notion that she could be Paulette, as George told him it was the work of his overanxious mind, but he harboured a strange feeling that he had met or seen her before.

Chapter 11

• •

Ricardo's continued indifference worried Annabelle. Since the night of the dance, she had concocted numerous schemes to lure him, but he did not respond to any. Could it be that she was wrong and that it was Sally whom he loved? But she could still recall the lust in his eyes when she moved around the dance floor. It had to be Pa, she concluded. As far as Ricardo was concerned, it would be offensive for him to have a relationship with the daughter of a man he considered a father.

The only thing left to do was to cast pride aside and approach Ricardo herself. She must tell him how she felt. He must be convinced they could have a relationship without George ever finding out. As for Zaid Baksh, she would continue to see him to please her father, but in any event, he was due to depart for England soon and may never return.

A brilliant idea struck her; she would send Ricardo a letter.

She scribbled the letter and handed it to Miss Simon and told Miss Simon that her pa asked that she deliver it to Ricardo. Miss Simon took the envelope and placed in on the sewing machine and continued stitching the curtains.

The letter which Annabelle wrote with her left hand to feign the penmanship was supposedly written by Rosabelle. It read:

Dear Ricardo,

Annabelle loves you very much but is embarrassed to openly tell you. I have arranged for both of you to meet tonight under the immortelle tree at 8.30.

Sincerely,
Rosabelle

Annabelle felt that her scheme was foolproof. If it worked, Rosabelle would never find out. If it didn't or if she were caught, she could not be implicated, as the handwriting was not distinctly hers. Or she could say that Rosabelle was out to make mischief.

The moon was partially covered with thick clouds lined with hues of gold and a veneer of violet as Annabelle cautiously crept from her bed with eyes focused on Rosabelle, who pretended to be asleep. She slipped on a dress and tiptoed out of the house with her slippers held tightly in her hands.

A rush of excitement flowed through her body when she approached the tree and caught a glimpse of a dark outline of a figure perched on the dense root of the immortelle. She felt nervous as she timidly approached. A rush of emotions propelled through her virgin body.

The night had never appeared as magical as it did then. The dewdrops twinkled in the light of the moon.

As she neared the figure, her excitement turned to curiosity and then fear. The figure was not that of Ricardo. She attempted to turn around and run, but the mysterious stranger called out to her.

"Annabelle, Annabelle," he whispered.

"My gosh, it's Zaid Baksh. How did this happen?" she muttered. She was baffled. Her heart pounded; her feet grew weak as she sauntered toward him.

He took her gently in his anxious embrace and whispered softly in her ear, "Oh, Annabelle, I have waited a long time for this. I love you so much."

He rubbed his lips against hers and kissed her gently. He mistook the tears in her eyes for joy.

Then, suddenly, the silence was broken by the sound of approaching footsteps. Annabelle stood in the arms of Zaid Baksh with profound fear. Her jaw dropped in disbelief. She wished the ground would open and swallow her up. Ricardo stood staring blankly at the couple. Annabelle freed herself from Zaid's embrace and ran as fast as she could, passing Ricardo on the way.

Rosabelle pretended to be asleep when Annabelle came rushing through the door and jumped into bed, crying hysterically. A broad, malicious smile emerged on Rosabelle's face. She pulled the blanket over her head and gloated. Her plan had worked.

Rosabelle was sweeping the scraps of cloth from the curtains when she came across the envelope addressed in a strange handwriting to Ricardo Simon. She closed the door and proceeded to open the sealed envelope with a nail file. She hurriedly scanned through the letter.

"That bitch! I'll fix her good," she said.

A twinge of hatred edged her teeth as she retrieved the pen from the drawer of the sewing machine and a pad of paper from the wardrobe. She tried her best to forge Annabelle's handwriting.

Dear Ricardo,

I must see you tonight at 8.30 p.m. under the immortelle tree. I love you, and I long for you to hold me in your arms. Please be there.

Love,
Annabelle

She placed it in the same envelope and carefully resealed it. Miss Simon had not yet left; she was downstairs conversing with Rosey.

Rosabelle took the letter to Annabelle and said, "Annabelle, I found this letter addressed to Ricardo on the table. Miss Simon must have left it there."

Annabelle was relieved to find Miss Simon downstairs and handed her the envelope.

Rosabelle scribbled another letter addressed to Zaid Baksh. The content was the same except for the time. She asked Zaid to meet Annabelle at eight, under the immortelle tree. She had not figured out how to get the letter to Zaid Baksh in Rio Claro. She overheard Miss Simon saying to Rosey that she would be going to Rio Claro later in the evening. She waited until Miss Simon was almost home and hurried behind.

"Miss Simon! Miss Simon! Pa asked if you could deliver this letter to Rio Claro, please."

The next day, Annabelle swore that she would get even with Rosabelle. In a fit of jealous rage, Rosabelle had gloated to Annabelle what she had done.

Annabelle, however, had a bigger problem to deal with. How was she going to explain Zaid Baksh to Ricardo?

Rosabelle snickered provokingly as she left the room, slamming the door behind her.

Chapter 12

· ·

Sticks was propped against the large wooden door of the Chinese shop in Rio Claro, pulling on a cigarette butt. The hustle and bustle of Christmas shoppers with bags and boxes did not occupy his consciousness. His thoughts were far away. He had come to Rio Claro to locate his family and saw at least five young men who could be his son and half a dozen women who could be his wife. His son, Ray, would be in his late twenties now—a young man, perhaps with wife and children of his own. Ray was no more than two years old when Sticks last saw him. His little girl, Christine, was even younger. Sticks could not picture what Christine looked like, except that she had inherited his dark features and had curly hair.

In the midst of his reverie, a distant memory came rushing through. He recalled the night Paulette had given birth to Ray. It was a wet Friday night when he sat playing a game of cards at the club. He had just pulled the much-needed four of clubs and was about to stand in triumph when news of the birth of his son reached him. He felt a kind of happiness which he had never felt before. He ordered drinks for everyone with his winnings. A few days later when Paulette came home from the hospital with the child, he lifted him high into the air and called him Ray. It was then that he noticed a heart-shaped birthmark on the left buttock of the child. That birthmark would confirm his suspicions that Ricardo was his son, he thought to himself.

He jumped into a taxi and headed to Bristol Village, excited.

Over the next few days, Sticks carefully monitored Ricardo's routine but was yet to figure out how he would observe whether there was a birthmark on Ricardo's buttocks. After all, Ricardo had to be practically naked for him to observe this. Also, the bathroom was an enclosed area located outside the house.

Together with George, Sticks had worked all evening preparing the land to extend the cocoa field. He had observed that once water was available, Ricardo would take a bath before he went home. It was the third week of December, and the days were now shorter. George signalled the end of the workday, and they all gathered their belongings and headed toward the house. Sticks led the way and took a seat on a small bench in the shed, removing his rubber boots. Ricardo arrived soon after, while George stayed behind to tend to the cattle.

This was an ideal opportunity to converse with Ricardo, as they were alone, Sticks thought. He looked at Ricardo and said, "Well, we got a lot of work done today."

"Yeah," Ricardo replied in a brash tone.

Ever since their first meeting, Sticks had detected that Ricardo did not care for his company. But he had to try to befriend him.

"How's your ma's cold? Is she feeling better?" Sticks enquired.

"Yep," Ricardo replied harshly and got up and left.

George returned to the house and breathed a sigh of relief as he threw his tired body on a stool near to Sticks. Sticks stared at Ricardo as he made his way home, unaware of George's presence.

George's voice startled Sticks. "You're still filled with thoughts of that boy being your son?" George asked.

Sticks reflected for a while before responding. "I remember something today which can help in finding my son."

George waited to hear what Sticks had remembered. "Well, what?" George asked.

"A heart-shaped birthmark on his buttocks," Sticks replied. "Do birthmarks fade away?"

"I don't think so," George said.

"Let me be blunt. Have you ever noticed a birthmark like that on Ricardo?" Sticks asked.

George searched the far corners of his mind and then replied, "No, I don't think so."

A look of disappointment reflected in Sticks's eyes.

Christmas was less than two weeks away. Danny was vamping up the Morris chairs in the yard with Brillo pad, sandpaper, and polish, closely supervised by Rosey, who occasionally slapped his hand when he missed a dirty spot.

Rosabelle, armed with bucket and rag, washed the windows with a look of frustration on her face. Annabelle was downstairs slouched over a basin, grating dried corn. She would have ordinarily fussed over being given the hardest task, but this year she didn't. Not because George would pity her and do most of the work himself; there was another reason. Around this time of year, Ricardo usually spent a lot of time downstairs assisting George with repairing the furniture and odd jobs. She waited eagerly for him to show up.

Work on the preparation of the land had stopped until after Christmas. Sticks returned to Port-of-Spain for a day or two to take care of business, while George and Ricardo retreated to the forest for a hunting expedition.

George had a small shack about a mile and a half into the forest accessible from the back of his house. It was surrounded by mahogany tress which he sold to the sawmill owner and furniture makers. Every Christmas, George went to the shack to hunt wild game, which was a traditional Christmas delicacy.

While George busied himself with the hunt, Ricardo cleaned the shrubs from the citrus orchard and harvested the bananas and fruits, as it was against his nature to kill anything. The copious stretch of ground provisions which flourished alongside the narrow tributary yielded plenty this year. George would distribute some of the provisions and wild game to his neighbours, who all looked forward to George's treat on Christmas Eve.

The sky was suffused in hues of peach and purple as George made his way back to the shack with a stuffed bag slung over his shoulder. From a distance, George spotted the naked body of Ricardo having a bath. He carefully rested the bag down and cautiously approached. The luminous yellow light of the evening sun reflected on the wet, naked body of Ricardo as he bathed from a barrel outside the hut. The shimmering water bounced off his tan skin and rolled down his firm back and bare buttocks. George was now close enough to see if there was any birthmark on Ricardo's body as described by Sticks. When he was sure that his curiosity was satisfied, he retreated and pretended as though he had just arrived. He called out to Ricardo, who hurried behind the barrel to conceal his nudity.

A heavy feeling weighed on George's mind.

Chapter 13

• •

The morning sun had begun its ascent in the cloudless sky over Bristol Village. It was Saturday and market day—the busiest day of the week. The sleepy village came to life with a flurry of activity as farmers prepared their produce to take to market in Rio Claro. The lonely figure of Ricardo, decked in his usual three-quarter-length brown trousers and striped jersey, made his way up the street. He walked a bit slower than his usual swift stride, with a heavy look etched on his face. Ricardo had awakened from sleep three hours before in profound fright, his heart still palpitating from the petrifying dream. It was so vivid that he could not erase it from his mind.

He was digging the earth to sow seeds as he usually did, when the most grotesque-looking face he had ever imagined emerged from the hole, staring at him with bloodshot eyes. He recoiled in horror before gathering his strength to run, but when he tried to move, he realized that his feet were transfixed to the ground. On reaching the level of his eyes, the face transformed itself into a white, angelic-like figure. He lifted his head and followed it with his eyes as it flew high in the sky, and then suddenly, the object pitched across the dark sky like a falling star.

Ricardo quickened his pace as he approached the Castellos' house and headed for the shed where he found George securing the baskets of produce to take to market. A figure perched behind the curtains of the bedroom window caught his eyes. He first thought it was Annabelle and responded by smiling at her. But as he looked closer, he realized that it was Rosabelle. Her dark features became apparent in the increasing light. She responded to Ricardo's smile by blushing before concealing herself behind the bright, flowered curtains, giggling shamelessly.

Ricardo observed that Rosabelle was beginning to blossom—her broad face, large eyes, and flat forehead somehow seemed attractive. Although she looked a lot like Rosey, traces of George emerged when she smiled.

Ricardo went to work assisting George with the baskets. Thoughts of the nightmare began to dissipate, and flashes of an earlier half-forgotten dream emerged in his mind.

He was walking along a lonely but beautiful road with Annabelle. The path was lined with pink and white roses, and she stopped to pick the flowers, which she placed in a basket. They never spoke to each other, but he recalled quite vividly the sparkle in her eyes. At this point, the dream was suddenly railroaded by the terrible nightmare.

Ricardo attributed the dream of Annabelle to thoughts he had before going to bed. Seeing her with Zaid Baksh was distressing, but in his mind, he had confronted the fact that George had arranged for her to marry Zaid Baksh. But try as he might, he could not dismiss the strong, lustful feelings he harboured for Annabelle. He developed a strong urge to hold and kiss her, like the old feelings he had for Sally Francois, but these feelings for Annabelle were more intense. But he knew he could not allow himself to feel this way about Annabelle; George would never approve of him as a husband for his precious daughter. He had often heard George say that he wanted a better life for Annabelle. Zaid Baksh was her future, and George wanted this more than anything else. He didn't stand a chance more than a snowball in hell.

When he was through with his chores, George called out to him in a serious tone. It scared him. After all, George had never spoken to him in that tone of voice before.

"Ricardo," George said, "we need to talk. I have something to talk to you about."

Ricardo's jaw dropped; his heartbeat accelerated. He tormented himself with wild thoughts. *Maybe it's about my feelings for Annabelle. Maybe he found out. He probably saw the strange way I looked at her.*

He walked up to George. "Yeah?" he asked timidly.

George looked at him and couldn't bring himself to tell him.

"It can wait till later. Let's hurry to the market. We already late," George replied.

Ricardo felt like asking George to get on with it right away, as the wait might surely kill him. But George looked so distant and cold. For the rest of the day, Ricardo's heart was heavy. Few words were spoken between him and George at the market.

The weight of the basket, which Ricardo carried on his head from the truck to the shed, was heavy but more bearable than the anxiety which weighed on his mind. It was just about dusk when they returned from Rio Claro. Ricardo could not contain his anxiety any longer. He moved timidly toward George, who was sitting in the shed, unbuttoning his shirt.

George was visibly nervous when Ricardo approached. He retrieved a pack of cigarettes from his pocket and proceeded to light one while he avoided making eye contact with Ricardo. He cleared his throat and said, "Sit down, we need to talk."

This is it, Ricardo said to himself. *This is about Annabelle. He twitched.*

George continued, "I want you to know that I love you like a son, hence the reason I must tell you this. I'm going to say things to you which I have never repeated to anyone else."

Ricardo grew scared.

George proceeded with a slur in his voice. "That man called Sticks, he is not who … We used to be friends a very long time ago when we were young in Port-of-Spain. There was an accident involving me and Sticks; a man lost his life. Sticks was held, and I went into hiding. That's how I come to live here. Sticks confessed and was charged for manslaughter. He went to jail for a very long time. His confession got me off the hook."

George paused to catch his breath. Ricardo was puzzled.

Why is he telling me this? What is it leading to? Ricardo asked himself.

George continued, "He, Sticks, believed he had nothing to live for. His wife left him and took their two infant children with her. His search for them over the years turned up empty."

An ominous silence ensued.

Ricardo anxiously broke the silence. "What is this about, Mr George?" Ricardo asked.

"Sticks feel that his family is around here somewhere," George said.

Ricardo was more puzzled than before. "Mr George, why you telling me this?" he asked.

George paused to light another cigarette and turned around to face Ricardo with a harrowing look in his eye.

"Ri-car-do, you may be Sticks's son," George mumbled.

Ricardo grew numb. He rose to his feet and said, "No, my father is dead. Whatever that man told you is a lie."

He gathered his things and left. George lit another cigarette.

Ricardo felt weak in the knees as he made his way home, assailed with agonizing thoughts. He remembered his mother saying to him and his sister a long time ago that their father was dead. She was responding to questions from him about his father, whom his mother never spoke about. After that, no mention was ever again made about a father.

He tried to console himself with the notion that Mr George could be wrong. But he knew that George would not say something like that without good reason. He lay on the bed, gazing up at the ceiling with a harrowing look in his eyes, thinking that he should have told Mr George not to say anything about this to his mother, at least not yet. He still hoped that George was wrong or this was another nightmare from which he would awaken.

George sat in the shed in deep thought. He felt responsible for the welfare of Ricardo and Miss Simon, as though it was his duty to protect them, but from what? He wasn't quite sure. He was also almost certain that Sticks's intentions were good. He saw the callous look in Sticks's eyes falter into that of an innocent child at the mere mention of his wife and children. There was little doubt in his mind that Sticks genuinely wanted to make amends. George lifted his head as though in prayer for a happy ending to this unfolding drama.

George observed that Sticks had become withdrawn since he returned from Port-of-Spain two days ago. He sat on a bench in the work shed, absorbed in self-pity. He told George that maybe it was time he left Bristol Village for good; after all, finding his family seemed hopeless. Whatever his wife and children had achieved in life, they did it without him. Why would they need him now? They would hate him anyway, and he deserved it. He was a cruel father and husband. His eyes grew red.

He passed the back of his hands across his eyes when George came over and sat beside him.

"What would you do if you were to find your wife and children?" George asked.

"You really want to know what I'd do?" Sticks replied with a teary slur in his coarse voice. "I'd run up to them and hold them in my arms and never let them go." He paused and tried to smile. "But I'm only fooling myself. It's too late for that. But to be more real, I'd try telling them how sorry I am. George, I really am. I would not force myself on them; I would be out of place to do that. I would do anything to make up for … if it means taking my life. If they don't want to see me, I'll walk away." Choked up with emotions, Sticks got up and walked to the other side of the shed.

George was now even more convinced that Sticks's intentions were good. It was time to tell Sticks. George got up and shuffled toward him, "I have something to tell you. Just promise me that you will not do anything foolish. You have to think about what you will do. We must decide together."

Sticks froze. He instinctively knew that George had found his family. He turned to George with deep compassion in his eyes. "Anything you say, anything, I promise."

George was blunt. "Ricardo has a birthmark exactly as you described."

Sticks became weak and speechless. He sat on the stool and buried his head in his lap.

George walked away wondering if he did the right thing by telling Sticks.

Chapter 14

•••

The old clock on the wall, a wedding present from Rosey's father, began its chime to herald in the six o'clock hour. Darkness was progressing quickly in Bristol Village—the first quarter moon was barely visible among the blanket of shimmering stars. In the street, noisy children skipped around a group of boys engaged in the seasonal sport of bursting bamboo, their ecstatic faces illuminated by the raging flames of flambeaus belching streamers of black smoke in the still atmosphere. The loud, agonizing explosion of the bamboo echoed through the peaceful ambiance, agitating elderly villagers and dogs.

Annabelle strolled down the stairs of the house and made her way along the muddy track leading to the road, occasionally stroking her loose, wet hair. It had become an evening routine for Annabelle to take a leisurely stroll in the street to dry her hair after her evening bath, but Rosabelle knew that it was just a pretext—a scheme to meet Ricardo, who also took a stroll at this time to smoke a cigarette. Rosabelle gaped at her from behind the curtain, feeling pleased with herself that her plan had worked.

That fool! That stupid fool! Rosabelle said to herself. *Ricardo found out about you and Zaid Baksh. Ha ha ha ha ha!*

Rosabelle harboured thoughts that she would be the one to win Ricardo's heart. Soon he would be her boyfriend, and Annabelle would be jealous. She smiled deviously at the thought.

Danny was one of the boys bursting bamboo. Rosey had often warned him that the sport was dangerous, for it had claimed the eye of a village boy a few years ago. Annabelle spotted him from the corner of her eye but pretended not to see; she was quite aware that Danny knew all about her scheme. Annabelle too had her suspicions about Danny's involvement with a gang of delinquent boys who went about stealing fruits and chickens from the villagers.

In their naive minds, the boys in the village were aware that Annabelle harboured some sort of feelings for Ricardo. They would often tease her in a sing-song chorus—"Annabelle like Ricardo, na-na na-na na"—but not in the presence of Ricardo, whom they feared.

Annabelle stood gazing up the street where earlier, from behind the curtain, she had seen Ricardo. By her timing, he should have returned a long time ago. Wild thoughts engaged her. *That bitch Sally's probably keeping him from returning home.* The thought caused her to gnash her teeth.

She had stopped speaking to Sally. Whenever they crossed paths, Annabelle turned her head away or scowled her face. Sally felt hurt, as she considered Annabelle to be her friend. Sally was naive to any wrongdoings on her path that would cause Annabelle to act in such a hateful manner toward her. She searched deep in her mind for even the slightest notion that would cause Annabelle to act this way. But as far as she knew, Annabelle was in love with Zaid Baksh and that both he and Annabelle planned on getting married. She told Annabelle that she was happy for her. Perhaps Annabelle thought that she was jealous of her. But she wasn't. Maybe she should have a talk with Annabelle, letting her know that her feelings were for Ricardo. Then she'd know that she was not jealous of her and Zaid Baksh.

"I'll get even with that bitch!" Annabelle exclaimed. But for now, she must plot to get Ricardo. *That bitch, Rosabelle, I hate her! I hate her! Now Ricardo thinks that I love Zaid Baksh.*

The thunderous sound of the bamboo continued its raucous echo throughout the village, but as the noise momentarily ceased, the loud cry of a woman attracted the attention of the villagers.

"Help! Help me! Please, somebody!"

The children abandoned their sport and scurried in the direction of the scream. Men and women gathered outside their homes to investigate the commotion. Rosey detected that the scream was coming from Miss Simon's house and quickly alerted George, who was relaxing in bed. He sprang from a mild slumber, pulled on a shirt and pants, and instinctively reached for his cutlass, which he kept under the bed. He ran down the stairs and hurried to Miss Simon's house. When he arrived, he encountered a small crowd outside. They were afraid to venture inside and heaved a sigh of relief when George arrived with cutlass in hand.

The scream subsided, and the house appeared ominously tranquil. Everyone assumed the worst. The flickering light of a shadeless lamp shone through the open window as George cautiously crept up the rickety stairs, tightening the grip on the cutlass, as he was prepared to face the worst.

He took a deep breath and composed himself as he entered through the open door. His eyes required a moment to adjust to the dim room, but as his vision became clearer, George was angered by the sight which confronted him. He relaxed his grip on the cutlass and exhaled loudly. The room was plastered in lambent shadows and black smoke from the naked flame of the lamp, which emitted a smoky scent. George's face was blank as he stared at the statuesque figure of Sticks standing over the lame body of Miss Simon, which was sprawled across the bare floor.

George walked slowly toward Sticks and took him by the arm and led him away from Miss Simon. He lifted the lame body of Miss Simon and carried her to the bedroom and placed her in bed. He then took Sticks, who appeared dazed and disoriented, by the arm and led him gently down the stairs. The crowd of curious onlookers was mystified as George led Sticks like a child up the street.

From the instant George had confirmed the existence of a birthmark on Ricardo's buttocks, Sticks was overly excited. Those eyes piercing through the veiled face could only belong to Paulette. He was sure beyond the shadow of a doubt that it was she. In spite of George's warning, he could not wait to reveal himself to her. He felt a compelling urge to comfort her, to protect her, to make amends. The burden of self-pity weighed heavily on his mind. He yearned desperately to be a part of their lives again, so he cast aside good sense and headed to Paulette's home. He tiptoed up the narrow stairs and stood for a moment on the landing, staring at the open door. He pulled the curtain aside and stared inside the dimly lit room. No one was in sight. His curious feet led him inside. He called out softly, his voice choking with anxiety.

"Paulette? Paulette?" he muttered.

Miss Simon came cautiously from the kitchen. "That voice sounded like ... Oh no! It must be my imagination playing tricks on me," she said to herself. The last she had heard of Sticks was that he was sentenced to prison for murder.

As she entered the living room, he moved toward her. Her jaw dropped. She placed her hands over her face and muttered, "My God, Sticks—the man staying—George—"

The light of the lamp illuminated his scarred face. He reached out his hand to touch her. Distant memories and fear rushed through her mind as she recalled images of Sticks with fire in his eyes, lifting his hands high into the air beating her until she bled. The pain and the fear came rushing through the years. She stood transfixed. She tried to scream but was speechless. She tried to run but could not move. Then in an instant, she regained her strength and started to scream as loudly as she could, over and over until she fainted on the floor.

It was a rainy night a long time ago when Paulette decided that she had had enough. Sticks had just come home from the club, his face somnolent from alcohol and his eyes red with rage. He had just lost all of his money in a gambling game. She was half asleep with the children when she felt his heavy hands pressing against her breasts and shouting, "You bitch! Get up right now. I want food!"

Her eyes collided with his hateful eyes, and she turned to the other side of the bed, ignoring him. In a fit of rage, he held her by the hair and pulled her from the bed. Her loud screams awoke the children. He retrieved a thick leather belt from the chair next to the bed and, lifting his hand high into the air, he beat her until she fell to the floor, bleeding from her mouth. The children began screaming loudly. He hurled obscenities at them before rushing out of the house, slamming the door behind him. It was the verge of dawn when she struggled to get up from the floor. The children were seated next to her with teary eyes. She hurriedly gathered some clothes and stuffed them into a bag. She then lifted the children from the floor and rushed out of the house. She slung the bag over her shoulder and cradled the small girl in her arm; she took the boy by the hand and hurried for the train station in South Quay.

She had no idea where she was going; all that concerned her was escaping from Sticks and that hellhole, not only for her sake but for the children's.

The streets of Port-of-Spain were dark and deserted, and she avoided the main streets for fear that Sticks might see her. The train station was desolate. Departure of the morning train was more than two hours away. She sat in the back bench to conceal herself. For the children's sake, she pretended to be strong and composed, but her battered body wrenched in pain. Blotches of blue-black marks were visible on her fair face.

It was a midmorning in September when the train arrived in Rio Claro. The provincial southeastern town was under heavy rain, and Paulette reached into the small travelling bag for garments to shield the children from the downpour. The squalid structure, which served as the town's train station, was cramped with people seeking refuge from the weather. The little girl was fast asleep on her shoulder, and the boy bent his tear-stained face in disgust. He was hungry and desperately needed to go to the bathroom. Paulette scoured the station for a less-cramped area where the children might be more comfortable.

As she looked around, she noticed a woman staring at Ray with motherly compassion on her face. When the woman realized that Paulette had seen her staring at the boy, she walked up to her and asked, "What's wrong with the boy, madam?"

Ray turned to look her in the eye, and she bent down and caressed his face.

"Oh, you sweet little thing," she said endearingly. Paulette smiled at the woman, for she needed someone to speak with whom she could trust. "You must be new to this town. I don't recall ever seeing you around," the woman said.

"Yes," Paulette replied.

The crowd which had gathered in the train station started to disperse as the rain subsided. The woman was about to leave when Paulette called out to her.

"Madam, I don't mean to impose on you, but I'm wondering if you could assist me, please," Paulette said.

The woman turned around with compassion in her eyes. Judging from the ragged appearance of the children and the marks on Paulette's face, the woman had already assumed that something was wrong.

Paulette continued, "I'm in search of an aunt of mine. I don't know her address. All I know is that she lives in Rio Claro and that her name is Mildred Simmons."

The woman drifted off in deep concentration and then responded, "The name sounds quite familiar. Do you know anything else about her?"

"No, not really," Paulette replied.

"I'll ask around. This is a small town. It should not be difficult to locate her," the woman said. "In the meantime, let's go to the market. We can ask around there," the woman suggested.

Before long, the entire marketplace was aware that a woman with two small children was in search of a woman named Mildred Simmons. It was not long after that the identity of Mildred Simmons was known.

Paulette was drained of energy when she finally arrived at the home of Mildred Simmons, which was located approximately a half mile from the market. It was a small, unpainted house on wooden stilts, partially hidden by a thick growth of trees and shrubs. A rusty bell protruded from behind a fence of loosely draped chicken wire. She tapped the bell gently and waited for a response. A dark woman with broad nostrils, attired in a bright, flowered headtie, emerged from behind gauzy curtains and curiously approached the strangers.

"Good day, madam. Can I assist you?" the woman asked.

"Are you Mildred Simmons?" Paulette asked.

"Yes," the woman replied.

"I'm sorry to impose on you like this, but I'm in a crisis," Paulette said, pausing to catch her breath. "I'm hoping that you can assist me. My name is Paulette Simmons. I'm the daughter of your half-sister from Port-of-Spain, Jocelyn, and these are my children."

Paulette need not have said more. The ragged appearance of the children, her battered face, and her wistful voice told the story.

Mildred Simmons had lived alone following the death of her husband three years earlier. She had no children of her own, and her niece's children would fill her lonely home with joy. After a few days, Paulette began sewing for a few villagers, earning her keep.

A few months had flown by, and Paulette felt the need to create a new life for her children. Mildred Simmons was kind to her, but she felt that she had overstayed her welcome; after all, it was a temporary arrangement. She longed for a place of her own where she could open a dress shop and perhaps rear poultry and raise a vegetable garden.

It was by coincidence or fate that her wish was granted. An old friend of Mildred Simmons's came visiting one Saturday evening. He was an elderly man decked in dark suit and black fedora. He came to say farewell to Mildred Simmons; his daughter had sent for him to live with her in America. He said that he had grown old and feeble, and she felt uncomfortable with the idea of him living alone. Paulette was seated behind the sewing machine in the bedroom when she overheard him mention that he was looking for someone to take care of his house, and she had previously spoken to Mildred about of her plans to find a place of her own. Paulette rushed out of the bedroom and sat on the sofa in the living room.

"Pardon me, sir, but I overheard you say that you have a house for rent," Paulette said.

A week later Paulette was hanging newly made curtains in the two-bedroom house in Bristol Village. For fear of Sticks ever finding her, Paulette assumed her godmother's first name, Besey, and she altered the name Simmons to Simon. She introduced the children as Ricardo and Elsie.

It was Christmas Eve, and the small hamlet of Bristol Village stood still under a star-studded sky. The three-quarter moon played hide-and-seek among balls of drifting white clouds. Small fires shone from the backyard of every home as women were busy baking black cakes and sweet and salt breads in ovens made from steel barrels fuelled by coal pots. The men were boiling their Christmas hams in oil tins which rested on stones.

For George Castello, it would be a long night. Together with the parang group, he must serenade each household in the neighbourhood with traditional parang songs before the break of dawn on Christmas Day. He promised Miss Simon that he and his family would prepare her ham and cakes, as she was weak and needed to rest. Ricardo stayed close to his mother, nursing her back to health. They were both recovering from the shock that Sticks had brought to their lives. Annabelle went about the task of hanging new curtains, devoid of the Christmas spirit. She was disheartened by the thought of never capturing Ricardo's heart. It was useless. She was better off dead, she concluded.

The night was progressing swiftly. George retrieved his mandolin to serenade the villagers, but before he departed, he went to check on Sticks, who had not left his room since the incident with Miss Simon. George knocked on the door, but there was no reply. George cautiously opened the door, and to his surprise there was, no one there.

George retrieved a note addressed to him attached to a large cardboard box. George eagerly opened the note to discover that Sticks was gone for good.

Chapter 15

• •

The crowing of cocks heralded Christmas morning in Bristol Village. The ambiance was alive with traditions of the season that excited the senses—chilly air, scrubbed walls and stairs, new curtains, colourful balloons, sharp smell of paint and varnish, distinctive scent of the red-patterned oil cloth on the kitchen table, aroma of ham and cakes, the glow in the eyes of children anticipating gifts from Santa Claus. But above all, it was a spirit, a Christmas spirit which manifested itself from the heart and mind—a harmonic blend of the tangible with the intangible.

Annabelle was up an hour before, while everyone else was asleep. She meticulously dressed herself for the six o'clock mass with the light of the lamp. Everything must be perfect.

Her hair and make-up had to complement her new dress. It might be the last chance she had to seduce Ricardo, as Sally was gaining ground and beating her at her own game, without even trying or even being aware that she was in a love triangle.

Annabelle was perplexed at Ricardo's coldness toward her. Instinct told her that he had feelings for her. She could still recall quite vividly the seductive manner in which he looked at her at the dance. She suspected that he was stifling his feelings to please George. He could not really believe that she could be in love with as dowdy a boy as Zaid Baksh, she thought. Ricardo probably felt inferior to Zaid because he was not wealthy and that George was always harping about a better life for her. She was enraged. After all, money was not everything. She swore that Pa was not going to get away with his scheme to marry her off to someone she didn't love.

She brimmed with excitement as she slipped the dress over her head and stepped back to look at herself in the mirror. She turned in all directions, twisting and twirling and fixing the dress until she was satisfied that it was a perfect fit.

It was two days ago when she encountered the dress spread conspicuously across the bed. She knew that Pa would eventually buy her the dress. But in the midst of her joy, she felt guilt, like it was a bribe for keeping his secret. George was up in the nick of time to assist with the zipper. She looked like a princess. He smiled. He could not wait for her to marry Zaid Baksh; he wished Mr Baksh could see her now. She would be a worthy daughter-in-law to Mr Baksh. George gushed with pride.

The sun had not yet risen. It was dark and chilly when Annabelle stepped regally down the stairs, beaming with self-confidence. The lime-green dress trimmed with white lace edging, which she had secretly adjusted for a tighter fit and lower neckline, hugged her slim, shapely figure. The broad hat trimmed with white roses and green ribbons matched the white high-heeled shoes. Her slim, defined face was radiantly attractive with red rouge and signal-red lipstick, although she looked more like a precocious child than a young woman.

The flickering lights of lamps and candles gleamed through the windows and crevices of the wooden houses. The noisy sound of crackers and whistles penetrated the atmosphere, as the children had awakened earlier than usual to claim their gifts from Santa Claus.

The soft light of the morning sun began to emerge in the cloudy sky as Annabelle approached the church. The wooden windows and front door were draped in palm branches, and a conspicuous red poinsettia plant leaned against the banister of the uneven wooden stairs. The ground was muddy from the December rains as Annabelle cautiously negotiated her steps across the boulders which lined the soggy path. She preened her dress and hair with her hands before stepping up the aisle in a stylish manner, consciously swaying her hips. She walked toward the front of the church to the stares of the yet small congregation. She turned around and scoured the pews to see if Ricardo was there, but she did not see him. Ever since she could recall, Ricardo always attended Christmas morning service, though he rarely attended church during the year. She wondered whether he would attend the service, owing to the scenario with Sticks and Miss Simon. She said a silent prayer that he would show up. If he didn't, her efforts would be wasted. She also prayed for George to change his mind about her marrying Zaid Baksh and to accept Ricardo as a son-in-law. He meant well, she knew, but she was in love with Ricardo. She was consoled by the fact that she had time on her side, as Zaid was scheduled to depart for England for a year after the holidays.

A dim light shone from the front window of Miss Simon's house as Ricardo reluctantly dressed himself for church. He did not want to leave his mother alone after the trauma she had been through, but she insisted that he go to church. He kissed her and made her promise that she would not attempt to get out of bed until he returned. He slapped on some aftershave lotion and hurried over to meet Sally Francois. The fresh air and Christmas ambiance revived his spirit as he stepped out of the house.

Miss Simon lay in bed in deep contemplation. Perhaps she had overreacted. Maybe Sticks had changed and wanted to make amends. Deep inside, she wished that he'd return so they both could make peace with each other. After all, he was Ricardo's father, and she was a professed Christian.

She tediously lifted herself up and sat on the bed, praying for strength and guidance. When she was through praying, she got out of bed and put on the slippers which Ricardo had given her for Christmas. She shuffled to the living room and eased herself into the Morris chair. The room was lit by a lamp which Ricardo had placed on the table before leaving. Miss Simon stared at the small pine tree decorated with strips of coloured paper. She was confused by the countless gifts strewn beneath it. Maybe it was another one of Ricardo's gestures to cheer her up. But the presents looked old and faded. As she surveyed the presents, she noticed a small envelope lodged between the branches of the tree. She thought of waiting until Ricardo returned to ask if he had anything to do with the presents and the envelope, but curiosity got the better of her.

She reached for the envelope and discovered that her real name, Paulette, was scribbled on it. She cautiously opened it and almost fell to the floor in profound shock. It was an old bank book. She grasped it tightly in her hand and pressed it against her bosom as her thoughts wandered through the corridors of time to her distant past.

Sticks was elated at the birth of their firstborn son. He spent all of his money on a lavish christening. She was dead set against the celebration and told Sticks that they could not afford to spend so much money, as they were behind on the rent. Besides, she knew that the celebration was bound to include alcohol, which transformed Sticks into a demon. But to her surprise, Sticks refused to consume any alcohol, even though his friends harassed him to have a drink. It was a wonderful occasion, she recalled. She twisted her lips into a sentimental smile as she remembered how loving Sticks was to her and their baby son. She was convinced that the baby had changed Sticks for good. It was one of the few memories which she held dear to her heart. The next morning after the christening, Sticks delightedly escorted her to the bank. She had no idea what he had planned. When he got to the bank, he walked up to the clerk.

"Madam, I'm here to open an account for my son," he said.

"How old is the child?" the clerk asked.

"A few weeks," Sticks replied, feeling proud of himself.

The clerk suggested a joint account with him and the child.

"No," replied Sticks, "the other person will be the child's beautiful mother."

The memory caused Paulette to blush the same way she did back then.

She was stunned beyond her wildest imagination at the current balance on the account. She opened the small book again to verify whether her imagination was playing tricks on her. The figure she read the first time was the same figure she was seeing now: eighty-seven thousand, seven hundred fifty-five dollars and fifty-two cents. She could not help but wonder how Sticks had earned all that money. It could change her life, but she would have to think about that when she felt better.

She leaned back in the chair and drifted off to sleep.

The ringing of the church bell incited spasms of excitement in Annabelle. The church was filled to capacity, but Ricardo was not there. The choir of children walked slowly in procession, pausing to light their candles from a larger one on the table. Annabelle hardly noticed the procession; she was preoccupied with thoughts of Ricardo. *Is he coming? He has to come!* She stood up when the choir rose to sing the opening hymn, "O Come, O Come, Emmanuel", while the congregation was supposed to remain seated. She sat down quickly, feeling a bit silly.

Annabelle breathed a sigh of relief when the prolonged sermon by Pastor Miles was finally concluded. The congregation rose to their feet for the closing hymn, "Silent Night, Holy Night", Annabelle's favourite hymn. She half mumbled the words of the hymn while constantly staring into the congregation to see if Ricardo was there.

The blush on her face when she spotted him was shameful. The man sitting next to her looked at her with disgust. She turned around again to stare at Ricardo with a silly blush on her face. To her surprise, Ricardo stared back at her with lust in his eyes. Although he was aware that she was looking at him, he made no effort to avert his eyes. She turned around to sing the final verse with renewed vigour in her voice. Sally sat next to Ricardo, unaware at the silent conversation between him and Annabelle. Her presence did not worry Annabelle;

after all, she was convinced that it was her Ricardo lusted over.

Annabelle was walking on air when she left the church. She walked all the way home, oblivious to the cheerful atmosphere which prevailed. Her thoughts overflowed with visions of her and Ricardo. Ricardo had gone in the opposite direction to escort Sally home, but Annabelle was undaunted. She realized that Ricardo's relationship with Sally was purely casual. This time, she could not be wrong; he looked at her in the same lustful manner as he did on the night of the dance. She was going to cast pride aside and throw herself at him.

Miss Simon had drifted off in a deep sleep on the Morris chair when Ricardo returned home. His eyes were drawn to the cluster of presents under the tree. As far as he knew, there were usually two presents under the tree, one for him and the other for his mother. He fell on his knees to investigate the presents. A deep, passionate feeling engulfed him as he opened one of the presents. It was a small red car with a faded note, "Merry Christmas, son, from your daddy". His jaw dropped. Tears rolled down his face. He hurried to the bedroom and buried his head in the pillow, grasping the car tightly in his hand. It was a moment in his life which was lost forever, a moment which was decades too late. For a moment, he wished he were a boy again and could rush into his daddy's open arms and say the words, "Thank you, Daddy. Merry Christmas."

Chapter 16

• •

Midnight was fast approaching when Annabelle slid out of bed. She listened attentively. A deathly silence echoed through the stillness of the night; even the slightest sound would be detected. Satisfied that everyone was asleep, Annabelle retrieved her slippers from under the bed and held them in her hands. She tiptoed from the bedroom and headed for the kitchen, where she carefully unbolted the door, taking extreme care not to make a sound. She looked over her shoulder with every movement of the rusty latch, until it was eventually unlocked. She cautiously stepped out on the landing, gently closing the door behind her.

She felt a profound sense of accomplishment, as she had successfully completed the first stage of her scheme. She tiptoed down the creaky stairs, stopping on the last slat to place the slippers on her feet. She looked over her shoulder before proceeding on the muddy track. She breathed a sigh of relief when she reached the road.

Her heart pounded nervously against her breast as she approached the towering immortelle tree, not knowing what to expect. All she knew was that she was in love, and the feeling was in a way forbiddingly exciting. She longed for Ricardo to take her in his arms and hold her until eternity. Suddenly, nothing else mattered to her but Ricardo. It was as though the rest of the world ceased to exist.

The blanket of stars against a cloudless sky shimmered more brightly than ever. An auspicious full moon hovered above, illuminating the dark silhouette of Ricardo sitting on the tangled root of the old tree, puffing a cigarette.

Upon reaching the tree, Annabelle rushed into his arms. He took a final pull of the cigarette before discarding it on the ground. Pangs of anxiety rippled through her body, and her knees grew weak. Ricardo placed his arms around her and gently stroked her hair.

Intense feelings of guilt overwhelmed Ricardo—but animal instinct and his adrenaline rush got the better of him. Annabelle's bewitching eyes forced his wavering mind into a state of unyielding passion. He responded to her trembling mouth by sucking her wet lips. They were both held captive in a tight embrace of ecstasy from which climax was the only release.

He grabbed her shoulders and pushed her to the ground. The strength of his muscles against her defenceless body released a torrent of passion from deep within. She felt like his willing slave, and the feeling was ecstatic. Her partially attired body was sprawled out on the cold, bare earth. She opened her eyes for a moment to see sparkles of moonlight seeping through the leaves of the massive immortelle tree. Then suddenly, without surrender, his naked body was ravishing her virginity. She moaned with sweet desire.

Nature's call had awakened George when he encountered the unlatched kitchen door. He distinctly recalled latching the door before going to bed. He proceeded to check on the children to see if any of them had gone to the latrine. Both Danny and Rosabelle were fast asleep, and Annabelle was missing. George assumed that she had gone to the latrine and he sat impatiently in the kitchen, smoking a cigarette, waiting to use the latrine when she was through.

George could no longer hold the call. He bolted down the stairs, headed for the latrine, and called out to Annabelle, but there was no reply. He unlatched the door and proceeded to ease himself with worrying thoughts about Annabelle's whereabouts. He cut short the prolonged time he would usually spend in the latrine and sat in the darkened kitchen waiting for her.

Annabelle threw her head back against the trunk of the tree, exhaling loudly through her mouth, while Ricardo released her and proceeded to light a cigarette. There was a moment of silence between them before Ricardo asked, "Are you all right?"

"Yeah, I'm all right," she said with an ashamed slur in her breathless voice.

Ricardo took her in his arms and planted a delicate kiss on her forehead. "You'd better go now before they notice you missing," he said.

"See you tomorrow," she replied.

The sound of barking dogs accompanied Ricardo's screeching bicycle as he rode down the street.

A feeling of guilt and fear consumed Annabelle as she cautiously made her way up the stairs. She gently opened the door, and with slippers in hand, she stepped into the kitchen. She was startled out of her wits at the sight of the red glow from George's cigarette. The slippers dropped from her hand, and her heart jumped to her throat.

"Where did you go?" George asked sternly.

She paused to catch her breath before responding, "To the la ... trine, Pa."

He lit the lamp, which illuminated her visibly guilty face and sweaty, dishevelled appearance. She knew that she wasn't fooling George. The sound of Ricardo's bicycle and the barking dogs incited a riot in the still night.

The silence which had developed between George and Annabelle was evident, and their avoidance of each other had fuelled curiosity in Rosey. She gnawed at George until he confessed to her what Annabelle had done.

"I keep telling you that girl is no good!" Rosey retorted.

George knew what he had to do.

Annabelle sat on the stairs seething with anger. *Pa's wicked and evil*, she thought to herself. *How could he force me to marry Zaid Baksh when he knows that I hate him? He said that Zaid would give me a good life, but he is just interested in Zaid's money. Not me! How could he say that Ricardo is not good for me?* She gnashed her teeth.

More and more, she thought of telling Rosey that her Pa had another woman. *Who does he think he is, telling me that Ricardo is not good for me when he himself is no good!* She dropped her head to her knees and began to sob.

But fate was working against her. Rosey was about to find out about George's mistress, though quite by accident.

George lay in bed, burning up with fever and struggling with a nagging headache. Rosey needed beef and vegetables from the market to prepare a pot of soup for him. She was dead set against sending Annabelle to the market, so she got dressed and hopped into a taxi headed for Rio Claro.

At the market, Rosey was greeted by a kaleidoscope of colours, a flurry of activity, and a blend of musty and redolent scents. She dodged the boisterous crowd and navigated her way through boxes, crates, and baskets brimming with vegetables and foodstuff. She paused for a moment to re-familiarize herself with the layout of the market. She recalled that the butcher was at the back of the cluster of thatched booths. As she made her way toward the booths, she was relieved to see cuts of beef hanging from a stall. She hurried to the butcher's stall, hoping that Mr Ramjohn would remember her. She had no money. George usually bought the meat on credit.

As Rosey approached the stall, she saw Mr Ramjohn immersed in casual conversation with a stout, cantankerous woman with a jowly face and round nose. Rosey stood to the side, unnoticed, as the woman blabbed on. Mr. Ramjohn, a thin-faced, bearded man either nodded or smiled at the woman's gauche tirades. Rosey heard the woman bad mouthing some poor soul. Her curiosity aroused, Rosey retreated to conceal herself behind a large cut of meat while she cocked her ears to listen to the woman.

"I is more woman than she! She don't even know how to take care of the man. I hear that she resemble a cow. You know, Ram, I hear that she can't even boil water to make a cup of coffee for George. If it wasn't for me, the poor man might be dead now. But you know Ram, it was me who encourage George to stay with the cow. What she name again? Rose? No, Rosey—yes, that's the name of the cow. Rosey!" The woman erupted in a bout of scandalous laughter that caused Rosey's blood to boil. The woman finally continued. "He wanted to leave she you know, but I tell him to stay and bear it out for the sake of the children."

Rosey had heard enough. She stepped out from her hiding place, her eyes red with rage. Mr Ramjohn turned in her direction and, as their eyes met, he flinched and the blood drained from his face. He cleared his throat before saying loudly, "Mrs Castello," distinctly enunciating each syllable. But the cantankerous woman was too engrossed in her vulgar discourse to take the hint.

Finally Mr Ramjohn spoke over her ramblings. "What brings you here? Where's George?" He glanced at the woman, then back at Rosey.

Rosey made no reply but simply stared at the woman with intense anger burning in her large bloodshot eyes. She dropped her basket on the counter as she took a step toward the woman, grabbing her by the neck of her dress. "You blasted whore!"

"Who the hell is you! Take your hands off me!" the woman shouted.

Rosey wrapped her hand in the woman's hair and yanked it as hard as she could. "You want to know who I is? Take a good guess, you slut! I is the cow, Mrs Castello."

The woman pushed Rosey away with her large arms and fired a cuff to her face. Rosey responded by twisting the woman's hand with all her might. A large crowd quickly formed around the women.

Mr Ramjohn shouted at the women. "Stop it, Millie and Rosey! You are making fools of yourselves!"

The crowd jeered. "Leave the women to settle their affairs!" someone shouted.

Soon the two women were rolling on the ground, a tangle of loose hair and tattered clothes. A police officer finally intervened and separated the two women.

Rosey quickly took a step back, brushed off her dress, then scurried off for a taxi back home. In the taxi, she realized that she had forgotten her basket at the stall. She was not going back for it. Now, she had only one thought on her mind, which was consumed by intense rage for George. She felt the urge to thrust a knife through him. In all her life she had never been so humiliated. She always felt as though she had the upper hand with George—until now.

The taxi ride seemed to take longer than normal, and Rosey's anger was gradually overtaken by feelings of guilt, loneliness, and insecurity. All these years she had taken George for granted, never sparing a thought that she could lose him to another woman. Once back at the house, she raced up to her bed, hiding the tears running down her face as she told herself what a fool she had been.

It was a Saturday afternoon in the new year when Annabelle slipped on the blue chiffon dress which George had bought for the special occasion, affixing the white frills with little enthusiasm. The rest of the family was already dressed and impatiently awaited her.

Rosey proceeded to the bedroom door in high temper and shouted, "Get yuh blasted ass out here right now. We ready to leave!"

She pushed the door to find Annabelle sulking on the pillow. She grabbed her by the hand and dragged her through the open front door and into the waiting car. Annabelle was relegated to sitting in the back seat while Danny took her place in the front seat with George.

The taxi stopped at the destination, and George alighted from the car, followed by Rosey, Rosabelle, and Danny. Annabelle intentionally remained in the car, pouting.

"This is slavery!" she said.

Rosey opened the door and pulled her out of the car. "Yuh ent see slavery yet!" Rosey exclaimed.

George looked away.

George's family followed him through a narrow doorway which led to a steep staircase and onto a spacious landing. George was greeted cheerfully by Mr and Mrs Baksh.

"Hello. Please come in. Oh, Rosey, you look nice. Rosabelle, you have grown into a pretty young lady. George, you'd better watch her closely."

Rosabelle blushed.

"And this must be Danny. You have a handsome young man there, George. And there she is, our Annabelle. She looks lovely. Oh, do come on in. After all, we are almost family now."

The large drawing room of the Baksh home was filled with well-attired men and women, engrossed in conversation. Large bunches of balloons and festoons of ornate decorations denoted a convivial occasion. The mahogany furnishings and glass vases of flowers—fresh and ornamental—shimmered under the large, ornate chandelier. For a moment, Annabelle forgot about her dilemma. She fantasized about living in this luxury. But she knew that her love for Ricardo exceeded everything else in the entire world. She consoled herself with the notion that this was only an engagement and that she was still free to marry or elope with Ricardo.

After Annabelle's "whoring", as described by Rosey, George went to Rio Claro in a desperate fit to convince

Mr Baksh that it would be best for Annabelle and Zaid to marry before Zaid went to England. "What if your son find another girl in England? What would become of my daughter?" George argued.

Mr Baksh called in his wife, and after a long discussion, it was agreed that Zaid and Annabelle would be engaged, as Mr Baksh refused to burden his son with marital responsibility while he was studying.

Thunderous applause greeted the placing of the conspicuous diamond ring on Annabelle's finger by Zaid Baksh. He was proud to show his sincere love for Annabelle with a passionate kiss on her lips. Everyone mistook the tears in Annabelle's eyes for joy. But George overflowed with happiness.

Rosabelle looked at Zaid Baksh and snickered. "That stupid ass!" she said.

Chapter 17

• •

An ominous silence echoed through the stillness of the black, sultry night. George sat in the couch in the living room, barely visible by the light of the moon which seeped through the cracks and crevices of the wooden house. He stared blankly into space with a sense of hopelessness on his face. His thoughts drifted deeper and deeper into the dark corners of his mind; his world had come crashing down on him. He concluded that there was nothing left to live for. He had lived through many disappointments in his life, but this one was too much for him to bear. Just a short while ago, he overflowed with joy at the engagement of Annabelle and Zaid Baksh. Now all that was left of that most gratifying moment in his life was a hollow feeling in his heart.

Rosey could not sleep either; she sat on the bed with a worried look on her face, not so much for herself but for George. She knew how he felt. Annabelle was his favourite child, and he wanted to give her the world. Rosey also reached into the far corners of her mind. She felt somewhat responsible. Maybe if she had been a more supportive wife and mother, she agonized.

She thought of going to the living room to comfort George, but she felt uncomfortable in expressing emotions, and too, their relationship was distant and cold.

It was early morning of the previous day when Annabelle awoke, vomiting profusely. George dismissed her illness to an upset stomach and treated it with home-made remedies. He became concerned when the vomiting persisted into midmorning. He hurriedly dressed himself and lifted a weak Annabelle into a car en route to Dr Deo Ramnath in Rio Claro.

The small office was cramped with people when they arrived. George pleaded with the patients to allow Annabelle to see the doctor right away, fearing that it might be food poisoning or some life-threatening illness.

He paced the waiting room, agitated, while Annabelle was being examined. George rushed over to the doctor when the door opened, and Annabelle emerged from the examination room.

"Is she all right? Is she all right?" George asked, excited.

"How are you?" Dr Ramnath replied. "Don't worry. She will be all right. Come into my office. Let Annabelle wait outside."

George hurried into the office with an anxious look on his face.

"So, how's the family? You look well. Since you're here, let me check your blood pressure," Dr Ramnath said.

"But I want to know about Annabelle. What's wrong with her?" George asked.

Dr Ramnath's facial expression morphed from callous to concern. "Is Annabelle married?" he asked.

"No," George replied with a curious look on his face, "but she's engaged to be married to Mr Baksh's eldest son."

"Oh yes, I was at the engagement party," Dr Ramnath replied. "George's pretty daughter and Baksh's brilliant son."

"But, Doctor, you're still not telling me what is wrong with Annabelle," George lamented.

"Well, your daughter is a healthy, normal young lady. She is experiencing what is commonly called morning sickness. Let me be the first to congratulate you," Dr Ramnath said.

George was perplexed as Dr Ramnath extended his hand to him. George reluctantly shook his hand.

"You are going to be a grandfather," Dr Ramnath quipped.

George's face dropped; his heart became weak. He stepped out the door like a zombie, oblivious to everything and everyone. Annabelle sauntered behind him as he headed for the taxi stand. They neither exchanged words nor eye contact from Rio Claro to Bristol Village. For the next few days, Annabelle remained in bed, mortified and shunned by her family; she was the target of reproach. Rosey warned the children not to say a word of this to anyone.

Two weeks later, Annabelle threw herself on the bed with a blank expression on her face. She propped her frail body against the stuffed travelling bag that had been prepared for her long journey to George's brother in a small village tucked away in the island's northern range. She had never seen her uncle in all her life; the only thing she could recall of him was the occasional faint mention of his name.

George had sent a message to his brother a week before, telling him that Annabelle would be visiting with him for a while. It was the only safe place that George could think of to hide Annabelle's shame. He was desperate. Since she was born, George wasted no time in boasting to everyone how pretty and well bred his daughter was. His shame was even more magnified by the recent engagement he had imposed on Rafeek Baksh. George would rather die than to face Mr Baksh ever again.

The day after Annabelle's visit to the doctor, George's worst fear was realized. He was seated in the shed at the rear of the house, when suddenly, like a raging bull, Mr Baksh confronted him with a tirade of insults.

"You bastard, George Castello! You bastard! You tried to stick me and my son with someone else's child. What kind of man are you?" Mr Baksh blared.

George turned his head in shame. Tears gathered in his tired eyes. He could not remember the last time he cried.

Mr Baksh shouted, "What the hell! You think you could have gotten away with that? Trying to make my son the laughing stock of Rio Claro?" Mr Baksh paused before declaring, "That whore—"

Before he could finish his statement, George flew up in a fit of rage, knocking Mr Baksh to the ground with his fist. As Mr Baksh lay on the ground, George reached for a shovel and began to beat him. A few villagers arrived in the nick of time to rescue Mr Baksh from being badly hurt or even murdered. George was arrested and charged with inflicting severe bodily harm on Mr Baksh. He was released on bail to appear in court in two months. But three weeks later, Mr Baksh, who had suffered a fractured arm and rib, dropped all charges. He told the police that George had suffered enough.

It was by accident that Mr Baksh learned about Annabelle's pregnancy. He ran into Dr Ramnath at the grocery store. The doctor shook his hand and congratulated him on the expected birth of his first grandchild. Mr Baksh rushed home to interrogate his son.

The blunt sound of a car horn echoed through the stillness of predawn. Annabelle, whose eyes were heavy with sleep, lifted her languid body from the bed and headed for the car, straining under the weight of the heavy travelling bag. No one, including George and Rosey, went to bid her farewell. As the car negotiated the darkness with its dim headlights, Annabelle glanced at Ricardo's abandoned house. Miss Simon had left to visit her daughter in England to recuperate, and Ricardo had disappeared after the confrontation with George.

Ricardo was unaware of Annabelle's condition when he paid a friendly visit to George the evening following the visit to the doctor. Rosabelle pushed her head through the window to gesture him away with her hand. He mistook the gesture for a friendly greeting and continued toward the shed.

"Good evening," Ricardo said.

There was no answer from George. He sat staring at Ricardo with contempt in his eyes.

"Is something wrong?" Ricardo asked.

George rushed up, grabbed him by the neck, and choked him until he gasped for breath. Lucky for him, Rosabelle sounded an alarm, and George was restrained by a villager. Ricardo began to shiver. He had never seen George this angry in all his life and instinctively knew that he had found out about him and Annabelle.

Ricardo got up and ran as fast as he could.

The crowing of cocks heralded the dawn as the car stalled for the second time. Annabelle sat in the vehicle, pondering her life. She felt alone and depressed and that she would have been better off dead. She heard the driver say that he would get the car started in a jiffy, but she didn't really care. As far as she was concerned, she should have ignored everyone, including her pa, and eloped with Ricardo.

The car had driven a far distance when it again started to jolt before coming to an abrupt halt. The frail, elderly driver lifted the bonnet and hollered, "I'll get it started in a jiffy, don't worry."

After fidgeting with the engine for nearly a half hour, he declared, "Sorry, miss, but the car won't start. We'll have to walk the rest of the way."

The morning sun cast shadows in front of them as Annabelle and the driver, whose name she had only just learned was Joseph, made their way along the main road of the small town of Arouca. After passing the Catholic church, Joseph suggested that they rest for a while.

"How far again?" Annabelle asked.

"My child, we have just started our journey," Joseph replied.

He pointed to a narrow track which meandered up the mountains.

"We're going up there?" Annabelle asked.

"Yep, we are," Joseph replied.

Annabelle hung her head in utter frustration.

They had walked for about a half hour when Annabelle lamented, "I can't walk another inch. This is terrible. Is there another way to get to my uncle?"

From the distressed look on her face, Joseph decided to rest. They took refuge from the scorching sun under a mango tree.

"How far are we from my uncle's house?" Annabelle asked.

"About three, four miles up the mountains," Joseph replied.

"Are you mad? I can't walk that distance," Annabelle carped.

"Wait here, miss. I'll be back shortly," Joseph said.

Just when Annabelle began to worry about Joseph's whereabouts, she spotted a donkey cart coming up the hill with Joseph sitting next to the driver.

He hailed out to her as they approached. "Get in. We'll be chauffeur driven all the way," he jested. "And the driver know your uncle."

Annabelle heaved a sigh of relief.

Joseph had offered the donkey-cart driver some money to transport them up the tedious track. He confessed to Annabelle that he himself could not make the journey on foot.

As the soothing breeze hit her face, Annabelle's mind drifted off to Bristol Village. She wondered where Ricardo was hiding and if she'd ever see him again.

The driver, whose name was Pablo, was a thin, middle-aged man with missing front teeth and wrinkled skin. His lips were stained by the pipe he carried in his shirt pocket. He was a talkative, affable man who knew everybody in the village. He earned his livelihood by transporting cocoa and coffee down the mountains to the main road with his donkey cart, from where it was transported by lorry to the buying agent in Port-of-Spain. He tried to amuse Annabelle with funny stories about the village, but she hardly heard a word he said. He pointed to the rivers and streams and exotic creatures, but that didn't interest her either. The bottomless precipices did, however, scare her.

"What if we fall over?" she asked. Both men laughed at her remark.

Between her wavering state of mind, Annabelle heard him mention on a few occasions, "She treat him like he was her own son, and he loved her the same as if she was his real mother." and wondered who Pablo was talking about.

Pablo continued, "It was a real sad occasion when she dead. She hold on to him on her dying bed, saying, 'You are my son. Don't let them tell you anything different! You're my son, and you'll always be my son!'"

Tears filled Pablo's eyes as he related the story to Joseph.

"Who is he talking about?" Annabelle asked.

"Your uncle Kelvin, of course," Pablo replied.

"But my pa said that Kelvin has no children," Annabelle said.

Pablo did not answer. He remained cautiously quiet.

Perhaps he's just a silly old man, Annabelle thought.

The sun was high in the sky when the donkey cart reached the village of Lopinot. Annabelle stared in awe at the quaint little village tucked away in the forested mountains. There was something eerie about this place, she thought. It was as though it belonged to another era. Over to her right stood a large, abandoned estate framed by towering, old trees with a huge, dilapidated estate house at one end and smaller structures scattered throughout the grounds.

"What's that building?" Annabelle asked.

"That, my child, used to be La Re-con-na-is-sance—in English, it mean 'the Lookout.' It used to belong to the owner of the estate, Charles Joseph Comte de Lopinnot.

He was a Frenchman with royal blood who came here in 1800 with family and slaves," Pablo related.

The story intrigued Annabelle, but she was too daunted by her dilemma to pay it any mind. The donkey cart came to an eventual stop in front of a thatched cottage. A slim, sprightly man emerged and headed toward them.

He pelted his cigarette stub on the ground and, with a big smile, greeted Pablo. "I see you come up the hill again," he said.

"Yeah, boy, Kelvin, and this time I bring you a surprise visitor," Pablo replied.

"Yes," Kelvin said, "George daughter. I was expecting her."

Kelvin wiped his hand on his trousers and reached out to shake Annabelle's hand. "Welcome to Lopinot," he said.

Annabelle responded by nodding her head. She observed that he looked nothing like her pa. He was slim, tall, and darker than George, with a straight nose and piercing hazel eyes. He retrieved Annabelle's bag from the cart and invited the men inside for a cup of coffee.

It was, without a doubt, the longest and most tiring day of her life, Annabelle carped.

She lay on the small, uncomfortable bed, feeling alone and depressed. The night was pitch-black—ten times darker than Bristol Village, she observed.

She would give anything to be in her own bed in Bristol Village. It was the first time in all her life that she was away from home for more than a day. She consoled herself with the notion that George would come and take her home. He loved her too much to torture her like this.

Annabelle had just opened her eyes from a shallow sleep to the sound of crowing cocks. She was in a state of disorientation, thinking for a moment that she was at home in Bristol Village. It was the most uncomfortable night she had ever experienced, and she could not bear the thought of spending another night there.

She lay in bed feeling sorry for herself, conjuring up sad memories from her childhood. She remembered going to Rio Claro with her pa and getting lost. She felt scared and helpless and started to cry. Then from nowhere, George came running to her, holding her in his strong embrace. She felt safe again in his arms. He was probably on his way to Lopinot right now to get her.

Tired from lack of sleep, she drifted in and out of slumber. Then suddenly, she sprang up and sat on the bed. She thought she heard the sound of George's voice. She listened attentively. She distinctly heard George's voice. She frantically pulled on a dress over her nightgown, brushed her hair, washed her mouth in the basin, and bolted for the living room.

"Pa, Pa!" she shouted.

But to her dismay, she came face-to-face with a young man who not only sounded like George but looked like him.

She froze in disbelief. Her mouth remained agape.

"Good morning. Did you sleep well?" Kelvin asked.

Annabelle stood transfixed, gawking at the young man.

"This is your cousin Gerald," Kelvin said.

Annabelle did not respond, her eyes riveted on the young man.

"I'm Gerald, your cousin," he replied with outstretched arm.

"Oh, I'm sorry. Just that you look so much like my pa," Annabelle said as she shook his hand.

Annabelle gulped down a cup of coffee just to please her uncle before returning to her room. She felt ill at ease in the company of two strangers who kept asking embarrassing questions. Gerald, whom she had never met before, asked about her husband. It was obvious to her that she and her pregnancy were discussed, perhaps in a sordid sort of way, between them. She knew that her pa had told Kelvin that she was pregnant but wasn't sure what else Pa might have disclosed.

As she lay in bed, staring aimlessly at the dingy ceiling, she recalled that she had heard the name Gerald before, but try as she might, she could not find the connection regarding the name. Then, like a bolt of lightning, it hit her. "Oh my gosh!" she said to herself. "Gerald is not Kelvin's son." Then in dawned on her what Pablo meant when he said, "Don't let them tell you that you were not my son." He was talking about Kelvin's dying wife.

Miss Queenie was not an old, silly woman after all; she knew exactly what she was talking about. Annabelle's mind drifted back to her engagement party at the Baksh's home in Rio Claro.

Most of the guests at the party had departed, leaving a small group of relatives and close friends behind. Annabelle threw her tired body onto a sofa in the gallery when the frail, raspy voice of an elderly woman called out to her.

"Come over here, my child. I didn't get a chance to speak with you," the woman said.

Annabelle, not wanting to appear rude, forced her languid body from the chair and went over to the woman.

"Sit down, child. Let's chat a little," the woman insisted.

Annabelle recognized the woman as Miss Queenie— she was widely known among the townspeople for her midwifery skill. She must have delivered half the people at the party. In fact, she boasted to Annabelle that it was she who delivered all of George's four children. *Silly woman,* Annabelle thought—*there are only three of us.*

"Child, do you know the true meaning of marriage? Nowadays you young people treat marriage like a game. I hope you are aware that you have to be submissive to your husband and do as he says. You young people want to have your own way, but that don't work. In my days, you had to respect your husband as though he was your father."

Annabelle let out a yawn, hoping that the woman would take a hint and leave her alone, but she continued in her husky, almost manly tone.

"I remember when your brother was born; I delivered him. Child, that was a sad, sad day. I could still hear his cry as he came into the world. Oh, but his mother, poor thing, she did not even get to hold him. The good Lord called her away."

Annabelle stared at the woman, perplexed and annoyed. She couldn't be talking about Danny. After all, Rosey was still alive. Then it dawned on Annabelle that perhaps Miss Queenie mistook her for someone else.

Tears rolled down her dark wrinkled face as she continued to relate the incident to Annabelle.

"By the time the doctor came, she had already died. Some folks blamed me for her death, but there was nothing I could do—but I felt so helpless. That was the only mother I ever lost. Joan, wherever you are, I'm so sorry."

She paused to dry her eyes with a white handkerchief tied to a keychain and continued.

"Child, your father cried like a baby. He didn't want to hold the child. He said the child was a bad omen, for he killed his mother. I took the child home, and the first thing

I did was to take the child to Father Christopher for him to christen. I called him Gerald Paul. But I was in no position to care for a newborn child. When he turned three, four months, I sent for George. He took the child and sent him for his brother in Lopinot to care for."

That old woman has to be insane. I have no brother by the name of Gerald Paul. And who the hell is Joan? Poor thing, age has taken its toll on her, Annabelle thought.

Annabelle now knew what the melancholy look on her pa's face meant. Later that evening when she related the old woman's story to Pa, she was puzzled by his response. He never responded in words, but she noticed how sad he became as she rehashed the old woman's tale to him.

George had just gotten married to Rosey, whom he despised. He found respite in a bar in Rio Claro, which he frequented almost every night. Shortly after, he became acquainted with a waitress by the name of Joan. Perhaps it was vulnerability, intoxication, or both, but one thing led to another, and soon George became intimate with her. A few months later, she told George that she was pregnant. George had planned to leave Rosey and move in with her when the child was born. After Joan died in childbirth, George was devastated and fell into the arms of another waitress at the bar by the name of Millie, who had recently separated from her husband. Her husband found out that she was sharing a house with George, where he later dropped off their four children. A week later, news came that Millie's husband had fatally shot himself. George blamed himself for the suicide and felt obligated to take care of Millie and her children.

The weeks and months passed slowly by, and Annabelle had finally begun to adjust to life in Lopinot and had grown fond of her uncle Kelvin and her cousin Gerald, who visited his father more frequently now. She never did disclose to Gerald that he was actually her brother, though someday she perhaps would. She was now ripe with the features of expectant motherhood and no longer went traversing the valley with Gerald. She spent most of her time in the house doing chores, but Uncle Kelvin would scold her and insist that she spend more time in bed until the baby came.

As she lay in bed pondering over how much her life would change when the baby came, she thought about Gerald and the secret about his life that he didn't know and might never find out. She wondered too if her baby would ever know its father and if she'd ever see Ricardo again.

It was an overcast morning when she accompanied Gerald on one of their walks in the valley, when they shared their innermost thoughts with each other. They went to the Lopinot cemetery, where he showed her the old grave, which contained the remains of the count and his family. Annabelle saw the sorrow in his eyes as he picked a wild flower and placed it on a grave. She instinctively knew it was his mother's grave. If only he knew—but she cast aside the thought. It was the wrong time and place to tell him, and perhaps it was not her place at all.

She walked up to him, placed her arm around his shoulder, and held him tenderly for a moment. Just then, a drizzle of rain caused them to begin their journey back to the house. Annabelle kept her arms around his waist until they were home. There was so much of Pa in him, Annabelle thought.

It was a lazy Saturday afternoon when Annabelle's routine was interrupted in an unanticipated turn of events. She was sitting on the step daydreaming when she heard the gentle voice of a child calling out to her,

"Miss, miss." She looked up and came face-to-face with a little boy staring at her with a note in his outstretched hand. Annabelle took the note from the boy with a smile of appreciation on her face. She brimmed with curiosity as she eagerly opened the note. Streams of excitement engulfed her as she tediously lifted her bloated body from the stair. The little boy waited for her as she slipped on her shoes. "Are you going to take me to the gentleman who sent you with the note?" Annabelle asked.

He nodded his head in agreement and proceeded to lead the way. She lumbered behind, grimacing her face in discomfort from her pregnancy but filled with excitement. The note was from Ricardo, who waited by the river for her. He said that he had only recently discovered where she was.

She had walked only a few yards when she spotted the figure of a man walking briskly toward the house. As he approached, she recognized the man to be Joseph—the man who had brought her to Lopinot. He had such a menacing look on his face that Annabelle turned around and followed him, leaving the boy behind. She stood behind Joseph as he knocked on the door.

"Kelvin! Kelvin! Where are you? I have something urgent to tell you," he said.

Kelvin opened the door, frantic. Before he could say anything, Joseph blurted, "Get Annabelle ready right away. I come to take her home. George want to see her. He fall sick. She must come right away!"

Annabelle placed her hand over her mouth and cried, "Oh my gosh! Pa! What's wrong with Pa?"

Joseph turned and stared at her in shock, as he did not recognize her. "Pregnant?" he asked.

In less than fifteen minutes, Annabelle and Joseph were on their way to Bristol Village. Ricardo, unaware of what had transpired, sat by the river, anxiously awaiting Annabelle. He held a gold ring in his hand, staring at it with a smug look on his face. Darkness had fallen when he slowly got up and walked away with a profound look of dejection on his face. He was swallowed up by self-pity. Annabelle had turned him down, he thought.

It was night when Annabelle and Joseph approached the hamlet of Bristol Village. She was filled with anxiety as the car negotiated the sharp bends with its dim headlights and noisy exhaust. She prayed for Joseph to hurry, but he was doing the best he could. Her heart flipped as he cleared the bend and the house came into view.

Who are all those people? What are they doing there? Why's there a tent? Her mind was filled with a barrage of questions. She tried to remain calm as she stepped out the car. Maybe it's a thanksgiving service, she consoled herself. Her feet were, however, weak as she approached the gathering. All eyes were fixed on her as she approached. When she reached inside, she felt the life in her body drain to her feet. She fainted in the arms of a woman. The sight which greeted her was too much for her to bear.

The cold body of George lay in an icebox illuminated by burning candles.

Chapter 18

• •

A loud pounding on the front door jolted Annabelle
Johnson Reed from her nostalgic reverie into the
past. She took a few moments to compose herself before
proceeding to the door of the beachfront villa, moving
at her own pace amid piles of boxes and unpacked
furniture. The light which pierced through the undraped
window illuminated her face and exposed the age marks
and wrinkles. It was one of those rare moments that she
showed her face without make-up. She ran her hand
through her ruffled hair before opening the door.

A crew of men in blue coveralls stood on the large
gallery, straining under heavy boxes.

"Good afternoon, Mrs Reed. These are the last of your
things from Port-of-Spain," a member of the crew said.

She opened the door and gestured them inside, where
they deposited the cartons.

She hurried back inside to tidy up the bedroom before
Joyanne returned from Bristol Village, where she had
gone to tend to her home. She opened a box and retrieved

a small leather case, which she placed against her cheek, and smiled endearingly.

She opened the case, which was lined with red velvet, and gently removed a tiara of glittering rhinestone and placed it on her head. She looked at herself in the mirror and twisted her lips into a bittersweet, contemplative smile. *This crown changed my life forever,* she said to herself as her mind wandered off into a montage of memories.

It was two weeks after George's funeral. His untimely loss created a void in the home and had relegated Rosey into a hysterical maniac. All her life, she had always relied on someone else. First, it was her father, and then it was George. Now, there was no one, no money, and more mouths to feed. She would sit in the hammock and shout, "Oh God, why me? Why me?" Then she would erupt in a tirade. "George gone. Annabelle bring a fatherless child. Everyone leave and gone!"

With no one to tend to the garden, food was scarce, and there was Annabelle's baby to support. The baby, whom Annabelle named Joyanne Theodora, was born the day after George's funeral. Rosey carped to everyone that Annabelle and the baby had killed George. Annabelle was weak and sickly after the birth and could no longer sew. She too blamed herself for George's death and would lie in bed and sob. Rosabelle fought with her every day, blaming her for George's death and Ricardo's sudden departure from the village.

Rosey could not bear the fights and squabbling between her daughters and would shout at the top of her voice, "Oh God, I want to die! Please deliver me from this burden!"

To add to her woes, the little money she had saved in a brown bag under the mattress went toward paying legal fees for Danny. He—along with four other boys from the village—was held for the burglary of a store in Rio Claro and was made to stand trial. Rosey was relieved when he was incarcerated in an institution for delinquent boys in Port-of-Spain until he turned eighteen.

Annabelle was on her feet again and was able to sew and earn a little money for the upkeep of the home and her baby. She sat in the gallery, hemming a garment next to Rosey, who cradled the baby in her arms, while Ricardo, who had returned to Bristol Village a few days earlier, sat on the stairs with a distant look in his eyes. Rosey did not welcome him with open arms. In fact, no words were spoken between them. He too was burdened by guilt at George's death and felt a deep sense of obligation not only to Annabelle and his baby but to all of George's family. Although Rosey blamed him for George's death, deep inside, she was glad that he had returned. After all, the family needed a man around the house to tend to the garden and livestock. Ricardo stayed in the room downstairs. He had suffered a severe bout of depression when he thought that Annabelle had dumped him, and he piddled away the money Miss Simon had left him. The house, which had been left in his care, fell into a state of dilapidation.

The Saturday afternoon was bright and peaceful when a strong wind blew unexpectedly and rustled the trees, causing the heavy shadows cast across the yard to dance and sway. When the wind subsided into a gentle breeze, an exquisite-looking car pulled up in front of the house. All eyes stared with utter curiosity at the red, shiny car from which a tall, dark man in a cap alighted and proceeded to open the back door, offering his arm to a slim, elegantly attired, middle-aged lady. She wore a blue suit trimmed with white lace and a large blue hat, which shaded her well-manicured, attractive face from the sun. She was brown skinned with small eyes and a turned-up nose and wide mouth lined with red lipstick. All eyes followed her as she stepped gingerly up the stairs and into the gallery.

"Hello, everyone. You all are probably wondering who this stranger is," she said in a warm, refined tone. She giggled at their silence and the blank expressions on their faces. "Well, I won't keep you all in suspense any longer. I am Catherine, Rosey's half-sister." She turned to Rosey and asked, "Don't you remember me? We met at our father's funeral many years ago."

Rosey jumped to her feet and rushed over to the woman, impulsively planting a kiss on her cheek. "Oh yes, I remember. You and your sister came to the funeral. What's her name again?" Rosey asked.

"Oh, that was Gertrude," Catherine said. "She's now in England but asked me to convey her sympathy to you and the children."

Rosey offered her a chair and said, "Sorry to have you standing. Please, sit down."

"Thank you," Catherine said as she dusted the chair with her hand and sat down. "Oh, I'm so sorry to learn about the death of your husband. I'm sorry I could not be with you, but I was in Europe at the time and only recently returned home."

"Thank you," Rosey replied, wondering how Catherine knew about George's passing, but she felt that asking her might be impolite.

Catherine looked around and deduced that things were not well with Rosey and the family—their ragged clothes, the squalid surroundings, and the dingy clothes on the baby. She felt that offering money to Rosey might offend her, but in any event, Catherine's visit had an ulterior motive. She wanted a naive country girl to work at her home in Port-of-Spain, and she remembered that Rosey had a daughter or two. She revealed that in the past year she had dismissed three maids for either stealing or having adulterous relationships with her partner. Rosey immediately suggested Annabelle, which delighted Catherine. She assured Rosey that, in return, she would educate and provide opportunities for Annabelle and that part of Annabelle's salary would be sent to Rosey each month.

Rosey was elated.

Before Catherine left, Rosey called her aside and told her, "Can we talk about a private matter?"

"Certainly," Catherine said.

Rosey said, "I will send Annabelle under one condition—and that is you keep her in Port-of-Spain for at least a year or so. Don't allow her to come back home. You see, the child she has is from the boy sitting on the step. He not working nowhere and can't see about the child. I want to keep Annabelle away from him. I'm afraid that she might have another child, and things already hard around here. In any event, George had plans to send her away, to keep her from seeing that boy, but George died."

Catherine empathized with Rosey and agreed to keep Annabelle in Port-of-Spain for a while.

A week later, a slight drizzle from the overcast sky greeted Annabelle as she alighted from the car in front of the train station in Rio Claro. Ricardo followed behind with a large travelling bag in one hand and the baby in the other. Her fat cheeks rested against his neck, partially lifting the pink bonnet off her head and exposing her closed eyes and the thumb in her mouth.

Annabelle sat next to Ricardo with the baby in his lap inside the choked building, waiting to board the train. Her eyes lacked the eagerness of a week before when Aunt Catherine invited her to Port-of-Spain. The reality of leaving Ricardo and the baby behind quelled the excitement of the fabulous life in the city she had daydreamed about.

She was consumed by sadness and distressing thoughts. What if she never saw them again? What if her baby forgot her or Ricardo found someone else? She held on to Ricardo and the baby as though she did not want to let go. Choked up with sadness, she hesitantly boarded the train, promising that she would soon return.

The atmosphere felt different when she awoke in Port-of-Spain. It was intimidating and lonely. Her ambivalent mind drifted back to Ricardo and Joyanne; she desperately wanted to go home, but everyone was depending on her to survive—even her baby.

She was at first excited by the ambiance which greeted her in Port-of-Spain. She felt like a princess in the fairy tales with which her pa regaled her as a child. This was the life she had dreamed of; she could not believe it was unfolding right before her eyes.

It was late evening when the train had arrived in South Quay, Port-of-Spain. She was chauffeured to her destination in Aunt Catherine's car. Her eyes pierced through the window to capture the sights of the capital city, which she was experiencing for the very first time. She felt as though she were in a foreign land as the car made its way around the Queen's Park Savannah with its stately buildings and picturesque landscape.

The car stopped in front of a large colonial-styled house in the posh neighbourhood of St Clair. The chauffeur opened the door, and she stepped out on a pathway lined with colourful shrubs and flowers. She stared in awe at the house with its ornate gallery and carved balusters. The chauffeur pressed a button, and a man decked in dark trousers and white shirt opened the door and beckoned her inside. She was greeted by a large, shimmering crystal chandelier which reminded her of the picture of Cinderella's castle in the storybook. A large hat stand with a huge mirror occupied the lily-white wall which faced her, and a large painting of a dark-skinned woman with her breasts partially exposed, which caused Annabelle to blush, occupied the opposite wall.

She was led inside another room where her feet became submerged in lush red carpet. This has to be a dream. This could not be real, she thought. The soft light from a smaller chandelier illuminated a large piano to her right and two polished cabinets filled with expensive plates and glasses. A three-piece living room suite stood around an ornate coffee table topped with candles and magazines. Annabelle hesitantly sat on the edge an armchair facing a painting of a woman who resembled Aunt Catherine. She twitched at the sound of approaching footsteps and nervously awaited the opening of the door.

The door was pulled open and she was now facing the woman whom she had seen for the first time a week before in Bristol Village. Only this time she looked serious and haughty.

"Come with me," Aunt Catherine said in an abrupt tone. "I'll show you to your room. We'll talk at dinner. I know you must be tired; you can freshen up and have a short nap before dinner. Dinner is at seven thirty. Don't be late."

Annabelle followed Aunt Catherine to a spacious corridor and into a large bedroom where a woman was making the bed. Aunt Catherine introduced them.

"Miss Boxhill, this is Annabelle, whom I told you about. And, Annabelle, this is my housekeeper, Miss Boxhill. You may call on her should you need anything."

It was already close to seven o'clock when Annabelle came out of the bathroom in awe. It was the first time in her life that she actually stepped out of a shower and into her bedroom. This was a welcome change from the outdoor bathroom in Bristol Village where she had to carry water in a bucket and pour it on her body with an enamel cup. It was her first taste of the good life, and she revelled in it. The full image of herself in the tall mirrors fascinated her. She twisted her body in photographic poses and gazed at herself in the four mirrors. She suddenly got a notion to look at herself completely naked. She looked around to ensure that no one was there and walked to the door to ensure that it was locked. She dropped the towel in the middle of the room and waltzed across the floor stark naked, imitating a ballet dancer. She was pleased with what she saw in the mirror and called to mind an expression she had heard from a women in the village: "A woman's looks and body can open doors."

But in the midst of her indulgence, she was overcome with guilt; she wished Ricardo and Joyanne could be here with her.

It was 7.20 when she remembered that dinner was to be served in ten minutes. She quickly opened her bag, pulled out a duster coat, and hurriedly dressed herself. She followed the direction of Aunt Catherine's voice and found herself in the entrance of the dining room. She was about to enter when she was distracted by busy footsteps behind her. She turned around to find Miss Boxhill gesturing her to stop.

"Miss Annabelle, where are you going?" she chided.

"To dinner," Annabelle replied.

"Are you mad? Please come with me back to your room!" Miss Boxhill said.

She treaded behind Miss Boxhill with a confused look on her face.

"Sit down, miss!" Miss Boxhill said. "You can't go to dinner dressed like that! You'd embarrass Madam. She has her friends over to meet you. Dinner is a dress-up occasion!"

Annabelle felt embarrassed, but Miss Boxhill was sympathetic. She went through her clothes and picked out one of her church dresses.

"This one would do fine," Miss Boxhill said.

"But this is my church dress," Annabelle protested.

"Don't argue with me, child," Miss Boxhill retorted.

Annabelle slipped on the dress, and Miss Boxhill assisted her with her hair and make-up. Annabelle left the room, beaming with self-confidence.

It was the dead of night when Annabelle eased herself off the bed and into the chair in the corner of the bedroom. She was rankled with sad and nerve-racking thoughts. She wondered what Joyanne was doing. Was she missing her? She felt an enormous urge to hold her in her arms. And Ricardo? Was he thinking of her as much as she was thinking of him? She wondered what Aunt Catherine and her hoity-toity friends thought about her. She felt like a slave, having to do what other people wanted her to do. She was afraid to even come out of her room without permission. She thought of Bristol Village where she was free to do as she liked.

The mortifying experience of her first night in Port-of-Spain besieged her.

Four women were engrossed in conversation when she arrived in the dining room. She stood in the entrance for a moment until Aunt Catherine spotted her in the corner of her eye and gulped down the drink from her glass before springing to her feet.

"Ladies, this is my niece whom I told you about," said Aunt Catherine.

Annabelle lifted her head timidly and nodded to each of the ladies as she was introduced. She was afraid to speak for fear that she might say something stupid.

The plump woman in the group declared in a deep masculine tone, "She's prettier than you described, Catherine. A bit shy, but pretty."

The other ladies walked up to her and kissed her on the cheek.

Annabelle felt inept and clumsy throughout dinner—it was like some sort of rich people's ritual which she knew nothing about. The setting of the table was intimidating, and she had no idea of what she was eating. She observed the women and tried tediously to follow what they did. The fork fell from her hand; she choked on the sherry, bringing it up on her dress; she could not comprehend the vocabulary the women used and spoke out of context. She had never felt so humiliated in all her life. In addition to which, there was a significant age difference between her and these women. The conversations were either above her learning or the people and situations were foreign to her.

The women sickened Annabelle; she found them obnoxious but had to tolerate them and show them respect. She was in a strange environment, and they were Aunt Catherine's friends. They drank until their tongues became heavy, gossiping and badmouthing their husbands in the most shameful manner. Through their conversations, Annabelle gleaned that Aunt Catherine was in some sort of relationship with a man whom they referred to as T.J., but Aunt Catherine remained silent whenever his name came up.

Annabelle stared repulsively at the fattest of the three women, known as Dorothy. She was well attired in a blue silk dress, white shoes, and a string of pearls around her stumpy neck. She looked at Annabelle with drowsy eyes and spoke in a heavy tongue about a relationship she shared with her gardener, explicitly describing her sexual encounters when her husband departed for the office. The youngest of the women, a slim one with bony feet and a thin, long face, laughed in the most scandalous manner at the crude discourse, sipping her sherry with a look of ecstasy on her face.

That drink tastes awful, Annabelle thought to herself, squirming her face. *How can they drink that terrible thing without vomiting?*

The oldest among the group, Mary, a stout woman with large ears and freckled face, occasionally gawked at Aunt Catherine, whose face was flushed with embarrassment. She stared at Annabelle with compassionate eyes and said, "Ladies, there's a young girl in our midst. Have some respect."

"She has to learn the facts of life, you old prune," Dorothy said. The comment incited a fit of laughter from the group; the bony one spilled the glass of sherry on her lap.

Aunt Catherine intervened and said, "Annabelle dear, you look tired. You are excused."

Annabelle jumped to her feet with relief and left the room. As she headed up the corridor, she looked back and mumbled, "You old shameless bats!"

Morning came too soon for Annabelle. She wished she could stay in the safe sanctuary of her bedroom forever. She wondered if she had to be up by a certain time, as there seemed to be a rule for everything in that house, she grumbled. She got up with little enthusiasm, assailed by thoughts of Joyanne and Ricardo, and went to the bathroom. She dressed herself in a duster coat and headed for the kitchen.

"Oh my gosh," she said. "This might not be appropriate for breakfast."

She turned around and frantically searched the house for Miss Boxhill, whom she found in the laundry room.

"How am I supposed to dress for breakfast?" she asked.

Miss Boxhill looked at her from head to toe and said, "You can go as you are; there are no guests except for Madam's gentleman."

"Madam's gentleman?" Annabelle asked.

"Oh, go on along. Madam will introduce you. He's a member of the household, you know," Miss Boxhill said.

But Annabelle rushed back to her room and sat in front of the mirror, fixing her face and hair. She sprayed some perfume behind her ears before proceeding to the breakfast table. She paused for a moment as she entered the room. Aunt Catherine's back was facing her, and seated opposite was a tall, strapping figure of a man, holding a newspaper directly in front his face. His powerful hands wore a thick, gold watch, and an enormous ring with a red stone protruded off his right index finger. Only the top of his balding head fringed with light brown hair was visible. It appeared to Annabelle that whatever relationship Aunt Catherine and this man, whom she assumed was T.J., shared, it was not—she searched her mind for an appropriate word—friendly, romantic, or whatever, for there was absolutely no communication between them. Or perhaps they had talked all morning long and were now exhausted.

Catherine sat with a distant look in her eyes, sipping a cup of coffee and smoking a cigarette as Annabelle nervously entered the room and, trying to sound as polite as she possibly could, said, "Good morning."

"Good morning, dear. Did you sleep well?" Catherine replied, sounding more cordial than before.

"Yes, Auntie, I slept okay," Annabelle said.

Catherine turned to T.J., who was still holding the newspaper in front his face, thoroughly absorbed by whatever he was reading, while Annabelle anxiously awaited an introduction.

"Tom, this is my niece from Bristol Village, whom I told you about," Catherine said.

He moved the newspaper slowly away from his face and stared at her for a while.

Annabelle was uncomfortable at his gruff and imposing appearance. He folded the paper, rested it on the table, and looked at her.

"Hello, dear," he said. "I'm Tom Johnson. Pleased to make your acquaintance."

His voice was quite cordial and directly contrasted with his grim appearance, Annabelle observed. Her tense demeanour eased, and she smiled affectionately at him.

He removed his spectacles, placing them in his pocket, and continued to stare at her through piercing blue eyes.

"Your aunt omitted to tell me how beautiful you were," he said. "I can tell that we'll get along very well. You may call me T.J.; all my friends do."

Aunt Catherine looked at him with repulsion in her eyes.

He continued to leer at Annabelle, making her uncomfortable. She couldn't find the word to describe the manner in which he looked at her, but it was the same way Ricardo looked at her at the dance. Then the word came to her—lustful.

Despite his age, for he could be her father's age or even older, he was a strong, strapping, handsome man, she thought, with a long face and a straight nose. She especially admired his imposing personality. She was sure that no one was brave enough to oppose him, not even Aunt Catherine.

She noticed the uneasiness on Aunt Catherine's face when T.J. spoke or looked at her. She couldn't help but wonder why.

Aunt Catherine got up and poured herself another cup of coffee and scolded herself for bringing Annabelle to Port-of-Spain. From the way T.J. looked at Annabelle, she was sure that it would be the same thing all over again. She must find an excuse to send Annabelle back home, soon!

Chapter 19

• •

The evening sun cast a mélange of shadows beneath the Poui trees—resplendent in pink and yellow hues against the distant, forested Northern Range. Annabelle felt like Alice in Wonderland as she strolled hand in hand with T.J. around the Queen's Park Savannah. She no longer felt uncomfortable around him. She had discovered that behind the sinister façade was a funny and thoughtful man who made her feel comfortable and at home. He brought her chocolates and fashion magazines whenever he visited Aunt Catherine, for she had told him that her pa used to buy her chocolate on special occasions, such as birthdays and Christmas. And he observed that she possessed a penchant for sewing as she spent much of her leisure time behind Aunt Catherine's Singer machine creating fashionable clothing for herself and her aunt. On Saturdays, the two climbed into his jeep for tours of the city. Sometimes, he took her to the bookstores to peruse the latest books and novels. He told her that reading expanded the mind.

She could tell that Aunt Catherine was opposed to T.J.'s generosity by the disdainful expression that often emerged on her face. Annabelle wasn't quite sure whether Aunt Catherine was jealous or protective, although her instinct leaned more toward jealously.

She had sensed Aunt Catherine was most times "aloof"—a word she gleaned from T.J. Aunt Catherine often treated her like a stranger, almost like one of the servants. Although she knew that her aunt had brought her to Port-of-Spain to help around the house, she expected to be treated like family.

T.J., on the other hand, treated her like a friend—a much-needed friend in a strange and intimidating place, far away from home. She felt secure in his company, the same way she felt in Pa's arm as a child. Memories of George flashed through her mind—she conjured up childhood moments when George took her to Rio Claro and held her firm in his strong hands. There was this one time when she pulled away from him, darted across the street, and narrowly escaped being knocked down by an approaching car. George dropped his bag, sprinted toward her, and lifted her against his chest with tears in his eyes.

She was intrigued by the history and legends of the places of interest with which T.J. regaled her as they strolled along, looking like father and daughter, or even grandfather and granddaughter. His hand was now wrapped around her shoulder, and her face mirrored sheer ecstasy.

T.J. told her the names and history of the magnificent buildings which they passed on the way: the Roman Catholic Archbishop's Palace in a Romanesque-Irish-style architecture with a gallery of medieval arches, constructed at the turn of the century; the fairy-tale castle which was home to the eminent Stollmeyer family; the grand townhouse known as Hayes Court was home to the Anglican Bishop; the German Renaissance style of Queen's Royal College; the French Provisional architecture of Mille Fleurs, home to Dr Prada, who once served three terms as mayor of Port-of-Spain; Ambard's House, in fine Baroque style, stood as a testimony to the well-respected French family who earned their fortune from cocoa; Rosenweg—constructed in the style of a Venetian palace, home to Joseph Agostini, who made his fortune from sugar and cocoa.

Annabelle was intoxicated with excitement. She placed her arm around T.J.'s waist, and he responded by removing his hand from her shoulder to around her waist.

Upon reaching a bench beneath a Poui tree, T.J. suggested that they sit for a while. Annabelle felt as though she had known him all her life. She felt comfortable sharing her thoughts and secrets with him, as though he were her father. She knew no one could really take the place of George, but he filled a void in her life she thought no one could.

She was aware that Aunt Catherine was appalled at the friendship which had developed between T.J. and her, but she was not about to let anything come in the way of the gratifying feeling which engulfed her. In any event, Aunt Catherine was haughty toward her, especially when they were alone. She only pretended to be nice in front of company. Come to think of it, she really didn't like Aunt Catherine very much.

Annabelle and T.J. sipped coconut water as they chatted about his homeland of England. He told her about the royal parades, the horses and carriages, and he promised to take her to England to see the castles.

T.J. noticed that she had suddenly grown quiet and pensive and was no longer listening to what he was saying. He moved closer to her and placed his powerful hand behind her neck.

He asked, "What's wrong? You can tell me."

"I'm thinking about Ricardo and my baby," she said with a twinge of emotion in her voice.

"Are you uncomfortable with me holding you?" T.J. asked.

"I'd rather that you not hold me so close," she said.

He removed his arm from around her and asked, "What were you really thinking about?"

"I'm thinking about home," she replied.

"Anyone in particular?" he asked.

"Yes, I told you Ricardo and my baby," she replied with a hint of irritation in her voice. "And my father who died because of me."

"How could you say such a thing?" he exclaimed.

"'Cause it's true," she said with a slur in her voice.

"Do you want to talk about it?" he asked.

There was no response. She retrieved a handkerchief and blotted tears from her eyes.

"Why do people fall in love? It is as though love is a form of punishment," she carped.

His discourse which followed was well planned to play her naive mind like the strings of a guitar; after all, he was years ahead of her and extremely experienced in the ways of life.

"You seem to be the type of woman who aspires to be the best that she can be. Look around you. Can you honestly tell me that you would want to go back to Bristol Village? Fate has brought you here to Port-of-Spain and to me. You were born for bigger things. But of course you must make certain sacrifices in life if you want to get ahead.

You can't allow a man who cannot give you anything to stand in the way and prevent you from achieving your dreams. Your daughter is better off with your sister. I'm sure your sister will give her love and everything she needs. If you truly love your daughter, you will aspire to be successful, not only for yourself but for her. I'm sure you'd want to give her all of the things you didn't have. Don't look back, look ahead."

The words "you were born for bigger things" resounded in her mind as she headed back for Aunt Catherine's with T.J. by her side.

Dusk had fallen over the city of Port-of-Spain when Annabelle and T.J. arrived home. Annabelle proceeded to her room while T.J. went into the kitchen for a drink of whisky. He found Catherine at the dinner table with a faraway look on her face. She held a cigarette between her fingers in one hand, and her forehead was propped against her other hand. A cup of coffee next to her elbow was untouched. T.J. retrieved the newspaper from the dining table and eased his large frame into the recliner. He took a sip of the whisky and placed the glass down. No words, not even a glance, were exchanged between them.

The silence was eventually broken by the loud ringing of the telephone which was within arm's reach from T.J. Catherine glanced at him after the third ring, but he remained unperturbed. She angrily got up and proceeded to answer the telephone, and in a hushed tone, she responded to the caller, "I'm sorry, Dorothy. I don't think I'll be going. Something came up. Bye."

T.J. folded the newspaper and turned to look at her. "You've cancelled your trip to Tobago?" he asked.

She looked at him with revulsion and scampered out of the room. She returned a few moments later with a drink in her hand. "You think I'm so naive that I don't know about your plan?" she retorted.

He flung the newspaper to the ground and sprang from the chair with profound rage.

"What the hell are you talking about, woman?" he shouted.

She slammed the glass on the table and shouted, "You think I don't know that you are anxious to get me out of the house so you can be alone with my niece, to take advantage of her. You monster!"

He sprang up at her and slapped her so hard that she fell to the floor, hitting her head against the wall. His ring cut a deep incision on her face, and blood gushed from it.

The flight from Tobago was an uncomfortable experience for Catherine; there were anxious moments in the midst of what appeared to be a thunderstorm. It was an unrewarding trip. She was as daunted and jaded as when she had left home. Her morale was not uplifted as the doctor said it would be. Dorothy and the other ladies tried unsuccessfully to amuse her. A haunting premonition caused her to shorten her stay by a few days. How could she have been so stupid and naive? She wished the driver would go faster. Her heart pounded profusely against her chest. Her only consolation was that she could be wrong about her notion. Visions of desperation in T.J.'s eyes kept flashing through her mind. She too was just about Annabelle's age. The pain and turmoil came rushing through the years, as though it were just yesterday. She felt angry. She would kill him with her bare hands. That nasty vagabond! That rapist! As the car approached her home, her heart sank, and her feet grew weak as she forced herself from the car. She was right, but how she wished she were wrong. T.J.'s jeep was parked in the garage.

T.J. had concocted a scheme to dupe her into believing that he was going to London on business. She was sceptical at first, but when she saw the ticket and his packed suitcase, she was convinced that he was really going to London. She called Dorothy and told her that she would be going to Tobago after all.

It was past the hour of seven when a stunned Annabelle stumbled into the kitchen to find Aunt Catherine in tears, with a lit cigarette in her hand, spewing ash all over the table.

Annabelle was consumed by profound shame and guilt and retreated to the bedroom.

The repulsive manner in which Aunt Catherine looked at her was daunting.

Chapter 20

....

1949

The thick drapes in the bedroom of the townhouse blocked the light of the midmorning sun from seeping though. Annabelle had only just awakened with a nagging headache from the champagne she consumed the night before and wondering what time it was. She switched on the lamp to look at the clock and exclaimed, "Ten twenty!" She bolted from the bed and rushed to the bathroom, stripping off her clothes on the way. She scurried out of the apartment without breakfast and sped off for downtown Port-of-Spain, applying her make-up at the traffic light and constantly glancing at her watch.

"I hope the sales clerks have the sense to wait," she said to herself as the traffic light turned green.

She breathed a sigh of relief when she finally arrived at the store and saw the clerks waiting on her. She got out of the car and hurried toward them.

"Ladies, forgive me for being late, but the plumbing in the apartment developed a leak and flooded the entire place," she lied.

She opened the door to the exclusive store with a large sign above—Annabelle's Exclusive Fashions—and proceeded inside with the sales clerks tailing behind. After opening the cash register, she went over to the café across the street from the store for a cup of coffee. She sat sipping the coffee and watching the people passing by in the street, wondering what their lives must be like. She lit a cigarette and pondered over her own life.

Her relationship with Aunt Catherine had deteriorated to a state of disrepair. She could still vividly recall the repulsive look in Aunt Catherine's eyes and the intense guilt which she herself felt for coming between Aunt Catherine and T.J. But she was not about to give up T.J. He had promised her the moon and stars, and she was determined to get whatever she could from him. After all, he did tell her that meeting him was destined. There was no love between Aunt Catherine and T.J. anyway. Besides, Aunt Catherine treated her like one of the servants.

She pressed the cigarette butt in the ashtray and ordered another cup of coffee. The incident involving Aunt Catherine and her had happened a year ago. It was a quiet evening when Annabelle emerged from the safety of her bedroom where she was now spending most of her time. She tried hard to avoid Aunt Catherine and turned her head the other way when they crossed paths. She had gone to the kitchen to get something to eat, trying to be as quiet as possible. She was frightened out of her wits when she turned around to find Aunt Catherine standing in front of the doorway with visible affront in her eyes and tears rolling down her face. Annabelle stood transfixed with fear and shame. She made a bold move to walk away, but Aunt Catherine placed her hand against the doorway, blocking her from passing.

"You ungrateful bitch! You whore! After all I've done for you, you stole my man from me. He's old enough to be your grandfather! Bitch! Bitch!" Aunt Catherine screamed at the top of her voice, grabbing Annabelle by the hair, tugging it as hard as she could, and slamming her head against the wall.

Annabelle recoiled in horror and forced herself from Aunt Catherine's firm grip. She managed to free herself and bolted to her room, trembling. She could hear the rants of Aunt Catherine behind her.

"You whore! You ungrateful whore! Get out of my house! Get out of my house right now! Go! Go! Go!" Aunt Catherine ranted and raved like a madwoman, throwing anything she could find. Before long, the house looked as though it was ravaged by a storm.

Annabelle was sitting on the front stairs of the house with her head buried in her lap, sobbing hysterically, when T.J. arrived.

"What's going on here?" T.J. asked.

She did not reply.

He left her and hurried inside the house. The broken vases, overturned furniture, and ripped drapes strewn about the floor confirmed his suspicion. He hurried back to Annabelle and lifted her from the stairs with his strong arms. He placed her head on his shoulder and held her in a tight grip, stroking her hair.

"I'm so sorry; I should have taken you away from that insane witch a long time ago. Don't worry, I'll deal with her. Don't worry. Pack a few things, and I'll take you away from this hellhole," T.J. said.

The blanched moon hovered above in the dark sky as T.J. drove Annabelle to his home. There was absolute silence between them as the jeep travelled west of Port-of-Spain along the coastline. The fresh, pungent scent of fish from the nearby fishing village of Carenage wafted on the occasional breeze. Annabelle turned the window all the way up and proceeded to recline against the soft seat of the swanky jeep. She was not sure where T.J. lived. He visited Aunt Catherine at least five times a week. Sometimes he slept over, at times not. But he always departed for somewhere he called home. In the few years since she had been in Port-of-Spain, she had deduced a few things about T.J.: that his home was at least half an hour away from Aunt Catherine; that he had dogs which he often mentioned in his conversations; he spoke of a yard boy; he played golf; and he rubbed shoulders with politicians and businessmen.

Although he never spoke much about his profession, she knew that he either owned or held an executive position in the large motor car corporation, Sun Island Motors. Over the months, she had become quite friendly with his secretary over the telephone. They had never met in person, but they spoke for long periods on the phone. His secretary, whom she knew only as Suelyn, was especially pleasant to her. They spoke of fashion and people in the news and other things that young ladies spoke about.

A trickling of rain greeted them as the jeep came to a stop in front of a flat, plain house. T.J. went ahead to secure the large dogs which lurked about the bare yard. A few minutes later, he emerged from the rear of the house and gestured her to come inside. The loud barks of the dogs sent chills through her spine as she entered the compound.

"They are fierce animals," she said.

"They are only defending their territory," he replied.

"From a defenceless woman like me?" she said.

"To them, every stranger is an enemy. In any event, looks can be deceiving," he jested, slapping her bottom as she entered the house.

It was dark, perhaps the middle of the night, when she awoke. She found it difficult to fall asleep in a strange place. She turned on the lamp on and lay on the bed in deep reminiscence. Her life rolled through her mind in incoherent flashes, moving back and forth between Bristol Village and Port-of-Spain. Strong emotions engulfed her as she wondered about Ricardo and Joyanne and what they were doing. She realized at that moment that her love for Ricardo was just as strong as the day they made passionate love under the immortelle tree. She grabbed the pillow and held it tightly in her arms, conjuring up the passion she felt for Ricardo when she held him in her arms on that precious night. She had to write Ricardo a letter as soon as she knew where she was moving to.

It suddenly dawned on her that T.J. did not come into her bedroom. She was certain that he would have slept with her. It was the first time since the weekend at Aunt Catherine's that they were alone together. She recalled quite vividly how anxious he was to take her to bed. She had heard him say, "Life's challenges, my dear, lie in its pursuits", but she never understood what he meant. The more she felt she knew T.J., the more mysterious he became. He was prepared to give her the world, and it was all that mattered to her now. She must not confuse herself trying to understand him.

A week later, when he told her that he had a surprise for her, she could not imagine that it would be such an enormous surprise. He blindfolded her and drove for about fifteen minutes when he stopped and lifted her from the jeep and inside a building. When she removed the blindfold, she was surprised beyond words at the fabulous townhouse with every imaginable luxury. From the first glance, it was easy to deduce that it was an exclusive neighbourhood for the elite: the well-manicured lawn, the large swimming pool, the tennis court, the security guards, and the Mercedes Benzes. Annabelle wondered why T.J. choose to live in that plain, ordinary house when he had the money to enjoy this type of luxury. But she had already deduced that T.J. was more interested in using his money to wield power and influence than he was in material things.

"I'm sorry to kick you out of my house, but I like living alone. You women are too damn fussy," he jested. "Aren't you forgetting something, sweets?" he asked as he was about to leave.

"Oh, I'm sorry, dear," she said as she tiptoed to kiss him on his lips.

"What's that for?" he asked with a wicked grin on his face.

"I thought you said I forgot something," she replied.

He reached into his pocket and retrieved the key to the apartment.

"Oh, that," she said with a smile on her face.

When she opened the door to the bedroom, she encountered a large sign sprawled across the wall above the bed: "Welcome Home, Belle." A small envelope on the pillow caught her eye as she perused the decor in shades of lime-green and white. The furniture and bed were dark oak and the adjoining bathroom, pink. She retrieved the envelope, dropping herself carelessly onto the large sofa, and tore it open to find a card with a handwritten note.

My Dear Belle,

I'm requesting the privilege of your gracious
company to join me for dinner tonight, in honour
of your nineteenth birthday. Please wear the
green dress and the necklace, which you'll find
on the dining table. I'll pick you up at 7.30 p.m.

T.J.

She jumped off the chair, gleaming like a child on a
Christmas morning, and darted into the dining room.
She grabbed the small wrapped box and savagely ripped
off the paper.

"Oh my gosh. This looks expensive," she whispered as
she excitedly fastened the shimmering necklace around
her neck.

Then it suddenly struck her. *How did he know it was
my birthday? I don't recall ever telling him. T.J. seems to know
everything, and that is frightening,* she thought.

She was fixing her make-up when the horn sounded
for the second time.

"I'm coming! I'm coming!" she shouted from the
bedroom, knowing full well that he could not hear her.

She hurried out of the bedroom as T.J. sounded the
horn more aggressively.

"Men have no patience! Don't they know it takes time
for a woman to look her best?" she grumbled as she made
her way down the stairs and into the living room.

She knew that she looked fabulous and beamed with
self-confidence as she stepped gingerly toward the jeep.
She opened the door and sat next to T.J., leaning over
to plant a kiss on his lips, when he pushed her away

and scolded her, "Get back inside and change that dress! Didn't I tell you to wear the green one?"

She was shocked by his reaction.

"But I prefer this one," she said in a childlike tone.

Not realizing that he was dead serious, she closed the door. "Let's go. It's getting late," she said.

He switched off the engine and turned toward her. "Get to hell out right now and change that dress!" he blared.

She shivered with fear and shock; T.J. had never spoken to her like that before. She had seen him lose his temper at Aunt Catherine, even hitting her, but she never imagined that he would act that way toward her. She rushed out of the jeep in tears.

As she was about to close the door of the jeep, he shouted at her, "You have five minutes to get back into the jeep! Don't let me have to come and get you!"

When she finally got back into the car, hurt and angry, he was less aggressive. He gently warned her in a low tone of voice, "Don't ever countermand me again!"

It was past the hour of eleven when they got home. T.J. was not much company, and neither was she. He spoke about things that were uninteresting to her—politics, business, and horses. She, however, enjoyed the ambiance of the posh restaurant and the champagne, which she had too much of. She revelled in the attention she received from the patrons—she elicited envious glares from women and lustful stares from men. She could not help but notice the pride in T.J.'s eyes as he basked in the attention he received with an attractive young woman at his side. All eyes peered at them as they left the restaurant, hand in hand.

Annabelle could not help but wonder whether all she was to T.J. was a prized possession like his jeep, horse, or yacht. His terse reaction to her choosing her own dress instead of the one he chose frightened her. What next? she wondered.

She alighted from the jeep and headed for the door of the apartment and was about to wave goodbye to him, when to her surprise, he parked the jeep and followed her to the door. She was not sure what he wanted but was too tired to think about it. He reached over and opened the door for her. The lights in the townhouse were turned off, although she was certain that the lights in the living room were on when she left. As she neared the switch, the lights suddenly came on, and with it came a thunderous scream of voices: "Surprise! Surprise!" She jumped with fright and stared at the crowd of people, all of whom were strangers to her. They proceeded to sing "Happy Birthday" and passed around champagne. The apartment appeared strange with decorations and balloons everywhere.

T.J. came up from behind and placed his arms around her. "Happy birthday, Belle. Hope we managed to surprise you," he gushed.

She took a glass of champagne, which was offered to her by a waiter decked in white shirt and red bow tie, when T.J. called the attention of the crowd by clapping his hands.

"Your attention, please! May I have your attention, please!" He cleared his throat and proceeded with his speech.

When he was through conveying birthday wishes, he stated, "I have yet another surprise. I guess it's a night full of surprises. After all, one does not turn nineteen every day."

She stared at him with eager eyes as he continued, "Ladies and gentlemen, as president of Sun Island Motors, I would like to present my company's candidate for the upcoming Miss Trinidad and Tobago Carnival Queen Pageant."

All eyes navigated around the room to see who the lucky lady was. Annabelle stared into the crowd overflowing with excitement for this lucky young lady as T.J. continued, "Well, I've toyed with you long enough. Miss Sun Island Motors is …" He again paused, provoking a chuckle from the crowd. "Okay, okay, folks, I will not toy with you any more. The lucky young lady is Miss Annabelle Castello."

There was a moment of silence. Annabelle was confused. She thought she heard her name, but … Everyone huddled around her, kissing her on the cheek and shaking her hand.

Ever since she was a child, she fantasized about the carnival queens she saw on the front page of the newspaper. She would dress up in her mother's clothes and hobble around in her shoes, holding a swizzle stick for her sceptre and a bowl for a crown.

She rushed up to T.J. and placed her arms tightly around his neck. "I love you. I love you," she said. "This is the best birthday present anyone has given me. Thank you! Thank you!" Tears of joy shimmered in her eyes.

She swallowed the final sip of champagne from the glass when a soft, cultured voice came from behind, startling her, saying, "Congratulations, Annabelle."

The voice sounded very familiar. She turned around and encountered a petite young lady with simple yet sophisticated looks. Her distinct oriental face and flawless complexion framed by a mass of black hair gave her the appearance of a doll, Annabelle thought. The young lady smiled at her.

"Don't you know who I am?" she asked with a smirk on her face.

"You're T.J.'s secretary, Suelyn. Oh my gosh!" Annabelle shrieked.

Suelyn smiled and said, "You're good with voices, and you are so pretty."

Annabelle blushed and replied, "And so are you. T.J. should have selected you to represent his company at the pageant."

"I would not have met one of the major criteria, Annabelle," Suelyn replied.

"What's that?" Annabelle asked.

"Oh, I'm way over the required age limit, and in any event, I'm much too shy for that type of thing," Suelyn said.

Annabelle wondered how old Suelyn was, as she did not appear to be much older than she was.

The conversation between the two young ladies was interrupted by T.J. "What are my two favourite ladies talking about?" he asked.

"Oh, nothing important," Suelyn replied.

T.J. pulled Annabelle aside, asking Suelyn to be excused.

When they were a safe distance away, he said, "Belle, there is something important I must tell you."

She listened attentively, detecting a hint of seriousness in his voice. "I just learned that there are a few criteria that each queen contestant must meet, the major ones being an age limit of between sixteen and twenty-four years," T.J. said.

"But I meet that criteria," Annabelle replied.

Yes, I know, but that's not all," he continued. "You must be single, which you are." He paused for a moment as she listened with keen attention to his following remark. "And you cannot be a mother."

Annabelle stared at him with a blank expression on her face before saying with profound disappointment, "What does that mean? Do I have to drop out of the pageant?"

"No, you don't have to. No one except you, me, and Aunt Catherine knows that you are a mother. No one will find out," he assured her. "You must not mention this to anyone; as I told you time and again, your past is behind you now. You must look forward if you want to progress. Don't you want to move your life forward?" T.J. asked rhetorically.

Annabelle felt as though she would be abandoning Joyanne if she lied about not having a child.

Chapter 21

••

Carnival was a mere month away, and the perennial spirit of revelry permeated the island—the ping-pong sound of steel pans reverberated through towns and villages as pan men practiced their renditions with a sense of religious pursuit for the upcoming steel pan competition. Craftsmen busily created costumes, some bending wire, others affixing sequins, tinsel paper, and brightly coloured plumes on frames. Entwined in the spirit of merriment was another spirit—that of intense competition. Everyone yearned to win a title: Carnival Band of the Year, King and Queen of the Masquerade, Steel Band Champion, or some other title at stake.

It was in this spirit that Annabelle awoke brimming with excitement as she prepared to compete in the Trinidad and Tobago Carnival Queen Pageant. It was a title that most young girls fantasized about, as it was the epitome of regal splendour—the closest thing to royalty on the island. Annabelle's imagination was rife with thoughts at the attention she would receive if she won the title. She would achieve instant fame, and her picture would appear on the front page of the newspaper. She would be the envy of all women, and men would drool over her. She harboured an intense desire to win the crown.

She was snapped from her daydreaming by the voice of T.J. calling out to her, "Belle, it's time to get out of bed. The luncheon with the press is in a half hour."

She jumped out of bed and into the shower with great haste.

Spasms of anxiety engulfed her as she stepped gingerly into the posh restaurant with T.J. at her side.

"Are you nervous?' T.J. asked.

"A bit," Annabelle replied.

The restaurant was crowded with elegantly attired people. Annabelle felt ill at ease and intimidated by the other pretty contestants who were all white. Her optimistic spirit dwindled into a vortex of despair and scepticism. Throughout her life, she was referred to as fair skinned or Spanish by the people in her village. Now she appeared dark among these girls who were either the daughters of expatriates or descendants of the eminent French Creole group. Her mind was assailed by doubts about entering the contest. She felt like leaving the restaurant.

She stood alone, feeling foolish, while T.J. walked around the room, fraternizing with the other sponsors and the contestants. He seemed to know everyone there while she sat like a fool. She breathed a sigh of relief when she saw him coming toward her.

"So, what do you think?" T.J. asked.

"I feel like the ugly duckling," she replied.

"What's wrong? You don't seem excited any more," T.J. said.

"Look at the other contestants. They are white high-society girls! Come to think of it, no black girl has ever won this contest! You didn't mention that criteria to me! Let's get out of here!" she retorted.

"You are more beautiful than all the other girls here! Look at that one over there. My dog Rover stands a better chance of winning than she does," he quipped.

They both laughed.

When he caught his breath, he continued. "Do you know that a few of the sponsors were hinting to me that I have a winner in you? They want to know where I found that beautiful princess," he said.

"You're just saying nice things to amuse me," she replied.

"You should know me by now that I never back a loser. You have a unique look, and that will take you places," he said.

She retrieved the glass of juice from the table, brimming with renewed self-confidence. She knew that T.J. was an honest and very influential man. Her determination to win was revived.

As the pageant drew closer, Annabelle's fervour to win grew more intense. She herself wasn't sure whether she wanted to win for the sole joy and reward of winning or to prove a point to the other contestants who snubbed her.

It was the first day of rehearsal; the stage of the amphitheatre at the Queen's Park Savannah was bigger than she had envisaged. As intended, she arrived earlier than the other girls; no one except for three men working on the lighting system was there. Rehearsals were more rigid than she had thought they would be. The dance instructor was meticulous and demanding, and Annabelle strove to be better than the other girls. The remark by the dance instructor, that she possessed natural rhythm, incited jealousy among the other girls. They gave her the cold-shoulder treatment, but she was no longer intimidated. She knew that they were all jealous of her.

After rehearsal, she slumped her tired body into a chair and awaited her driver. As she was about to shut her eyes, a voice startled her and caused her to twitch.

"Tired, little country girl?" the young lady said sarcastically.

Annabelle turned around to see Sandy, one of the contestants—a carnival queen prototype: white skin, blue eyes, and blonde hair. Annabelle remained silent as T.J. told her to do, but Sandy persisted, "Why don't you drop out of the competition while you can still salvage some pride? Can't you see that you don't belong?"

Annabelle could no longer contain her anger. She jumped to her feet and retorted, "Do you feel threatened by me?"

"Threatened by a slut like you? I know your type, sleeping with a rich, old man to fulfil your ambitions. Get real, little girl!" Sandy shrieked.

Annabelle seethed with rage. She felt like slapping Sandy but changed her mind. She was not about to be provoked into a situation which might result in her being disqualified from the pageant. Then Sandy would win, she reasoned. Instead, she retrieved her bag and walked away. Sandy's blue eyes were filled with affront as she looked at Annabelle walking away.

That night, Annabelle lay awake pondering over statements Sandy made: "Sleeping with a rich, old man to fulfil your ambitions."

Maybe that's what everyone thinks of me, she thought. *Maybe they are right.* She buried her head in the pillow, wallowing in self-pity.

She had drifted off into a shallow sleep when she was startled wide awake by the loud ringing of the telephone.

She jumped up and sat on the bed for a moment in a disoriented state before picking up the receiver.

"Hello," she said in a sleepy voice.

"Well, hello, Annabelle," replied a young lady.

"Who is this?" Annabelle asked.

"Don't you recognize my voice?" the young lady replied.

"No, I don't! Don't you know what time it is?" Annabelle replied angrily.

"Yes, I do, but this can't wait. I know your little secret. Let me rephrase that. I know your big secret," the young lady said.

Annabelle hung up. She knew it was Sandy and that she knew about Joyanne. It had to be Aunt Catherine who let out her secret. Annabelle walked languidly to the kitchen for a cup of coffee with a glum look on her face. She took a sip or two from the cup and went back to bed.

She lay wide awake, feeling defeated, and when she reached for the telephone to call T.J., there was no answer.

It was 4.53 in the morning when she awoke with an annoying headache. She struggled out of bed and went to the bathroom for an aspirin. When she returned, she sat on the bed and dialled T.J., but still there was no answer.

She lay in bed looking up at the ceiling with a blank expression on her face when she heard the door open. She eased herself off the bed and sauntered to the living room where she found T.J. "Thank God you're here! I'm going mad!" Annabelle exclaimed.

"Why? What's wrong?" T.J. asked as he walked up to her and held her head against his chest.

"They know! They know!" she cried.

"Know what?" he asked.

"They know I have a child," she said.

"Who knows?" T.J. asked.

"Sandy, the girl I told you about," she replied.

She was sobbing profusely when T.J. took her to the bedroom and gently laid her on the bed.

T.J. knew that this was cause for concern. After all, he had countersigned the contestant agreement which specifically stated that Annabelle Castello was single, nineteen, and had no children. But he wasn't overly worried. Who could doubt that the child wasn't her sister's?

Chapter 22

• •

The long-awaited night was here. Annabelle took deep breaths and exhaled slowly as she sat in her dressing room, awaiting the hairdresser. T.J. told her that breathing in and out would quell her anxiety. The confidence she had harboured an hour before turned into bouts of manic anxiety.

T.J. used his money and influence to get her the best dress designer and costume maker on the island; he hired and fired designers until Annabelle was satisfied.

The hairdresser was just about finishing up her hair when T.J. entered the dressing room and stared at her in awe. He could not believe his eyes. She looked exceptionally beautiful with her hair twisted in a roll at the back, her dark eyes lined with make-up, her red lips matching her rosy cheeks.

"My God, Belle, you look stunning!" T.J. exclaimed, beaming with pride. But there was no reply from her. He detected a look of deep sadness in her eyes. "What's wrong? You look sad," T.J. asked with deep concern.

"Oh, I wish my pa could see me now. He always wanted the best for me."

T.J. tried to console her. "I'm sure he's looking down at you right now from heaven with a big smile on his face."

Passionate feelings for Ricardo also occupied her mind, but she was careful not to mention his name to T.J. She was consumed by a deep sense of guilt for lying about not having a child; she felt like she had abandoned Joyanne. But soon she'd make amends. She was determined to. She wondered if Ricardo had received the letter she posted two weeks ago giving him her new address and pleading with him to bring Joyanne to visit her very soon. She planned on telling T.J. that Ricardo was her cousin from Bristol Village who had come to bring Joyanne to visit her.

She wiped the wistful look from her face and stood up in front of T.J. with more enthusiasm than before. "How do I look?" she asked.

"Like a million bucks," T.J. replied.

"I meant to ask you, whatever happened to Sandy? I've heard that she was replaced by another girl," Annabelle asked with curiosity in her voice.

There was a devious grin on T.J.'s face as he tried to avoid the question.

"Well, what happened to Sandy?" Annabelle insisted.

"Well, my dear, as I have often told you—money can buy almost anything. Maybe she and her mother are in Europe enjoying the good life."

Annabelle's face morphed into a perplexed expression.

The loud call from a man in a dark suit with a clipboard in his hand sent waves of excitement rushing through her body.

"Get ready, Miss Castello. You are next," he said.

The thunderous applause from the audience for the previous contestants incited a bit of anxiety in Annabelle. She took a deep breath as she heard her name called over the PA system. She timidly made her way on stage in her costume; there was no applause. Her nervousness resurfaced, but as she approached centre stage, she gushed with pride at the screams and applause which greeted her. She could see the audience on its feet. She looked refreshingly different from the previous contestants. Unlike the other girls, her costume reflected a local theme. It was titled "The Bird of Paradise" with large wing-like spans, in hues of blues, greens, white, and gold. Each span represented some aspect of the island. The blues for the Atlantic Ocean and Caribbean Sea; the gold for the natural wealth of the land—oil and asphalt; the white reflected the peace and tranquillity of the island; the greens for the waving coconut palms. When she departed the stage, she knew that she had left the audience spellbound.

She rushed into T.J.'s waiting arms. "How did I do?" she asked, beaming with confidence.

"You knocked 'em dead," T.J. replied.

Brimming with enthusiasm, she entered the dressing room to prepare herself for the next round of the competition—the evening gown parade.

She approached the stage with verve and élan in her long white gloves and radically slim-fitting gown with glass beads and silver sequins, which shimmered under the bright lights. The gown, called "Moonlight over Maracas Bay," elicited thunderous applause from the large crowd of elegantly attired men and women—the upper echelons of the Trinidad society.

She must have consumed a bottle of Moët when she collapsed into T.J.'s arms, intoxicated. When she came to, it was the middle of the night, and she was in her bed. She had no recollection of how she got there but reasoned that T.J. must have brought her home. It all appeared so unreal to her. A few years ago, she was a simple country girl satisfied with her life. Now, she was one of those carnival queens whom she fantasized about in the newspaper. But in the midst of her happiness, she was overcome by a feeling of sadness. The people who meant everything to her were not around to share in her happiness: her father, whom she disappointed and never got the chance to make amends; Ricardo, whom she loved with all her heart; and Joyanne. She felt immense guilt for saying that she didn't have a child. But in her sadness, a glimmer of hope surfaced at the thought of Ricardo visiting her with Joyanne in Port-of-Spain. There was absolutely no reason she could think of that would prevent Ricardo from visiting her.

She lay in bed, replaying the events of the previous night in her mind. She was overflowing with anxiety when the emcee announced the third-place winner. She fought with all her might to contain her emotions when she and another contestant remained centre stage awaiting the announcement of the second place. It was a close fight, Annabelle thought; the other girl had as much support as she had, and she was a white high-society girl. No coloured girl had ever won the title before.

The drums began its roll; the emcee placed the mike to his mouth and said, "The first runner up to this year's carnival queen title is—Betty Smith."

Twinges of anxiety ran through Annabelle's body. She stood transfixed. "Oh my gosh, I won," she whispered. Tears filled her eyes as the rhinestone tiara gently touched her head. The crowd roared in approval as she made her traditional walk around the stage. Bright flashes of camera bulbs captured her every movement.

Annabelle revelled in the attention she received at the victory celebrations at the Mariner Inn. Everyone— politicians, police commissioners, businessmen, and the media—was there to toast her, Annabelle Castello, the carnival queen.

She was on cloud nine.

It was after ten in the morning when she awoke to the sound of T.J.'s voice talking to someone on the phone. As she approached, he handed her the newspaper and continued to talk on the phone. She smiled, elated, at the large picture of her on the front page with the headline, "Annabelle Castello, New Carnival Queen Crowned".

Butterflies filled her stomach. It was too good to be true, she thought as she waited impatiently for T.J. to hang up the phone to share her ecstatic feeling.

He eventually hung up the phone, and with a haggard look on his face, he blurted, "It was the hospital calling with bad news."

It was the story of her life, she lamented. For everything good, something tragic followed.

She looked at him with profound anxiety. "What?" she asked.

"It's about your aunt Catherine; she wants to see you. She suffered a stroke and might not make it," he mumbled.

She got up and went to the bedroom, shutting the door behind her.

T.J. called out to her, "Get dressed; let's go. We don't have time."

There was no reply.

He opened the door and saw her sitting on the bed, sobbing. She turned and looked him in the eye. "I can't go; she hates me. I'm too embarrassed to face her. Please don't make me go," she pleaded.

He sat next to her on the bed, stroking her hair. "You have to go. You'd never forgive yourself if you don't," he said.

Annabelle was too immersed in grief and guilt to notice the stares and whispers from admirers at the hospital as she forced her weak feet up the stairs with T.J. by her side.

"Isn't that the carnival queen? She's beautiful!" one woman told another.

Aunt Catherine's face was turned against the wall when they approached the bed. Annabelle was overcome with anxiety at the thought of facing Aunt Catherine. She recalled the anger and contempt in her aunt's eyes on the last occasion they had crossed paths. The nurse came over and touched Aunt Catherine on her shoulder to alert her that she had visitors. She turned around slowly until her pale eyes met with Annabelle's teary eyes. They stared at each other for a few moments before Aunt Catherine's face twisted into a sad smile. She painfully reached out her hand to Annabelle, who responded by gently holding her cold hands. Her mouth trembled to speak, but no words came out. From reading her lips, Annabelle swore that she was trying to say, "I forgive you."

Tears rolled down Annabelle's face as Aunt Catherine's lifeless head fell against the pillow.

T.J. stood in the corner of the ward with a callous look on his face.

Chapter 23

••

Annabelle stared conceitedly at her reflection in the mirror; she felt as though she were looking at someone else, as she herself could hardly believe the transformation. She looked like a picture out of a Hollywood magazine. She, however, eagerly counted down the remaining weeks of her reign as carnival queen. The engagements, public adulation, and scrutiny were becoming burdensome for her, but she harboured no regrets. The experience was exhilarating and the adulation intoxicating—she rubbed shoulders with the elite of the Trinidad society and earned the admiration of the mundane. The heartfelt editorial in the newspaper, captioned "Simple Country Girl Captures Trinidad Society", assisted in earning her tremendous respect and popularity. The writer slanted the article along the line of a "rags-to-riches" story. In the eyes of the ordinary people, she represented a new hope to the oppressed and neglected in the society.

Among her achievements, she was particularly proud of her business, Annabelle's Exclusive Fashion. She was looked upon as the authority on fashion and style on the island. Everyone, from the wives of politicians and businessmen to carnival queen hopefuls, came to her for advice on the latest fashion trends. T.J. provided the capital, but it was she who made it the success it had become. As far as she was concerned, it was her creative mind, her fashion sense, and her status as carnival queen that had propelled the business into immense success. But it was not the only accomplishment she felt proud of. It took her close to three years, and after quitting and then resuming her studies at business school, she graduated. For once in her life, she felt a sense of self-worth.

But in the midst of her accomplishments, she was burdened by a heavy feeling. Why didn't Ricardo respond to her letter? Perhaps Rosabelle got it and tore it up, or perhaps it got lost in the mail. She refused to believe that Ricardo didn't want to see her again and that he was really in love with Rosabelle. Rosey only said that out of spite, she hoped.

She was heartbroken and mortified when Rosey practically threw her out of the house when she paid her a visit—together with Suelyn and T.J.'s driver—a few weeks after winning the title. Suelyn had observed that Rosey's mind was contaminated with hate, envy, and reproach. Rosey greeted her with a tirade of insults.

"You only come back home to show off for yuh sister. She and Ricardo happy together, and they minding yuh bastard child!"

Annabelle was mortified, more so because Suelyn and the driver were there.

She did not meet Joyanne. Rosey had told her that Rosabelle and Ricardo had taken her out for the day but refused to say any more.

Annabelle left another letter for Ricardo, along with money and clothes for Joyanne.

Before leaving, Rosey reminded her to send the monthly cheques in her name to the bank in Rio Claro.

Annabelle recalled the wise voice of her father saying to her as a child, "Everything in life has a price." Her callow mind never understood what he meant until now. T.J. had given her everything she had dreamed of, but she paid a dreadful price—her freedom. She had become T.J.'s slave: he controlled who she saw, where she went, and perhaps even her thoughts. She felt like a prisoner in her fantasy world. Nothing belonged to her, she lamented—the clothes in her wardrobe, the car she drove, the posh house, even her own boutique. All she got from Annabelle's Exclusive Fashions was no different from the salary which the hired employees received. She knew that T.J. was not interested in the money from the business; he was more interested in holding on to power and control.

She sensed that T.J. was intimidated by her popularity and perhaps threatened by her ambition. He shrugged off her proposal to expand the business. She literally begged him, short of falling on her knees, to consider her plan to open another outlet of the boutique in the south of the island to capitalize on the growing expatriate population there. Each time, he mumbled in a nonchalant tone, "Come on, you have everything you need. Why burden yourself with additional responsibilities?" The conversation would usually end in him saying, "You need a rest, dear! Why don't you run off to Paris or New York and see what's new in the fashion world?"

This agitated Annabelle to the point of her coming close to hurling the closest object at him. There was yet another repulsive thought that crossed her mind. Marriage! She knew that it was just a matter of time before T.J. proposed marriage, as he had subtly alluded to it before. Soon, her one year reign as Miss Carnival Queen would end, and she would be free to marry. She dreaded the thought of being married to such an old and possessive man. She wished for a way out of her predicament.

At times, she felt like rushing back to Bristol Village into the passionate arms of Ricardo, but she knew she could not. Her life had become too complicated, and so had Ricardo's. Then suddenly, like a bolt of lightning it struck her. "Oh my gosh! Why hadn't I thought of this before?" she said to herself. Her face lit up, but her smile diminished when she heard T.J.'s approaching footsteps.

"How's my Belle?" he asked as he entered the bedroom, slapping her on her bottom.

She managed to force a grin.

"I have a surprise for you, dear," he said but was interrupted by the sound of the doorbell. "Who the heck can that be? Are you expecting someone?" he asked, agitated, as he headed for the door.

Annabelle felt a sense of relief when he left the room; he had become repulsive, and she hated when he was around. She fantasized about buying a big, fancy house where she, Ricardo, and Joyanne would spend the rest of their lives. Maybe she'd have another child or probably two or three.

The compassionate look in Aunt Catherine's eyes in the hospital was reassuring. She was sure that when Aunt Catherine's will was revealed, she would become a wealthy woman and free from T.J. once and for all. After all, Aunt Catherine had no close relatives, besides her sickly sister who was confined to a wheelchair and probably dead by now.

Annabelle's optimistic thoughts were again broken by T.J.'s footsteps.

"Who was at the door?" she asked.

"Just someone begging alms," he replied.

"Did you give the beggar anything?" she enquired.

"Yeah," he replied bluntly, in an attempt to change the conversation. "About the party," he said, but Annabelle wanted to find out more about the stranger at the door.

"You idiot!" he exclaimed. "You act as though you could change the world!" he fumed as he bolted from the room, slamming the door behind him.

Annabelle was surprised that he acted so angrily to her polite question. Maybe he was upset by the person ...

"Oh my gosh, could it be ...?" she wondered.

She rushed to the porch but was disappointed that she didn't see anyone walking away.

Whoever it was certainly made him angry, she concluded.

T.J. retrieved a cigarette from the pack in his pocket, nervously lighting it. He never thought he could be intimidated by anyone in this world. He was certainly caught off guard when he opened the door to encounter a young man with a sleeping baby in his arms.

"Who the hell could that be?" he asked himself. He, however, harboured an inkling.

He greeted the handsome young stranger. "Can I help you?" T.J. said.

"Sir, I'm looking for someone named Miss Annabelle Castello," the stranger replied.

"And who might you be, young man?" T.J. asked in an intimidating manner.

"Ricardo, sir," the young man said with a nervous slur in his voice.

T.J.'s jaws dropped. He froze for a moment before replying, "Miss Castello is inside making preparations for her engagement. She is to be married soon. Would you like me to get her?"

T.J. felt a sense of accomplishment as Ricardo's voice choked up with disappointment. "No, don't c-call her, it's ... it's not im-important," Ricardo said. He secured the sleeping baby and beat a hasty retreat.

T.J.'s face morphed into a wicked grin.

He wondered who the baby was. After all, Joyanne ought to be a toddler by now. The baby in Ricardo's arms was only a few months old.

Chapter 24

· ·

The melodious sound of "Moonlight Serenade" emanating from the orchestra in the gazebo wafted on the cool night air. The melody fluttered toward the full moon and twinkling stars which hovered above. T.J. had just announced their engagement to a cheering crowd of formally attired men and women, while Annabelle's emotions remained indifferent. She was peeved that T.J. did not tell her of his plan to announce their engagement; as far as she knew, the occasion was planned to celebrate the end of her reign as carnival queen.

Over the past few days, she had become more and more preoccupied with thoughts of Aunt Catherine's will and agonizing feelings about marrying T.J.

Annabelle emerged from the embrace of a young man as the music stopped, and she headed toward T.J., who was sitting with his feet crossed inside the gaily decorated gazebo, chatting with his buddies.

"Did you enjoy the dance, dear?" T.J. asked.

"Oh, I love the music of Glenn Miller," she said.

"He's all right, I guess," he replied.

"Do you want to dance?" she asked for the sake of mere courtesy, hoping he'd say no.

"No, you go ahead, dear. I don't feel like dancing. In any event, lots of men are looking forward to dancing with you," T.J. teased.

She heaved a sigh of relief, affixed the feathered mask on her face, and rushed off toward the crowd. She had not walked far when a tall man emerged from the darkness and grabbed her by the waist.

"Would you like to dance, princess?" he asked.

She was about to pull away from his embrace but changed her mind when she observed how strong and handsome he was. She was intrigued with his light brown eyes that peered through his mask, his wavy black hair, and his dimpled chin. *How incredibly handsome,* she thought. *But who is he? I've never seen him before.* Her mind was bombarded with questions. In many ways, he reminded her of Ricardo.

When the music stopped, he led her to a cosy table beneath a huge tree.

"You are more beautiful than the picture in the newspaper," he said.

"Am I still making the news?" she replied.

"Haven't you seen today's newspaper?" he asked.

"No, I was busy preparing for this party," she responded. "What did they say about me?" she asked.

"Well, actually they said two things—that you'll be giving up your crown soon and your engagement to Tom Johnson, the wealthy business executive," he said.

His response provoked silence and a faraway look on her face.

"What's wrong? Did I say something wrong?" he enquired.

"Oh, it's nothing you said. It's those newspaper people, always prying into people's business," she said. "Please excuse me for a while. I have to powder my face."

He rushed over to offer her his arm, but she was swifter than he.

She searched the lawn until she found her best friend, Suelyn, whom she grabbed by the arms and said, "I need to talk with you, Sue."

"What's wrong? You appear angry," Suelyn replied.

"To hell I am! Tell me the truth; were you aware that T.J. would be announcing our engagement tonight?" Annabelle asked.

"No, I didn't know. But why are you upset with me?" Suelyn said.

"I'm sorry to take it out on you—but I'm so damn annoyed. The newspaper knew about it and I didn't. I'm sure it was that dog T.J. who gave the newspaper the information to print," Annabelle retorted.

Suelyn placed Annabelle's weeping head on her shoulder to comfort her but was confused by Annabelle's reaction. So what if the newspaper disclosed the engagement? Suelyn wondered. But Annabelle kept the real reason for her reaction to herself. She was afraid that Ricardo would learn about her engagement and marry Rosabelle on the rebound. The notion was distressing.

When the tears subsided, she eased her head from Suelyn's shoulder and stared her in the eyes, saying, "I need to ask you something, and I want the truth!"

"What is it?" Suelyn asked.

"Do you know anything about Aunt Catherine's will— like when it will be read?" Annabelle asked.

Suelyn stared at Annabelle with a perplexed look on her face and said, "Belle, why don't you ask T.J.?"

"You know how wicked and manipulative he is. He will not tell me anything," Annabelle retorted.

"Calm down. You know that I am T.J.'s confidential secretary. I would be risking my job to disclose any information about T.J.'s business," Suelyn said firmly.

"But we're friends. I would not do anything to jeopardize your job. I promise," Annabelle replied.

Suelyn contemplated for a while and then replied, "All right, but you must promise to keep it to yourself. The reading of the will is scheduled in two weeks. I'll have to confirm the date."

Annabelle hugged Suelyn in appreciation.

Suelyn glanced at her watch and said, "I have to go now. Mother is not feeling well. Thanks again for a wonderful party."

"Give her my love," Annabelle replied as she hurried back to the young man.

He sat tapping his feet and quickly affixed his mask on his face when he saw Annabelle coming his way.

"Are you going to remain a mystery all night long?" Annabelle asked.

"Well, maybe for a while longer," he replied.

"At least tell me your name," she said.

He smiled and looked up at the tree. "Should I tell you, or should I remain a mystery to you?" he said in jest. "Why are you interested in me, anyway? You are about to be married to Port-of-Spain's wealthiest and most influential man."

She twisted he mouth in protest.

"You don't seem quite thrilled," he teased.

"Can we talk about something else?" she asked. "Let's talk about you. Come on, tell me your name," she pleaded.

He smiled and paused for a while. "Okay, it's David," he said.

"Oh, that's a strong and powerful name. Wasn't it David who slew the giant?" she quipped.

"Well, for sure it wasn't me. I don't think I could even kill a mouse," he replied.

She laughed.

He glanced at his watch and declared, "Oh my! It's almost eleven. I have to go!"

He scampered off the chair and hastened toward the gate. Annabelle trotted behind. "Do you have to leave?" she asked in a tone of utter disappointment. "Please remove the mask so I can see your handsome face," she said, almost begging.

"Nope," he replied bluntly, "I'm going to remain an enigma."

When he was sure that they were out of view from the crowd, he pulled her toward him and kissed her passionately.

He left her spellbound. She stood statuesque for a while before catching her breath.

Months later, on a rainy day, a black Benz pulled up in front of the grey, stonework church in Port-of-Spain. Through the misty windscreen, Annabelle could see a small group of people peering inside the car. A man decked in a dark suit held a large umbrella at the door of the car to shelter her as she alighted. A volley of camera flashes illuminated her simple but elegant wedding ensemble and glittering tiara. She handed Suelyn her small bouquet of white roses and proceeded to pull her long white dress up to her ankle to avoid the puddle of water on the landing of the church.

Roland P. Joseph

The wide hat hid the callous look on her face as she made her way up the aisle. She could think of nothing else but her profound disappointment at the reading of Aunt Catherine's will. She was devastated.

Marriage to T.J. was now inevitable.

Chapter 25

• •

Annabelle and T.J. were among the first to arrive at the lawyer's chambers for the reading of Aunt Catherine's will. Annabelle had long waited for an opportune moment to tell T.J. that she was fed up with him running her life and that she wanted out of the engagement and his life forever. Today, when she inherited Aunt Catherine's estate, it would be the perfect opportunity. Her face morphed into a conceited smile.

The long wait before the proceedings got started was apprehensive and tedious.

"Have you any idea what's in the will?" Annabelle asked.

"Not a clue," T.J. replied. "You must remember that we were not exactly chummy with her in her final days."

She was tempted to say to him, "Speak for yourself, you old dog." She held her tongue, just in case.

Unknown to anyone, Annabelle was already making plans to move in to Aunt Catherine's mansion with Ricardo and Joyanne. The wedding would be a simple one on the lawn, she imagined. She could see Ricardo in a simple navy-blue suit and her in a lace dress and white hat trimmed with roses. She giggled at the thought of Joyanne as their flower girl.

She was startled from her daydream by the voice of the lawyer.

"Thank you, ladies and gentlemen, for coming," he began. "Catherine was a wonderful person and a dear friend of mine. I assure you this will not be very long, as I shall come straight to the point. As you all may know, Catherine, besides being an elegant lady, was also quite wealthy and need I say charitable. So I will start by disclosing that she has left a sum of two hundred and fifty thousand dollars in cash to her church. This money is to be used to set up a charity fund for unwed and abused mothers. To each of her friends—Dorothy, Mary, Elaine, and Sylvia—the sum of twenty-five thousand dollars. To her niece Annabelle, her car. The remainder of her estate, which includes her home in St Clair, cash in the bank, and stocks invested in Sun Island Motors, estimated altogether at two and a half million dollars, to her only child, David West."

Annabelle felt the life in her body drain from her head to her toes. *This is insane! This can't be happening to me!* Tears gathered in her angry eyes. *Aunt Catherine has a son? Who? Where?* she thought.

She turned around slowly to see a neatly dressed young man in a dark suit being congratulated by a few persons.

She turned to T.J. who was unusually quiet. "Did you know Catherine had a son?" Annabelle asked.

With eyes staring straight ahead, T.J. muttered drearily, "Yeah."

You dog. You knew all along, Annabelle said in her mind.

Annabelle turned around to look at David West and twitched. "Wait a minute," she said, astonished. "He looks familiar." She frantically searched her mind. "Oh my gosh! It's David from the party!" She placed her hand under her nose and bent her head in utter shock.

Her plan to escape the clutches of T.J. and reunite with Ricardo and Joyanne sunk into the gloomy recesses of her mind.

She was devastated beyond words.

Chapter 26

· ·

1921

The ornate door of the white colonial-styled house opened in response to a buzz of the bell. A woman, probably in her early twenties, emerged from behind the thick drapes. She was fair in complexion with dark brown hair rolled in an untidy bun on the crown of her head. She smiled at the stranger, revealing the deep dimples on her cheek.

"May I help you?" she asked.

"I've come concerning the advertisement in the newspaper, ma'am," the young, timid girl at the gate said.

"Oh yes, do come in, please. You are the first for the day," the lady at the door replied. She led the shy girl inside, showing her to a chair in the large drawing room. "I'm Jane. What's your name, dear?" the lady asked.

"Catherine, ma'am," the girl replied.

"Do you possess any experience, Catherine?" Jane asked.

"No, ma'am," Catherine said. "You see, my mother died a month ago, and my father is also dead—and I really need a job."

Jane looked at the hapless girl with compassion and said, "You can start right away, Catherine. We'll see how it works out. Fetch your bag and follow me."

Catherine's mother had brought her and her sister, Gertrude, to Port-of-Spain when they were infants. Their mother, Louisa, had left her home, which she shared with her their father, Sonny, in Mayaro. The girls had no recollection of their father; their mother told them that they separated when they very small and that she had married their stepfather. After their stepfather died, Catherine's mother disclosed the identity of their father and told them to contact him should anything happen to her and they were left alone. Louisa earned a living by doing odd jobs—washing and ironing, babysitting, and other domestic chores for families in Port-of-Spain. But Catherine was sixteen and her sister fifteen when Louisa died. They felt that they were too old for a father, especially one they never knew. But Gertrude was curious; she inveigled Catherine to travel with her to Mayaro to visit their father. Although Sonny was happy to see them and for Rosey to finally meet her sisters, he was in no position to assist them financially.

Madam Jane was patient and compassionate toward Catherine, almost motherly. Losing both parents at such a tender age was tragic, she thought. Over the weeks that followed, Catherine grew comfortable in her new surroundings. Jane was satisfied with her cooking and cleaning skills, and on evenings, Catherine attended commercial classes for which Jane paid.

But Catherine felt uncomfortable whenever she was alone with Madam's husband, Tom Johnson, a strapping man in his early to mid-twenties, with sinister blue eyes. He looked at her in a suggestive manner, which caused her to shiver in fear. Whenever she was alone with him, she found something to do. She would take up the watering can and water the garden, dust the furniture, or remake the beds.

She, however, harboured the terrifying notion that one day there might be an unguarded moment. It was not long after that her worst fear was realized.

It was a cold, rainy night with thunder and lightning, which sent chills through her spine. She was always afraid of the thunder. She and her sister would hide under the sheet of their mother's bed.

Catherine took refuge in her bed and covered her face with the pillow. The rain was pounding against the roof so that she could not hear the sound of the opening door and ensuing footsteps. When she moved the pillow from her face, she sprang up from the bed and screamed so loudly that she even startled Tom Johnson, whose tall, imposing silhouette stood statuesque alongside the bed. The lightning bounced off his grave face as he stared at her like a wild animal ready to pounce.

It all happened quickly. She was too weak and in shock to fight back. She was in extreme physical and emotional pain when he left. These encounters continued, but she was too scared to say anything to anyone, especially Madam Jane, for fear of losing her job.

Catherine awoke one morning at around five o'clock, while everyone else was still asleep, and rushed to the bathroom sink and began vomiting. When she was through, she sat on the toilet with her head propped against her hands. Jane came in and saw her.

"Oh my goodness! What's wrong, Catherine?" Jane exclaimed.

Jane held her by her shoulder and gently led her back to her bed, placing the bedspread over her lame body. Catherine could not believe how calmly Jane had accepted the news from the doctor the following morning that she was pregnant. She expected Jane to be abusive toward her, but she was not; in fact, she was sympathetic. In her usual composed manner, she simply said, "Let me take you home safely, dear! I don't want anything to affect the birth of a healthy baby."

A profound feeling of guilt consumed Catherine. She was carrying this woman's husband child; how could Jane be so gentle to her? She asked herself over and over again but could find no answer. Jane had to know that the child Catherine was carrying was fathered by her husband. The mere thought that Jane did not ask about the baby's father convinced Catherine that she knew.

Over the following months, Jane took care of Catherine the way a real mother would. She hired another maid so that Catherine would have all the rest she needed. For the duration of her pregnancy, she hardly saw Tom Johnson. Catherine noticed how tense the relationship between Tom and Jane had become. Catherine was also aware of how obsessed Jane had become with the child she was carrying. It petrified her.

The piercing cry of the newborn baby echoed through the stillness of the early morning. Catherine stared in awe at the little wonder she had given birth to. She had not held the child for more than a minute when Jane took it from her and held its tiny face against hers.

"Oh, isn't he a darling," Jane said. "What shall we call him? How about David? Yes, David is a blessed name."

Catherine stared at Jane in shock. *That's my child! How could she choose a name for my child?* She felt like getting out of bed and snatching her child from Jane, but she was too weak.

Two weeks following the birth, Catherine lay on the bed, playing with the child. She observed that Jane was no longer around as before and that she had the child more to herself. To Catherine, nothing else mattered; the child was her life. When the child turned three months, Jane came into the room all dressed up with Tom Johnson treading behind.

Jane came up to her and said, "Catherine, I've come to say that I'm leaving. I'm going away." Jane then handed her a document and a pen and stated, "I want you to sign this!"

"What is it?" Catherine asked curiously.

"I'm taking custody of the child," Jane said.

"What? No! No! You can't! He's mine! He's mine! You can't take him!" Catherine began to scream hysterically, holding the child as tightly as she could. "Mr Johnson! Mr Johnson! Tell her she can't take him! Oh, please! Please, Mr Johnson!" Catherine begged.

Catherine realized she was fighting a losing battle. Tom had already signed the document—the birth paper listed him as the father.

Jane had threatened to file a lawsuit against him and was intent on ruining his reputation and his job if he didn't comply. Catherine had nowhere to go and could provide no future for the child. In return, Catherine was provided with a deed of gift for the house and a large sum of money.

A few hours later, Jane West-Johnson and the child were airborne for Florida. Jane was aware that she could never conceive a child.

Catherine grieved for the child for many years.

Chapter 27

• •

1961

The shiny blue Cadillac negotiated its way through the ornate wrought-iron gate of the large, two-storey, plantation-styled house with intricate fretwork, large dormer windows, ornate balusters, and airy galleries. The huge trees, replete with flaming amber blossoms, cast dappled shadows against the newly painted walls and sheltered the driveway from the piercing afternoon sun.

The rear door of the car flung open before the car came to a stop, and a light-haired young boy scampered out and pelted a stone, which he retrieved from the garden, at the tree, inciting a flock of birds to scamper from within the branches.

A tall, medium-build woman scurried out from behind the steering wheel of the car and hurried toward the boy, slapping him behind his head and almost losing her balance in the process.

"I'm tired of your antics, Troy! Get into the house right now!" she shouted as she dispatched two hard slaps to his back.

He ran into the house crying, "I hate you! I hate you! I'll tell my daddy!"

She returned to the car and opened the trunk, hollering at someone inside, "Lionel! Lionel! I need some help with the groceries!"

A slim, dark man with large nose and thick lips hastened down the stairs. "I'm coming, ma'am! I'm coming!" he cried with extreme urgency in his voice.

He retrieved the bags and hurried back to the house. She closed the trunk and staggered behind with a handbag slung over her shoulder. She had hardly put her handbag down when the phone rang.

On the third ring, she shouted, "Could you get that, Lionel?"

"Hello, Johnson residence," he answered. "Oh, she's right here." He turned around and handed her the phone.

She covered the receiver with her hand and in a hushed voice asked, "Who is it?"

"It sounds like Miss Suelyn, ma'am," he replied.

She twisted her face in a vexed expression and placed the receiver to her ear, "Hello, Sue. I'm too tired to talk; I'll call you later," she said in an abrupt tone. She hung up the phone and threw herself on the sofa. "Lionel, could you get me a drink?" she said.

He returned a few minutes later with a glass in one hand and an almost empty bottle of Johnny Walker in the other. "This is the last drink left, ma'am," he told her.

"Last drink? There's another bottle in the cabinet," she insisted.

"You opened that two days ago, ma'am," he replied.

"Don't get beside yourself with me, Lionel!" she shrieked.

He mumbled a retort and left the room.

She placed the glass on the coffee table, hurriedly reached for the phone, and dialed a number. "Hello, Sue," she said. "If you're coming over later, could you get me two bottles of Johnny Walker and some cigarettes?"

She emptied the contents of the bottle in the glass with trembling hand and proceeded to light a cigarette.

It had been ten years since the wedding. Annabelle, now in her early thirties, had lost her girlish visage and optimistic outlook on life. She took a deep pull from the cigarette and threw her head against the sofa, contemplating her life.

She was elated when T.J. carried her across the threshold of the large, elegant house with a breathtaking view of the lush Queen's Park Savannah. The first two weeks of marriage were blissful. She saw a side of T.J. she never knew existed—he was loving and caring, and he fulfiled her desires. But after two weeks, she noticed a radical change in him; he began staying away from home for a day or two and then weeks at a time. He would suddenly appear and then disappear. She thought that marriage had tamed him but again realized that the more she thought she understood him, the more of an enigma he became. T.J. did not move out of his old home; he shared his time between his bachelor flats and his marital home. This was the same arrangement he had with Aunt Catherine, Annabelle recalled. She thought of how lonely and miserable Aunt Catherine had grown and wondered if she'd suffer the same fate.

At times when she grew lonely, she sought comfort by drinking herself to sleep and smoking. Many a morning, she awoke with a nagging headache on the sofa where she had been drinking the night before.

Her friendship with Suelyn had strengthened over the years, and she often called Suelyn to enquire about T.J.'s whereabouts or to unleash her burdens. The bond between her and Suelyn grew even closer during her tedious pregnancy.

The rain was pounding loudly against the tile roof and glass windows, and the whistling wind incited a riot among the trees. Annabelle awoke, disoriented in the middle of the pitch-black night, as the storm had disrupted the power supply. She called out to Lionel, but her voice was drowned out by the raging storm. She attempted to ease herself from the sofa, but her head was spinning out of control. Her stomach was queasy, and she desperately needed to go to the bathroom. With all her might, she forced her limp body off the sofa. As she pressed her hand against the chair for leverage, the contents of her stomach spilled all over the sofa and floor. She felt the room spinning faster and faster until her body slumped to the floor.

The ambiance felt strange as she slowly regained consciousness. She opened her eyes, staring around the room until the blurry faces which hovered above her became clearer. She felt a mild tapping on her cheek accompanied by the voice of a man.

"Mrs Johnson! Mrs Johnson! Can you hear me?"

She looked up to see a doctor standing over her, and she attempted to sit up but was too weak.

"Don't move, Mrs Johnson. Try to relax," the doctor said.

She recognized the faces of T.J., who moved closer to the bed, gently squeezing her hand, and Suelyn, who wiped the sweat from her face.

"How are you, dear? You scared the life out of us," T.J. said. "You'll be all right. I have to run off to a meeting, but Suelyn will take care of you."

When he left, the doctor asked Suelyn to wait outside, as he wanted to speak with Mrs Johnson privately. Suelyn squeezed Annabelle's hand gently and left the room.

The doctor pulled a chair next to the bed and sat facing her. "Mrs Johnson," he said. "You have been naughty. Drinking and smoking heavily—you have to stop that right away for both you and your baby."

Annabelle stared at him with a baffled look on her face. The doctor smiled back at her and said, "Yes, Mrs Johnson, you are pregnant."

He retrieved a file from the nightstand and left.

Suelyn hurried back to the room, and with a weak voice, Annabelle told her the news with a discontented look on her face.

Annabelle prayed for the weeks and months to hurry by. She could not recall being so sick and harassed during her first pregnancy. T.J. followed the doctor's advice and literally confined her to bed like a prisoner and insisted that Suelyn move in to the house to keep watch over her.

Annabelle sensed that the real reason Suelyn was there was to police her drinking and smoking. After all, Lionel and the maid could easily take care of her. A private nurse also visited twice daily. She felt like a prisoner in her own home.

There was, however, an upside to her pregnancy: T.J. was around more often. He was enthused at being a father and having an heir to carry on his legacy and boasted that he was going to be a real father to this child. Annabelle noticed the gleam in his eye and his happy disposition. She was optimistic about her, T.J., and the baby living together like a real family.

T.J., who was visibly edgy, was on his fourth drink of brandy and his third cigar as he waited in the living room for the midwife to open the door. But she didn't need to tell him the news. In the silence of the night, he could hear the squeal of a newborn baby.

His heart skipped a beat. The brandy snifter fell to the floor and shattered into little pieces. He rushed up the flight of stairs and walked briskly toward the bedroom, almost colliding with the midwife who was on her way to tell him the good news.

"You have a healthy baby boy," she gushed.

He pushed the door and rushed over to Annabelle, who looked like she'd been through hell. With a smug look on his face, he took her hand and gently squeezed it. He walked over to the nurse, who handed him the red, chubby baby, whom he clutched clumsily, and said, "You're going to be a blessed child, Troy Thomas Johnson. You'll be as powerful and wealthy as your old man." He planted a soft kiss on the child's forehead and handed him back to the nurse.

Annabelle was fast asleep when he left the room.

Annabelle beamed with pride at the site of T.J. holding their son; it rekindled the happiness she knew as a child in Bristol Village. T.J. was home every night and rarely travelled on company business. She was certain that this child had changed T.J. into a real family man.

It was Troy Thomas George Johnson's first birthday, and Annabelle and Suelyn planned a grand party. There were more than fifty children and their parents at the gala affair. The sound of crackers, whistles, and screaming children penetrated the atmosphere. Colourful streamers and balloons hung from every wall and entrance—inside and out. The following day, a picture of Troy in his birthday hat occupied the front page of the newspaper captioned, "Heir Turns One".

After the children had left and Troy retired to bed, a few friends of Annabelle and T.J. gathered for cocktails. Annabelle led Suelyn aside.

"Where's T.J., Suelyn?" she carped. "He didn't show up for the party; at least he could have the common decency to attend. This is embarrassing! What will the guests think?"

Suelyn tried to console her. "He left the office early today. Maybe he has a surprise planned for his son."

Two, three, four hours passed by, and T.J. did not show up. The next day, T.J. returned without any explanation. Annabelle was certain that he had reverted back his old ways. He waited until his son was one year old before moving out of the house. She was exactly in the same predicament as Aunt Catherine and couldn't help but wonder if there was a new "Annabelle". She resumed her drinking and smoking binge and felt lonelier and emptier than before.

The alarm clock in Suelyn's apartment was turned off to facilitate an extra few minutes of sleep, when the phone began an annoying ring and jolted her from a half-asleep nap.

"Who the hell can that be at this ungodly hour?" she said to herself as she reluctantly reached for the receiver.

"Please, Miss Suelyn, you have to come right away! Madam Annabelle is going mad! You have to come right now," the frantic voice on the other end of the phone shouted.

"Lionel, is that you?" Suelyn asked.

"Yes, Miss Suelyn. You have to come right away!" Lionel begged.

Suelyn sprang from bed and hurriedly brushed her teeth and threw on a dress before scampering out of the house, tidying her hair on her way to the car.

The distant, forested mountains were barely visible in the emerging light of dawn as Suelyn made her way around the Queen's Park Savannah, with silhouettes of lofty trees shimmering with dew.

An ominous silence greeted her as she stepped gingerly up the stairs and stood on the porch for a moment before gently pushing the door. She felt a sense a relief when she spotted a sedate-looking Annabelle lying on the couch, staring up at the ceiling. She treaded lightly among shards of broken ornaments and overturned objects strewn all over the living room and sat on the edge of the sofa. She took Annabelle's hand.

"Belle, are you all right?" Suelyn asked.

Annabelle turned to her slowly with intense affront in her teary eyes and handed her the newspaper, which was folded on the society page with a half-page picture of T.J. and Annabelle, captioned, "Couple of the Year". Suelyn was puzzled. She could see nothing disturbing about the newspaper picture and flattering blurb except that their age difference was distinctly obvious. They looked like father and daughter; after all, T.J. was some forty years older than Annabelle.

"You see what I'm talking about?" Annabelle said.

Suelyn was stumped.

"My marriage is a sham. We are practically living separate lives, but to the world, we are the couple of the year? What a joke," Annabelle retorted.

Annabelle's anguish was now becoming clear to Suelyn, who went to the kitchen and returned with two cups of coffee. "This might calm your nerves," Suelyn said as she handed the coffee to Annabelle.

Annabelle composed herself and lit a cigarette. "Sue," she said, "I want to ask you something. You told me before that you were T.J.'s private secretary and that you won't or can't tell me about his confidential matters. But I'm asking you as a friend—is there another woman in T.J.'s life?"

Suelyn was dumbfounded by Annabelle's brazen question.

She reached for her coffee cup and took a long sip while contemplating a reply.

"Annabelle, I don't think so. In any event, T.J. knows that we are friends and would play it safe around me," Suelyn said.

Annabelle, aware that she had found herself in the same predicament as Aunt Catherine—except that, unlike her aunt, she was married to T.J.—swore that she would not be made a fool of. She turned to Suelyn and asserted vehemently, "T.J. will become the sorriest man alive!"

Suelyn was scared for Annabelle. She wondered if Annabelle knew the tyrant of a man T.J. was. After all, she had known him much longer than Annabelle.

Chapter 28

• •

Puffs of cigarette smoke and the loud music filled the dimly lit bar as Suelyn negotiated her way through a brawl of drunken men. She was mortified by being in such an undignified place but was deeply concerned for Annabelle. As her eyes wandered through the squalor of drunken natives and sailors, she came upon Annabelle seated on a barstool puffing a cigarette and sipping from a glass in the company of a young Caucasian man.

Suelyn timidly approached Annabelle and tapped her on the shoulder. Annabelle turned around and was shocked out of her wits to see Suelyn standing in front of her.

"Let's get out of here, Annabelle," Suelyn said.

Annabelle looked at her with glazed eyes and blurted out, slurring her words as she spoke, "T.J. sent you to get me? Tell him I'm living it up, dear. For all I know, you could be the other woman."

Suelyn pretended not to hear what Annabelle said and held her hand to lead her out of the bar. "Let's go, Annabelle. You are drunk," Suelyn said.

Annabelle pulled her hand away, causing Suelyn to lose her balance and fall against a drunken sailor. She struggled to regain her balance and darted out of the bar to the obnoxious jeers and whistles of a group of disorderly men.

Annabelle returned to the barstool and hugged the young Caucasian man who asked her, "Who was the gorgeous chick?"

"My husband's secretary," Annabelle replied.

"What did she want?" the young man asked.

"What the hell is this, an interrogation?" Annabelle retorted and eased her arm from around his shoulder.

"Okay, I'm sorry. Let me buy you another drink," he said.

"No, I really must go now," Annabelle replied.

"Will I see you again?" he asked.

"If it is meant to be," she said and headed for the door.

He gestured the barman for another drink and asked, "Who was that lady?"

The barman snickered. "Come on, Bradley Reed. You mean to tell me that a man about town like you don't know who she is?" the barman jested.

"No, come on, tell me," he insisted.

"That lady was Annabelle Castello Johnson," the barman said.

The young man's jaw dropped. "I thought she looked familiar," he said.

It was close to midnight when Annabelle drifted into the house and threw herself onto the sofa, startling Suelyn, who had drifted off to sleep in the recliner waiting for her to come home. Suelyn got up and flicked on the light to see Annabelle sprawled across the sofa, fast asleep. There was an urgent matter she had to discuss with Annabelle, but it would have to wait until she sobered up.

The morning sun and the large basket ferns and tropical plants cast dappled shadows on the tile floor and against the white wrought-iron table and chairs in the veranda. The kitchen maid moved briskly about setting the table for an outdoor breakfast. Suelyn approached the porch with the newspaper in one hand and a blue headtie in the other, which she wrapped around her loose hair before sitting at the table. She poured a cup of coffee and was riffling through the newspaper for the second time, when Annabelle hobbled into the veranda and sat opposite her. With red eyes and puffy cheeks, she greeted Suelyn with a languid, "Good morning," which she blurted through a yawn. Suelyn rested the newspaper on the table and looked at Annabelle with an austere glare.

"What's wrong? Why are you looking at me like that?" Annabelle asked.

"Like what?" Suelyn replied.

"As though I'm a naughty child and you, the mother," Annabelle chided.

"I want to talk to you as a friend. I hate to come across as though I'm prying into your private life, but I care about you," Suelyn said.

Annabelle's face morphed into a scowl. "I'm fed up with everyone trying to tell me that I'm wrong when all I'm doing is giving T.J. a taste of his own medicine!"

Suelyn shook her head from side to side in disgust.

"Tell me, where's T.J.? Where the hell's T.J.? I've not seen him in days. I have to lie to Troy when he asks about his father!" Annabelle retorted.

Lionel rushed over and asked, "Is there something wrong, ma'am?"

Suelyn dispatched him. "Everything's under control. Please leave us alone," Suelyn said.

When he was gone, Suelyn dragged her chair next to Annabelle. "I'm sorry to upset you; I didn't mean to. I only want to put you on your guard. You must listen to me. T.J. has found out about your rendezvous at the bar and has hired a detective to spy on you. I'm not quite certain of his intention, but I have a hunch about this. He's out to prove that you are an unfit wife and mother. I believe he wants to file for a divorce. You could end up the loser. You cannot fight T.J.! Please be careful," Suelyn uttered.

Annabelle lifted her head from the table and stared at Suelyn with a bewildered look on her face. She apologized to Suelyn for her behaviour and said that she wanted to be alone. She got up and headed for her room.

Annabelle looked at herself in the mirror and gnashed her teeth. "This is the last time that T.J. will take advantage of a woman. I will bring him to his knees!" she said to herself. "After all, I am George Castello's daughter. Just who the hell T.J. thinks he is?" she muttered.

She sat on the bed seething with anger.

Chapter 29

• •

T.J. came to the house to take Troy to the Queen's Park Savannah to ride his bicycle. He passed Annabelle sitting on the porch, puffing a cigarette and reading a magazine. Neither she nor T.J. acknowledged each other. Troy came over to kiss her goodbye while T.J. walked ahead carrying the bicycle in his hand. When they left, Annabelle pressed the cigarette in the ashtray and went inside to pour herself a drink before her midmorning nap.

It was midday when she awoke, staring up at the ceiling, mulling over her miserable life and the letter she had surprisingly received from Rosabelle the day before. It had been over a year since she had last received any word from Bristol Village and thought that someone had died—Ma perhaps.

Dear Annabelle,

I am writing to let you know that I got your letter, and I can't send Joyanne to Port-of-Spain to see you, as Ricardo feels that it would not be good for her. He is fearful that you might tell her something to confuse her. Anyway, Ma is not too well, as her pressure and sugar are acting up. If you can send more money to take care of Ma's medicine, she will be glad. Please do not pay her a visit, as she still blames you for Pa's death, and seeing you might raise her pressure. I'm writing to ask you to send the money for Joyanne and Ma to the bank account number, which I wrote below. Ma can't always go to the bank to draw out the money, so we opened a new account under my name and Ricardo's.

PS—I and Ricardo got married two months ago. Pastor Miles said that we were living in sin for too long, and he married us.

Rosabelle

"Still spiteful after all these years, she and Ma! All they want is money, money, money!" Annabelle scoffed. "In any event, Joyanne is now a young lady and doesn't need anyone's permission to come to Port-of-Spain."

The letter evoked bittersweet memories of a time when life was simple and carefree in Bristol Village. Though she was now living the life she had dreamed of as a child, in a strange way, she was envious of Rosabelle. The words of her father—"Everything in life has a price"—reverberated in her mind and incited a sentimental smile on her face.

The ringing of the phone snapped her out of her reflection. Lionel hollered from down the corridor, "Ma'am, it's for you!"

"I wonder who the hell this could be," she mumbled as she reached for the phone.

"Hello, Annabelle. Why the hell don't you give T.J. a divorce? He doesn't want you, you know. He spent the last few days with me," the anonymous caller said and slammed down the phone.

Annabelle's jaw dropped, and her eyes stared up at the ceiling in utter shock as she clutched the receiver in her hand. She placed the receiver down and picked it up again to call Suelyn when she remembered that Suelyn had gone to Mount Saint Benedict with her mother. She got out of bed, seething with rage, and headed for the bathroom.

The clock was striking one o'clock when she told Lionel that she was leaving for an appointment and to ensure that Troy had a bath when T.J. brought him back home.

The club was unusually empty for a Saturday afternoon when she arrived and sat down at the bar.

"Hello, Mrs Johnson," the barman said. "Are you having your usual?"

"Yeah, but make it a double, and hold the chaser," she replied as she lit a cigarette.

She sat making small talk with the barman when she heard a voice behind her say, "Lucky me to encounter the beautiful carnival queen Annabelle Castello once again." She turned around to see the young Caucasian man from a few days before.

"So you knew who I was the first time we met?" she asked.

"Everybody does. After all, you are the most beautiful lady on the island," he said.

"So is that your strategy, to lure unsuspecting women with insincere compliments?" she replied.

"If you knew me, you would know that I have a reputation for fraternizing with attractive and classy women," he teased.

"Then I should consider myself lucky that Trinidad's most desirable playboy, Bradley Reed, finds me attractive," she quipped.

He furrowed his brow in surprise. "You know who I was all along?" he blurted.

"Well, like me, your reputation precedes you too," she said.

It was late evening when they left the bar in each other's arms to the stares and glares of the patrons.

Lionel, who sat on the porch eagerly waiting for Annabelle to come home, hurried down the stairs when her car turned into the driveway. He was surprised to see her emerge from the passenger's seat in a dishevelled state. She braced herself with one hand on the car to keep her balance and tottered over to the driver's side. The glass rolled down to reveal the face of a young man with light hair. Lionel's face froze in utter astonishment as Annabelle bent down and planted a passionate kiss on the young man's lips. The young man then carelessly reversed the car into the roadway, causing the driver of an approaching car to swerve to avoid a collision. She laughed and shuffled up the stairs with Lionel treading behind.

"Mr Johnson asked about your whereabouts, ma'am, when he dropped off Troy. He said he was going to track you down," Lionel disclosed alarmingly.

She laughed infernally before erupting in a coughing spasm. When she recovered, she turned to Lionel and said, "The next time you see T.J., tell him that I too am on to him."

Lionel looked at her curiously.

Chapter 30

· ·

It was a monotonous Monday at the office, and Suelyn heaved a sigh of relief when the clock struck 4.30. Besides, the anxiety to tell Annabelle what she had learned was killing her. She rushed out of the office and headed over to Annabelle's. Earlier in the day, Suelyn had accidentally heard T.J. through the intercom talking to a strange man who had come to see him. She heard T.J. telling the man, "A sleazy bar she goes to … evade persons who know her … a red sports car … a notorious playboy … I want to nail her in court." She put two and two together and gathered that the man was perhaps the detective hired by T.J. to spy on Annabelle.

Annabelle's nonchalant response to the grave news irked Suelyn.

"I know you mean well, but I can handle T.J.," Annabelle replied.

Suelyn flew up from the chair and yelped, "Are you listening to me at all?"

Annabelle got up and placed her arm on Suelyn's shoulder. "Listen to me. I know what T.J. is up to, and I can beat him at his own game. Besides, Bradley is a smart guy. He won't do anything to jeopardize me," Annabelle said.

"Can you honestly say that you love Bradley, or are you using him to get back at—" Suelyn retorted.

Annabelle turned her back to Suelyn, and with impatience in her tone, she interrupted her before she could finished her sentence. "Listen, all my life there was always someone there for me; I'm not meant to be alone. Can't you understand that I need Bradley? Why can't you be happy for me?" Annabelle said curtly.

Suelyn turned to her and said, "I've warned you, Belle! All that's left to say is, be careful." She retrieved her handbag and left.

Annabelle rushed to answer the phone and then headed for the shower. She came out of the bedroom looking sultry in a red, gauzy blouse and tight-fitting Wrangler's. She called out to Lionel, "I'll be out for a while. Keep an eye on Troy. You know how he can get into mischief at times."

Annabelle was assailed by doubts as she parked her car in the hotel's private car park—it was as if the air foreboded something tragic. "Perhaps it's just mind over matter," she said and proceeded to freshen her make-up and hair in the rear-view mirror before entering the hotel. Bradley was stark naked in bed when she entered the room. She stripped off her clothes and joined him in bed, but the tryst did not seem as exhilarating and sensual as previous times, and Bradley detected her apprehension.

"Talk to me, babes. What's wrong?" he asked with a sense of urgency.

"It baffled me that you would ask the barman to call me about meeting you here," Annabelle said with utter concern in her voice.

"Hell no, I didn't ask anyone to call you. Someone called and said that you were on your way to meet me here," he insisted.

"Oh my gosh. Suelyn tried to warn me! Brad! Brad!" she shrieked.

"What?" he exclaimed.

With extreme urgency in her voice, she cried, "Brad, Brad, we have to get of here! This is a set—"

Before she could finish speaking, the door was flung open, and two policemen, the hotel owner, and T.J. glared at the two naked people. T.J. had a sinister smile on his haggard face as a photographer appeared from behind them and triggered his camera. Bradley Reed erupted in stitches of infernal laughter.

The blue Cadillac slammed into the partially opened gate. Annabelle scurried from the car, sobbing hysterically, and headed up the stairs and into the bedroom, slamming the door behind her. Lionel immediately rushed to the phone and called Suelyn, who arrived in less than half an hour.

"She's in her room, Miss Suelyn. I tried to talk with her, but she won't open the door," Lionel related.

They both hurried up the stairs and stood outside the door. Suelyn tapped the door. "Belle, Belle, please open the door," she said.

There was no reply.

"Let me try," Lionel said.

"Oh my gosh!" Suelyn cried. "I wonder if ... No, she can't be that ..." Suelyn hoped.

Suelyn turned around to see Troy staring up at her with a sad look on his face. She took his arms and led him back to his room.

"Mummy's okay. Stay in your room, and she'll come and talk with you just now. Okay?" Suelyn said.

He nodded his head as Suelyn pulled the door shut.

As Suelyn and Lionel stood in the corridor, wondering what to do, they heard the door unlatch. Suelyn pushed the door and entered the bedroom to find Annabelle sitting on the bed. Lionel asked if she needed anything. He then left the room to fetch coffee.

Suelyn pulled a chair next to the bed and asked if the coffee was okay. Annabelle nodded her head and took a few sips.

"What's wrong?" Suelyn asked.

Annabelle bent her head in defeat. "You were right," she murmured, "T.J.'s out to get me."

"Well, now that you know, you'll be on your guard," Suelyn replied.

"You don't understand. He caught us—Brad and me—in the hotel. He got someone to call Brad to say that I was waiting for him at the hotel. To cut a long story short, he and the police kicked the door open and took a photograph of Brad and me. How could I be so stupid?" Annabelle rebuked herself.

Suelyn's mouth froze agape with shock as she took Annabelle gently in her arms and said, "It will be all right." She waited for Annabelle to fall asleep and left scared to death for her.

It was midmorning when Annabelle awoke. She sat on the bed for a while with a harrowing look on her face. After going to the bathroom, she pulled on a duster coat and headed downstairs for the kitchen where she encountered the maid.

"Where's Lionel?" Annabelle asked.

"He's at the gate, collecting the mail, ma'am," the maid replied.

She sat at the table, sipping her coffee, when Lionel came into the kitchen.

"Ma'am, Suelyn called earlier to ask about you," Lionel said. "And, oh, this letter was delivered for you; I had to sign for it."

Annabelle stared curiously at the typed envelope addressed to her with an instruction: "To Be Opened by Addressee Only". She got up and went into the living room, fearing the worst as she anxiously opened the letter and read it with profound anxiety. When she was through, she leaned her head against the sofa and closed he eyes tightly for a few moments. She opened her eyes and stared aimlessly at the wall until her coffee, which lay on the table next to her, was cold.

The ringing of the phone startled her. Lionel shouted that Suelyn was on the phone. Annabelle answered and asked Suelyn to come over right away.

"T.J. is hell-bent on destroying me!" Annabelle blurted as Suelyn came through the door. She handed Suelyn the envelope and pressed her head against the headrest of the sofa as Suelyn riffled through the letter.

"You have to get hold of yourself if you want to win this," Suelyn told her.

"But he has a photograph of me cheating with Bradley!" Annabelle exclaimed.

"Who knows? A good lawyer could get around that," Suelyn said.

"By the way, did T.J. say anything to you?" Annabelle enquired.

"He did not come into the office today, and he didn't call, either," Suelyn replied.

Annabelle turned to her with a look of defeat on her face and asked, "Do you think he could really take Troy away?"

"Let's not jump the gun. We need to find you a good lawyer," Suelyn replied.

"There's some ... something I always meant to ask ... to ask you and don't know how. It's kind of, well, kind of personal," Annabelle stuttered.

"Well, just ask," Suelyn blurted.

Annabelle fidgeted before building up the courage to ask. "Has T.J. ever made advances to you?"

Suelyn snickered and replied, "Even if he wanted to, he couldn't. Mother would have murdered him, and he knew that. Besides, it was the priest who spoke to T.J. about hiring me, and every day for a year, he would call or come in to check up on me. I guess T.J.'s reputation was well known."

Annabelle breathed a sigh of relief.

To divert her mind from her dilemma, Annabelle turned to Suelyn and said, "You never spoke about your father."

"Well, Mother never spoke much about him and got all choked up whenever I asked. Besides, my grandfather was like a father to me," Suelyn replied.

Annabelle assumed a philosophical disposition and turned to Suelyn and theorized, "It's so unfair, Sue. T.J. can have all the women he wants and no one even bats an eye. But as soon as a woman retaliates, she is called a whore. I mean it was T.J. who drove me in the arms of Brad."

"That's life. We can't change it," Suelyn replied.

"I feel so helpless," Annabelle mumbled.

"There's nothing we can do now. Why don't you get a good rest, and we'll talk about hiring a lawyer tomorrow?" Suelyn suggested.

Annabelle gulped down two glasses of Johnny Walker before heading off to bed. Suelyn tucked her in before leaving.

Morning came too soon for Annabelle. She wished she could remain in her bed forever, but the loud knocking on her door jolted her back to the stark reality of her wretched life.

"Ma'am, the lawyer will be here in a half hour!" Lionel bellowed.

Annabelle must have smoked five, six cigarettes when Suelyn finally arrived with the lawyer, who apologized for being late due to an unexpected matter. He was an impeccably attired, slim, greying Caucasian man with an English drawl, named Ward Donaldson.

He glanced at his watch and asked politely if he could use the phone.

While he dialed the number, Annabelle asked to be excused and gestured Suelyn to follow her.

"He's British! Are you sure that T.J. doesn't know him?"

"No. He's a highly reputed lawyer whom I met while attending a lecture," Suelyn assured her.

When they returned to the living room, he was finishing up his conversation. He hung up the receiver and asked if they were ready to proceed.

"Mrs Johnson," he said, "your husband is a tactful and influential man who's out to prove that you are a fornicator, an alcoholic, and an unfit mother. From the letter sent by his lawyer, he has stated his intent to initiate divorce proceedings."

Annabelle interrupted him, "Whose side are you on? That is not true! I received a threatening call from his mistress and was only using Bradley Reed to get back at him!"

"Mrs Johnson, I'm merely repeating what your husband has accused you of. You have to understand that you have to counter these claims with strong evidence. For example, can you prove that his so-called mistress harassed you on the phone? And what about the photograph of you and Bradley Reed in a hotel, witnessed by the owner of the brothel and a police inspector?" Ward Donaldson replied.

Annabelle stormed out the room in tears.

Ward Donaldson turned to Suelyn and said, "You'd better explain to your friend that this is a serious matter, and she has to learn to control her temper and emotions if she intends to land on her feet." He proceeded to scribble a note, which he handed to Suelyn, and said, "Also, I want you to give her this note."

Suelyn nodded her head in agreement and showed the lawyer out before proceeding to Annabelle's room.

Annabelle flew up from the bed, enraged. "Never! Never! I'd rather beg on the streets than to go to that dog!" she snapped after reading the note.

Suelyn tried to reason with her, "You have to look on the practical side, else you'll risk losing everything, including your son. Ward is a professional and is good at his job. Do as he says, and go to T.J. and talk things over. See if both of you can work something out instead of going to court," Suelyn suggested.

"I can't face him after all that's happened. He will humiliate me!" Annabelle exclaimed. "Besides, that's Ward's job; I'm paying him good money."

"Belle, remember what Ward said—that T.J. told you of his intention to proceed with legal actions; he hasn't yet. And having a lawyer go to T.J. will only agitate him. We both know T.J. Perhaps all he wants is for you to come crawling back to him," Suelyn reasoned.

Annabelle's silence spoke consent.

"I'll tell T.J. that you want to see him and set up an appointment," Suelyn said.

"Okay. Guess I have no choice," Annabelle replied sheepishly. The reality of losing everything, including her son and business, now seemed real. She had already lost her daughter, and now the thought of losing her son was heartbreaking.

Suelyn spent the next morning trying to muster up courage to approach T.J. about Annabelle's matter, rehashing in her mind the right words to say. After all, their interaction had always been reticent and businesslike. She was unsure as to how he would respond to a personal and sensitive subject such as this. She was almost certain that he would insult her.

T.J. had telephoned earlier to tell her that he would be in after 2.00 but instead came in at 3.20, accompanied by two men who were still in his office after closing time. T.J. was surprised to see Suelyn at her desk when the men finally left. He asked what she was doing there after working hours. She told him that she had some filing to do and would be leaving shortly. He returned to his office and shut the door behind him.

Suelyn detected that he wasn't in a pleasant frame of mind and thought it best to leave it alone. She was about to open the door to leave but changed her mind. There would never be a good time to approach T.J. about this personal matter, she thought, so without thinking about it, she knocked on his door and entered the office. His head was buried in a pile of documents sprawled all over the desk, and he was unaware of her presence.

"Excuse me, Mr Johnson," she said.

He raised his head and looked at her callously. "Yes?" he said sternly.

"I need to talk to you, if it's all right," she replied timidly.

He didn't reply; instead, he continued to peruse the documents on his desk.

She fidgeted with a bunch of keys in her hand.

"Well, go ahead, I'm listening," he said.

Slurring her words, she said, "Well … well, it's about Annabelle. She … she wants to make an appointment to see you."

With a look of indifference on his face, he continued with what he was doing and then sat up on his chair with a malicious grin on his face.

"Don't allow yourself to be used by Annabelle. She'll get what she deserves." He paused for a moment before continuing his discourse in a sterner voice. "I don't want to hear anything about this ever again! Do you understand?"

"Yes, Mr Johnson," she replied awkwardly.

He called her back into the office as she was about to leave. "Since you're so interested in Annabelle's affairs, let her know that I will be picking up Troy after I leave the office. Tell her to pack clothes for at least three days," he demanded.

During the weeks that followed, Annabelle grew more and more despondent. The reality of being caught between the devil and the deep blue sea had propelled her into a severe bout of depression, and she drank and smoked more than before. Her lawyer had cautioned her about seeing Bradley Reed until the matter was over. In a fit of rage, she threw Suelyn out of the house, accusing her of being a spy for T.J.

Suelyn did not take it personally, as she knew that Annabelle had become erratic. She continued to consult with the lawyer and called Lionel regularly to find out about Annabelle's health. T.J. had concocted a scheme with a social worker and the police to remove Troy from Annabelle's care, but Ward Donaldson challenged the motion, and Troy was allowed to stay with her, pending a final ruling.

One evening at around 5.15 when Suelyn had telephoned Annabelle's home, the phone rang without a response. Suelyn made repeated attempts to call but got no reply. She grew worried, as she had just been awakened by an ominous dream.

She and Annabelle were in a crowded park with people moving swiftly in all directions, as if to escape some disaster. They became separated, and Suelyn searched feverishly for her and was led to a maze of large trees, which she reluctantly entered, shouting, "Annabelle! Annabelle!" The place grew darker and darker until she could see nothing. She was about to faint when the sound of a flight of birds snapped her back to consciousness. As she turned a narrow corner, the sight of a flickering light was visible in the distance. She followed the light and came upon a brightly lit savannah. The birds emerged from within the branches of a tree and flew high up in the sky until they disappeared. She ran toward a building which looked like a church and accidentally wandered into a funeral service. She moved timidly up the aisle toward an open coffin. As she neared the coffin, she stared up at the ceiling to avoid looking inside. Then her eyes were involuntarily guided inside of the coffin. Her heart began to race. As she was about to look in the coffin, she jumped from sleep, terrified.

Suelyn made one last attempt to call Annabelle's home, but there was no reply. Unable to contain her anxiety, she jumped into her car and headed over to Annabelle's.

Her heart throbbed against her chest. The blood drained from her head to her feet. She instinctively sensed that something terrible had happened. A crowd had gathered in front of the house, and she could see the flashing lights from the emergency vehicles parked along the driveway. Then she saw the crowd of people rushing to get a view of something which was taking place in the driveway. She sat statuesque in her car as two men emerged from inside, carrying a stretcher with a draped body to an ambulance parked in front of the driveway. Suelyn felt light-headed. Her unconscious body fell against the steering wheel.

Chapter 31

∙ ∙

It was raining incessantly when the small funeral cortège made its way to the cemetery, following a church service for family members and close friends. Suelyn remained seated in the church, as she was too weak and distraught to attend the interment. She bent her head and said a silent prayer for Annabelle, who remained at home, heavily sedated. She also harboured deep empathy for T.J. as he held on to the coffin, sobbing hysterically. She never imagined that T.J. possessed the capacity to express his emotions so openly, let alone cry. This was so tragic! Troy dead at twelve! She bent her head in anguish and recounted the events of the past few days.

She recalled being slapped into consciousness by a police officer after she had fainted inside her car outside Annabelle's home and was taken inside and placed on the sofa. The kitchen maid handed her a cup of tea, insisting that she drink it all. She took a few sips and placed the cup on the table.

"Where's Annabelle?" she asked. "What happened? Who are all these people?" She turned to the maid for the answers.

"Don't you know?" the maid asked.

"Know what?" Suelyn insisted.

The maid sat down beside her and said, "Your godson is dead, Miss Suelyn!"

Suelyn felt faint. "Dead? Dead?" she repeated. "How? Where's Annabelle?" She placed her head against the sofa and began to sob. The maid patted her on her back and recounted the events to her.

"It was terrible, Miss Sue. I just finish hanging out the laundry when I went to the back of the house to get the bucket, when I come face-to-face with the body of Troy with head downward in the pool. I started to shout, 'Oh God! Oh God! Somebody come quick! Come quick!' Mr Lionel hastened from inside the house and asked me what the commotion about. 'You crazy or something, woman? You'll wake Ma'am.' I pointed at the pool. No one had the nerve to wake Miss Annabelle. Mr Johnson eventually come. He take the lifeless body of Troy out the pool and hold on to him like he don't want to let him go. It was the police who get him to hand the child over to the ambulance people. Imagine a man like Mr Johnson crying like a baby. He walk into the house like a madman, shouting curses at Miss Annabelle. He even call her murderer. She faint on the floor. The doctor give her injections. Poor soul, she yet to get over the shock. She say to Mr Lionel to give she a bottle of sleeping pills so she could end her life."

Suelyn was too devastated to cry.

Chapter 32

● ●

"We have to get this over with!" Ward Donaldson insisted to Suelyn.

"But it's just weeks following Troy's death!" Suelyn retorted.

"As far as the court is concerned, that's sufficient time, unless we produce a medical report saying that Annabelle's unwell. But I think it's time we bring closure to this matter, at least while she still has sympathetic support," Ward insisted.

Suelyn hurried up the stairs ahead of Ward and knocked gently on Annabelle's door. Surprisingly, Annabelle opened the door and beckoned Suelyn and Ward inside, looking a tad livelier.

"Belle, Ward has come to discuss an urgent matter with you," Suelyn said.

"I don't care any more! I deserve anything that happens to me," Annabelle said in a nonchalant tone. "My pa was right; success comes with a price." She paused to blow her nose. "For what it's worth, I have a big price to pay. I've lost my son; my daughter thinks that my sister is her mother.

The only man I ever loved I've abandoned for the high life. So whatever happens to me now, I don't really care."

"Come on, it's not the end of the world. There's so much to live for!" Suelyn exclaimed.

Ward intervened. "I have a strategy that will allow you to retain some substantial assets," he said.

"What, plead insanity?" Annabelle asked.

There was no reply from Ward.

"You're serious, aren't you?" Her eyes brimmed with anger. "You people don't get it, do you? I've lost my son, my daughter, and everything that meant something to me. Nothing, I mean nothing, matters to me now. Ward, send me your bill; I don't want to pursue this any more! And you want to know something else? All I wanted was to get custody of Troy to hurt T.J.!"

Suelyn went over to her and held her hand.

"I'm a bitch—an evil woman. You really want to stick around?" Annabelle said.

Ward walked out of the room, and Suelyn treaded behind to offer an apology. He turned to Suelyn and said, "I've seen that behaviour before, and I won't be surprised if she guzzles down a bottle of pills or slits her wrist. She doesn't need a lawyer; she needs a shrink." He slammed the door behind him and left.

It was 12.16 when the loud ringing of the phone penetrated the silence of the early morning, rudely awaking Annabelle from her sleep. A few minutes later, there was a knock on her door.

The voice of Lionel whispered, "Can I come in, ma'am?"

The door slowly opened. She got up and sat on the bed with a faraway look in her eyes, anticipating bad news from Lionel.

"T.J.'s dead, ma'am. He suffered a heart attack," Lionel blurted and walked away.

She stared up at the ceiling with her face void of emotion. A thousand thoughts rushed through her mind. The divorce matter had also died, she assumed, but it no longer felt like a victory. Her life, as far as she was concerned, was worse than death—her mind fermented with guilt, grief, and hopelessness.

Sleep came long and hard.

Chapter 33

•••

1967

A small group of elegantly attired people gathered beneath a white, ornate tent on the lawn of Annabelle's new home, west of Port-of-Spain, with a breathtaking view of the ocean. She was about to disclose "big news".

After spending time in an institution, she emerged renewed and revitalized. She took the advice of the therapist and purged herself of the past—she sold her three houses, her cars and her furniture, and paid off her former staff with the exception of Lionel, whom she considered an old, trusted friend. She was recently featured in the newspaper for her generous donations to charitable organizations for children, battered women, and animals.

Annabelle, now a tad pudgy around the waistline with an emerging double chin and chubby cheeks, looked a year or two younger than her thirty-seven years—the youthful sheen still glowed in her eyes and flawless complexion. Her impeccable style and panache were intact, as evident by her stylish, flowered gown and classy accessories. But she kept on carping to Suelyn about the wrinkles on her face and crow's feet under her eyes.

Bradley Reed, decked in a navy-blue suit, lily-white silk shirt, and burgundy tie, stood next to her, puffing a cigarette with an uneasy demeanour and an awkward look on his face. She clinked a tulip champagne glass with a fork to get the attention of the guests. Everyone gathered around, eagerly awaiting the "big news", which she blurted out without an overture, rousing the guests into a resounding chant, "To love, happiness, and health", as they raised their stemmed glasses, sparkling with Moët, in a celebratory toast.

But Suelyn's jaw dropped, and her heart grew heavy at Annabelle's news. She felt used and betrayed. At the very least, she thought she was attending an engagement party, not a wedding celebration.

Hours before the party, Annabelle came over to her home on her way to the hairdresser for one of their routine girls' chats. "This is strictly hypothetical; don't get worked up, but what do you think about me marrying again?" Annabelle asked.

Suelyn was taken by surprise. She wondered if Annabelle had already planned on getting married and was simply gulling her for an opinion. "I don't know. I guess if you feel ... or met the right person ..." Suelyn struggled for words.

"Well, I met someone, and it just feels right," Annabelle replied cheerily with a schoolgirl's blush on her face.

"Do I know him?" Suelyn asked curiously.

"Yep, you do," Annabelle said.

"What, you want me to play a guessing game?" Suelyn retorted.

"No, but I want you to be honest. Tell me what you honestly think," Annabelle said with a serious inflection in her voice. "It's Bradley Reed."

Suelyn's face morphed into an expression of disappointment, anger, and sheer surprise. She told Annabelle she needed to go to the bathroom and walked away.

Annabelle was not prepared for such a dramatic response.

But Annabelle was adamant that Bradley Reed was the answer to her prayer. She reminded Suelyn that she was not meant to be alone; she needed someone around to hold on to. But Suelyn's real concern was not Annabelle's vulnerability or even her marrying again. If it were anyone else, she would be ecstatic at the news, for as far as she was concerned, Annabelle needed a distraction in her life to sublimate the tragic events she had endured—losing her son in such a dreadful manner and her husband as well. But there was something sinister about Bradley Reed; she could not put her finger on it, but …

The fact that he was much younger than Annabelle had little to do with her notion. Annabelle's enormous inheritance was well publicized in the newspaper, and both Troy and T.J. were insured for millions. Suelyn was convinced that all Bradley Reed wanted was the money, in spite of Annabelle's claim that he had drafted a prenuptial agreement himself, which she said she tore up. Suelyn concluded that he was suave and versed in the art of seduction and that Annabelle was in a vulnerable trance, ripe for the picking. But there was nothing she could say or do; Annabelle was hopelessly in love.

Bradley Reed's reputation—a handsome, rich, dapper playboy—was widely known in Port-of-Spain. Women were flattered to receive even a glance from him. His red,

shiny Porsche was as adjunct to his character as his red
James Dean leather jacket. The sight of Bradley cruising
the streets of the city was in a way alluringly obnoxious.
He had earned a reputation for driving his Porsche stark
naked with the hood down and plunging into swimming
pools in his birthday suit. In some circles, he was seen as
a delinquent. He had no job and no known relatives but
lived a gilded life. He ascribed his wealth to inheritance,
but some speculated that he was a highly paid gigolo for
wealthy women. He was invited to the most elite social
events and held enviable memberships in prestigious clubs.
When he was missed from the circuit, it was assumed
that he had gone on one of his routine trips to Europe
or the United States. His membership to the Blue Island
Country Club was, however, revoked. He was ordered
out of the country club's pool by a group of formidable
old ladies for using foul language. He emerged from the
pool very obediently and sauntered toward the women
with droplets of water sliding off his lean, chiselled body.
One of the women fainted; the others beat a hasty retreat,
while their granddaughters giggled. Bradley Reed was
stark naked.

Besides his potent blend of youth, good looks, and
wealth, Bradley Reed possessed another attribute that
opened prestigious doors in the island's social circle:
he was white. But in spite of his fine physical assets—
chiselled jawbone which framed his androgynous face,
a strong Englishman's nose, wide mouth, dimpled chin,
and blond, curly hair—his rakish reputation preceded
him.

Annabelle was neither in the least perturbed about
Bradley's past life nor was she interested in his wealth. As
far as she was concerned, Bradley Reed rescued her from
the brink of suicide. She was taken by surprise when he

proposed marriage, as she considered their relationship a sordid fling that would soon come to an abrupt end.

They were on their way from a charity art event in Bradley's Porsche when he stopped the car and turned to face Annabelle. "Reach into my pocket, please," he said.

"Yeah, you're not wearing underwear, and I'll grope your cock," she replied, unamused.

"Babes, this is not a joke. In any event, you know I don't wear underwear; it's bad for the circulation. Come on, please," he insisted.

She shoved her hand in his pocket and pulled out a sparkling diamond engagement ring.

"Oh my gosh, Brad. Is this what I think it is? Rumours have it that you are not the marrying type. I'm stunned," she replied.

"I'm serious, babes. Getting old—need to settle down," he said in a serious tone of voice.

She placed the ring on her finger and held it up against the light. "My gosh, they're real diamonds!" she jested.

He turned toward her with a stern look on his face. "Babes, let's get married without anyone knowing. You know your friend Sue doesn't like the best bone in me," he carped.

"Well, she doesn't really know you well enough," Annabelle said in an attempt to dismiss his insinuation. "Besides, it's me who's marrying you, and no one else matters." She leaned over and sucked his lips.

He started the engine and sped off, saying, "Let's really go out and celebrate!"

Bradley was now an unofficial partner in Annabelle's Exclusive Fashions, which was renamed Annabelle's International Fashions. He sourced clothing and accessories from South America on his many visits there and took a keen interest in advertising the business throughout the region, even hiring an advertising agency. Before long, visitors to the island were flocking to Annabelle's International Fashions.

As a pre-wedding present, she bought a large house in a quiet, upscale neighbourhood in west Port-of-Spain, which she decorated herself with objects reminiscent of her mundane childhood—Morris chairs, hat rack, earthen goblets and vases ...

For the past weeks, thoughts of Joyanne, Ricardo, and even her old friend Sally flooded her mind. She planned on inviting them to visit her soon. Then, like a bolt of lightning, thoughts of her brother, Danny, rushed through her mind. No one seemed to know what became of Danny, now thirty-four or thirty-five. The last she heard of Danny was that he was released from the corrective institution around 1951—the same year she married T.J. She was choked up with emotion and regrets that she didn't visit him or spare him a thought. *You only realize how much people mean to you when it's too late,* she lamented.

A month after the wedding celebration, Annabelle booked a flight for Paris to see what was new in the fashion scene. At least that's what she told Bradley. She stood in front of the mirror, almost in a trance, staring critically at herself. She agonized at the emerging wrinkles on her face and was seriously contemplating cosmetic surgery, which she read was commonly done in Paris. The fact that Bradley was than ten years younger than her thirty-seven years incited intense insecurity in her.

"You'll be late for your flight, ma'am!" Lionel said as he glanced at his watch.

She hurriedly dabbed on her lipstick and rushed out of the room.

She boarded the plane and placed the backrest in a reclining posture as she contemplated her future with Bradley Reed. Months of therapy had helped to suppress her tragic past, but at times, she felt as though life had no purpose and that she was merely existing and not really living. Restoring her youth would renew her zeal for life, she thought. She felt a tremendous urge to be young and desirable again. In anger, she had told Suelyn that everyone was envious of her because a young and handsome man found her appealing. But deep down, she harboured intense feelings of insecurity and worthlessness. What if Bradley found that she was too old for him? What if he found a younger and more desirable girl? Maybe Suelyn was right—that she had become erratic and was casting caution to the wind, and that Bradley was an object to sublimate her fears and disappointments, just like some people eat to suppress their problems or drown their sorrows in alcohol. But she was not going to overanalyze life; Bradley made her feel good about her life and made her feel young again, and that was good enough for her.

The rumbling sound among the passengers to express their impatience at the prolonged delay to take-off prompted Annabelle to look at her watch, for she was immersed in thought and had lost track of the time. She turned to the man next to her.

"I wonder what could cause the delay?" she asked.

"I don't know," he replied angrily, "but I wish someone would say something soon!"

A few minutes later, an announcement came through the PA system: "We apologize for the delay, but we have experienced a slight problem and will be departing in ten minutes. Would passenger Annabelle Johnson Reed please exit the plane and report to the security desk."

The passengers craned their necks to gawk curiously at Annabelle Johnson Reed, a well-known name, wondering why she was being sought by security. She remained seated for a while and rummaged through her mind for a reason why she would be asked to report to security. She mustered up the courage to get up and leave the aircraft with her eyes focused straight ahead.

To her surprise, two police officers awaited her at the foot of the aircraft.

"What's wrong?" she asked nervously.

There was no response from either of them; they maintained a callous look and escorted her into a room.

She breathed a sigh of relief when she saw a police inspector whom she knew sitting at the desk.

"What's going on, Paul? What have I done?" she asked frantically.

He dispatched the two officers who had escorted her and called a Criminal Investigation Department officer into the room. The inspector's voice was crude; he acted as though he had never seen her before.

"Don't you recognize me, Paul?" she asked with desperation in her voice.

He ignored her and continued in his uncouth tone. She stared at him in disbelief as her eyes brimmed with tears. He proceeded to empty the contents of a suitcase on the desk and asked, "Recognize this suitcase, ma'am?"

"Yes, it belongs to me," she replied in a trembling tone.

The inspector retrieved a brown bag from the suitcase.

"Do you recognize this?" he asked.

"Yes," she replied, "I'm supposed to deliver it to someone in Paris."

"What's the name of the person?" he demanded.

"I don't know, I swear," she replied.

"You just said you have to deliver it to someone in Paris; now you don't know?" the police inspector blared and ordered an officer to handcuff her and take her down to CID headquarters in Port-of-Spain.

She began trembling profusely.

"Why, what's in the package?" she stuttered.

"Ma'am, there's a million dollars worth of illicit drugs in that package!" he said.

The embryonic light of morning peeped through a small opening at the top of the cell at CID headquarters in Port-of-Spain. The loud sound of approaching footsteps terrified her. She got up and sat on the hard bed and stared at the cell door with bloodshot eyes. The inspector instructed a guard to open the cell. She was escorted into the interrogation room a short distance away, where she was led to a chair behind a table. She sat facing a rugged-looking police officer and the inspector from the airport.

"Start talking!" the officer commanded.

"Please, sir, I don't know anything about the drugs! You have to believe me!" she insisted.

He looked her directly in the eye. "Then explain how it got in your suitcase and why you said you were going to deliver it to someone in Paris."

She bent her head down to avoid eye contact.

"Well?" he asked impatiently.

"My husband asked me to deliver the package to someone he described to me. He said it contained documents concerning a business deal and that the person would approach me in the airport," she whimpered.

"And you didn't find anything suspicious about that?" the officer asked.

"No, not at the time," she replied.

"Well, madam, your husband has put you in grave danger. You could be incarcerated for the rest of your life!"

She bent her head in shame and defeat as she was led back to the cell.

An hour later, she heard footsteps outside the cell, and the door unlock. She was again led to the interrogation room.

"Now, are you willing to strike a deal with us?" the inspector said.

"A deal?" she asked. "What kind of deal?" she asked curiously.

"Well, ma'am, by now I'm sure you realize that you don't have many choices. I'll put it bluntly; either you help us or you go to jail!" the inspector said brashly.

She half nodded her approval.

It was late afternoon when the aircraft touched down. Through the window she could see a light drizzle of rain amid the bright sunlight. She felt surprisingly relaxed—the trip was rewarding, as she had contacted new suppliers of clothing and trendy accessories for her boutiques. The Parisian fashion shows were as glamorous as the magazine features, and she met international designers and even some top celebrities. She managed to cast aside Bradley from her thoughts, although she felt betrayed and used, but life's many catastrophes had strengthened her, even rendered her callous at times.

A big hug and passionate kiss greeted her as she entered the door. "I missed you so," Bradley said with an eager grin on his face. "Did you deliver the contracts?" Bradley asked with a hint of anxiety in his voice.

"As planned, dear," Annabelle replied with an affected simile on her face. "I was so stupid not to confirm the flight and had to overnight in the airport for another flight."

"But, the package—I mean the suitcase—it remained with you all the time?" he asked with deep concern.

"Yes," Annabelle said, "didn't your business associate call to confirm delivery?"

With a faraway look in his eye, he said, "Strange though, he didn't call himself—someone else called the following day."

"What's so strange about that?" Annabelle enquired.

"He usually called himself," he said with a worried look on his face. "Are you sure ... never mind," he said and went into the bedroom.

Bradley got up earlier than Annabelle, pacing the house—from the bedroom, to the living room, and into the kitchen. The ashtray on the nightstand beside his side of the bed brimmed with cigarette butts. Between sleep and waking up, Annabelle could hear the shower running and the door to the closet open and close. It was around four when he roused her from sleep by gently slapping her face.

"Honey, honey, wake up," he said softly.

She looked up and through bleary eyes saw Bradley's face leaning over her.

"What's wrong?" she asked anxiously.

"I have to fly to Paris urgently. There's a flight departing for London at seven, and I'm going to see if there's room," he said.

She got out of bed. "Can't it wait?" she asked.

"No, it's urgent business which I must attend to," he insisted.

"Well, at least have something to eat, and I'll finish packing your suitcase," she said.

He kissed her on the lips and headed for the kitchen.

Annabelle hurried to the door and looked around to make sure that Bradley was in the kitchen. She came back to the room and frantically retrieved a neatly wrapped package in blue-and-white gift paper from under the bed and concealed it beneath the clothes in the suitcase. She looked over her shoulder to ensure that he did not see her put the package in the suitcase before slamming it shut.

It was still dark when he sped off for the airport.

Annabelle went back to bed and was awakened by the ringing of the telephone as it echoed through the quiet of midmorning. She covered her head with the pillow in an attempt to fall back to sleep, but the knocking on the door deterred her effort. She had anticipated the phone call and hoped that Lionel would not answer.

Moments later, Lionel came to the door and hollered, "Are you decent, ma'am?"

"Yes, come on in, Lionel!" she shouted through the closed door.

"It's Mr Bradley. He wants to talk with you," Lionel said.

She took up the receiver with a nonchalant look on her face. Before she could say hello, she was greeted with a tantrum of expletives.

"You bitch! You set me up! I'll get you—"

She hung up the phone and turned on her side, shutting her eyes. The words of the police inspector echoed in her mind.

"We have been trying to catch Bradley Reed for quite a long time, but I must say he is very conniving. He has evaded law enforcement for a number of years. Your husband, madam, is one of the biggest traders in illicit drugs in these parts. We have reasons to believe that he belongs to a ring called the South American Pirates, an organization with transshipment points in certain Caribbean countries. He never carries the drugs himself; he uses innocent and unsuspecting persons. I'm sorry to say this, but we believe that he married you for this very reason. You own a business which demands regular trips abroad. In other words, madam, you were a good and easy target for Bradley Reed. Here's the deal. We want you to plant this package in his bag or suitcase the next time he travels out of the country and call us."

She drifted off into a deep and much-needed slumber.

Chapter 34

• •

The weather forecast for Port-of-Spain was rainy with mild to moderate winds, but instead, the atmosphere was balmy with large balls of white clouds floating lazily above, shielding the city from the direct heat of the afternoon sun. An impetuous breeze spurred the young woman to impulsively press her hands against her dress to prevent it from blowing over her head as she alighted from the car in the bus terminus. Annabelle emerged from the driver's seat of the car and walked over to the medium-build young woman and embraced her.

"Joy, take care of yourself and your daddy, and don't forget to write to me," Annabelle said passionately. She planted a gentle kiss on her forehead and stared at her compassionately until she disappeared inside the bus.

Annabelle reclined in the back seat of the car on her way back home after taking Joyanne, who had paid her a short visit, to the bus station. She sat in the car, reminiscing about her early life in Bristol Village and what her life would be like if she hadn't come to Port-of-Spain. She was younger than Joyanne when circumstances led her to the city, but unlike Joyanne, she was enthralled by the large buildings, the hustle and bustle, and the intrigue and expectations that lurked about, ready to pounce at an eager and naive girl. It's funny, she thought, how different things seemed in retrospect. She remembered Pastor Miles saying, "When one is young and naive, the world is seen through a veil of rose-coloured glass, and life looks exciting and adventurous. When one grows old and faced with life's realities, the glass is removed, and he sees life through eyes of experience and familiarity, and life then appears tedious with many obstacles in the way."

A feeling of guilt and sadness engulfed her at the news of Rosabelle's passing from Joyanne. Ricardo must have posted the letter to her former address, as she did not receive it. She and Rosabelle were so different in every way, but regardless of their differences, Rosabelle cared for Joyanne as if she were her own daughter. Annabelle chided herself for not making an effort to reconcile the rivalry between Rosabelle and her.

Vivid memories of Joyanne, the little baby girl she held at the train station in Rio Claro, assailed her thoughts. She should have brought her baby with her to Port-of-Spain; perhaps her life would have been more fulfiling. But then again, she was not allowed to. Aunt Catherine was adamant that she leave the baby in Bristol Village. She wasn't sure if Joyanne was happy or not—she seemed so distant.

A tingling feeling enveloped her as she visualized Ricardo—those piercing, light brown eyes, curly hair, and muscular arms. Her face twisted into a silly grin. But that thought was short-lived. She was saddened that Joyanne felt like a stranger around her. It was distressing.

She was elated when she had opened the letter a few weeks before and saw that it was signed, "Ricardo Simon".

She was grateful to Suelyn, who inveigled her to write to Ricardo, asking him to consider sending Joyanne to Port-of-Spain to spend some time with her. She was hesitant to write, as her pleas in the past had all been turned down. Ricardo, Rosabelle, and Rosey were all afraid that she would say or do something to instil "quandary"—to use Rosey's word—in the girl's mind.

Come to think of it, she thought to herself, Joyanne never met her brother Troy, and Rosey never met her grandson and sons-in-law, all because of hate and envy, or perhaps Rosey wanted to punish her for her pa's death. Maybe Ma felt inferior and inept and thought that she would embarrass the gracious carnival queen and her "hoity-toity" friends and family. Or was it that her life had become too difficult to care about anyone else? She tried to evade the truth for too long, but lately, she harboured feelings of intense guilt for her father's death. The shame and disappointment was too much for him. Her mind was inundated with so many questions and no answers. Why didn't she cast pride aside and visit home more often? Why didn't she go to Ricardo and tell him how she felt? Why didn't she insist that she bring Joyanne with her? Why didn't she … The shrink at the institution was right—that latent guilt and sorrow are lodged in our subconscious minds, and as we grow older and vulnerable, those feelings begin to manifest and amplify themselves.

Lionel's voice snapped her out of her sojourn into her past. "Ma'am, we're home," he said and opened the door.

She retrieved her handkerchief from her lap, blotted the tears from her eyes, and headed for the bedroom. She lay in bed, feeling deeply depressed. Her mind was swamped with montages of her life.

She was panicky as she waited at the bus station for Joyanne just yesterday. A barrage of questions confronted her. *Will she like me? What has she heard about me? Is she happy? Will she trust me?* After the passengers alighted, she spotted a young woman stepping from the bus with her head bent, and she deduced that it must be Joyanne. She approached her.

"Hello. Are you Joyanne?" she asked.

The shy young lady nodded her head and forced a smile.

"I'm Annabelle. How was your trip?"

"Okay," Joyanne replied bashfully.

Annabelle sensed that Joyanne was tense, and on their way home, she pointed out key places of interest to lighten the mood. As she peered through the window, Annabelle took a long look at her in the car and thought how much she had changed. She no longer had Ricardo's tan complexion and brown, curly hair. In fact, her hair was now black and straight. And Joyanne's nose was no longer like hers. Annabelle was confused that she looked like Rosey.

Their interaction was awkward; Joyanne hardly spoke, and when she did, she was abrupt and obviously nervous. She eventually told Annabelle that she wanted to go back home. Annabelle took her into the kitchen and offered her a snack.

"No thank you," she said.

"You know, Joy, I want us to become friends—good friends," Annabelle said.

Annabelle's comment did not elicit a response from Joyanne. In utter frustration and disappointment, Annabelle led Joyanne to the bedroom and invited her to take a nap, after which she telephoned Suelyn.

"What should I do?" Annabelle lamented.

271

"Put yourself in her place. She's a simple country girl who's obviously intimidated by your lifestyle. You are only forcing her to stay when she wants to go back home," Suelyn replied.

"Joyanne and I are so different; when I was about her age, I was fascinated by the glamorous life. She prefers the simple country life. But where has that put me? I'm so unhappy and miserable. Maybe Joyanne is right not to be fascinated by this lifestyle. Life can be so deceptive. When I was at Bristol Village, I longed for the glamorous life. Now that I've lived the high life, I can't help but wonder whether my life would have been more fulfiling and worthwhile if I had remained in Bristol Village with my daughter and the only man I ever loved," Annabelle said.

"It was the best decision at the time, and maybe it still is. You're just being overly sentimental," Suelyn chided.

"But she is a decent and modest girl. I should be happy for that," Annabelle reasoned, trying to console herself.

"See how lucky you are? You have a daughter whom you are proud of," Suelyn replied.

"But she doesn't know I'm her mother," Annabelle retorted.

"One day she will find out. You're so lucky. Look at me; I don't have anyone except my mother," Suelyn said but immediately regretted saying that; she loathed anyone prying into her private life.

"Have you ever given any thought about getting married?" Annabelle asked.

"Maybe if I find the right person," Suelyn said in a brash tone.

"What about your lawyer friend, Ward?" Annabelle asked.

"Belle, it isn't that I have not given any thought to marriage; to be quite honest, Ward made some subtle hints to me, but I don't love him. And besides, he has been divorced twice," Suelyn said.

"I know exactly what you mean. That special magic never existed between me and T.J. or even Bradley. The only person I ever felt that way about was Ricardo. As far as love and relationships are concerned, there should be no compromise. It's either you love someone or you don't. It's as simple as that. You're a very nice person. You'll find the right person someday. Don't make the same mistakes as I have," Annabelle replied with a sentimental slur in her voice.

Suelyn grew infuriatingly uncomfortable with the conversation and tactfully changed the topic. "Have you decided to buy the beachfront property?"

"I'm thinking seriously—"Annabelle was saying when Suelyn interrupted her.

"I have to go. Someone's at the door," Suelyn said and hung up the phone.

Annabelle headed for Joyanne's room and told her she'd take her to the bus terminus tomorrow afternoon.

"At least spend one night with me; perhaps in the morning you'll change your mind about leaving so soon," Annabelle told her in an empathetic tone, hoping that she would warm up to her.

Try as Annabelle might to cast aside an extremely puzzling matter, it kept resurfacing in her mind. She was afraid that she'd find out something she wasn't prepared to face. But why would Joyanne say that she was nineteen years old when she was twenty-one? And why did she look so much like Rosabelle? Why did Rosey, Rosabelle, and Ricardo keep Joyanne away from her?

The true answers to these questions petrified her.

Chapter 35

· ·

It was a lazy Saturday afternoon; the gauzy clouds drifted slothfully across the cerulean sky. Annabelle was sprawled out on the sofa reading Danielle Steel while Suelyn sat in the recliner, perusing a *Cosmopolitan*. The serenity was interrupted by the buzzing of the doorbell. Annabelle sluggishly eased herself off the sofa and shuffled to the door, securing the buttons on her flowing cotton dress and fixing her messy hair. She opened the door to encounter a man in his thirties with streaks of grey interwoven in his curly black hair, decked in a dark suit and striped blue tie. They both stood staring at each other for a few moments before Annabelle broke the silence.

"No, it can't be!" she said, excited.

The man looked her in the eye with a sheepish grin. "I'm surprised that you recognize me at all. I thought I'd need to show you my ID," he jested.

"My gosh, Danny, this is like a dream. Let me pinch myself. Is it really you?" she gushed with excitement.

They rushed into each other's arms and embraced tightly.

"I've heard so much about you, big sister, the carnival queen. Let me look at you," he said.

Tears filled her eyes. "It's so good to see a blood relative! How long has it been?" Annabelle sobbed.

"Too long!" he exclaimed.

"Oh, please, come inside. I want to hear all about your life," Annabelle said as she took his hand and led him inside.

"You did well for yourself, Belle. Remember how Pa used to boast about his little Belle?" he asked.

The comment brought about a sad, contemplative look to her eyes.

"Those good old days in Bristol Village," she said with a sentimental slur in her voice.

"Well, yeah, some of it was good," Danny replied.

"Oh, where are my manners?" Annabelle said. "Sue, this is my baby brother, Danny; Danny, my best friend, Suelyn."

They shook hands and stared each other in the eyes for a lingering moment.

"Belle," Suelyn said, "I should rush off and leave you two to catch up on old times. In any event, I should check in on Mother."

She retrieved her handbag and proceeded for the door. Annabelle trekked behind and walked her to the car. "Wow, he's gorgeous. Where have you been hiding him?" Suelyn gushed.

"Well, it seems like a lifetime since we saw each other," Annabelle replied as Suelyn opened the door and sat behind the wheel. When she drove off, Annabelle rushed back inside, excited to find out about Danny.

Annabelle handed Danny a drink and sat next to him on the sofa, gawking in awe at his amazing transformation. His dapper looks and cultured mannerism took her by surprise and piqued her curiosity. Everyone thought that Danny would end up a reprobate. The last she knew about Danny, he was around twelve or thirteen years old and incarcerated in an institution for juvenile delinquents. It was almost like a dream that they would meet like this after more than twenty years.

"Pa's probably looking down at us and smiling," Annabelle said. "Do you ever think about Bristol Village, Danny?"

Danny noticed the passionate expression on her face and replied, "How could I ever forget Bristol Village? I went back only last week."

"How is it? Has anything changed?" Annabelle asked with vigour in her voice.

"Well, Ma died two weeks ago," he disclosed.

Before he could finish speaking, Annabelle yelled in shock, "Ma dead? No one told me a thing!"

"Well, I heard she wasn't in the best of health, and Rosa's death really shook her up," Danny said.

"I only learned of Rosa's passing two weeks after the funeral, when Joyanne visited me," Annabelle replied.

"Well, I went to the funeral. I had just returned from America, and she was very ill when I first visited. She died a few days later. I asked if you knew, and Ricardo said that he wrote you," he said.

She sat with a faraway expression on her face.

He got up and said, "Belle." She did not respond. "Belle, Belle," he repeated.

"I'm sorry; my mind was far away," Annabelle muttered.

"I have to go, but I live here now, so we'll meet again soon," Danny said.

"No, don't go, there are lots of room here. Why don't you stay with me awhile?" she begged.

"I have my own place, but let's meet for lunch or dinner soon," Danny suggested.

"Why not tonight, right here?" Annabelle insisted.

"Sounds good, but it would have to be after eight," Danny replied.

"Great. I'm looking forward to it," Annabelle said.

"Oh, why don't you invite your friend and make it a party?" Danny declared with a mischievous gleam in his eyes.

Annabelle looked at him curiously, recalling the glint in his and Suelyn's eyes when she introduced them.

After he left, Annabelle called Suelyn to invite her over, all happy and excited, but when she hung up the phone, she retreated to her room, said a silent prayer for Ma, and sobbed profusely for more than an hour.

Annabelle was about to pour herself a glass of champagne to start off what she envisaged to be an auspicious evening, when she put the glass down on the table and invited Danny and Suelyn to bow their heads and say a prayer for Ma and Rosabelle.

"I'm all right now," she insisted as Suelyn came over and gently hugged her. She composed herself, shrugged off her sad demeanour and, with renewed ardour, invited Danny to pop the champagne.

"A toast for health, happiness, and to my baby brother," Annabelle gushed.

They clinked their glasses in affirmation of Annabelle's toast.

Danny took one sip and rested his glass on the coffee table. "I steer clear of alcohol. Long story, but I didn't want to spoil the fun. So please, sis, would you get me a soda?" Danny asked.

When Annabelle returned with the soda, Danny and Suelyn were, to her surprise, immersed in conversation.

"I didn't know your brother was an engineer," Suelyn adulated.

"I didn't either," Annabelle replied brashly. "Dinner's served; let's go into the dining room."

Danny asked to go to the little boys' room and excused himself.

Annabelle was bursting with curiosity to find out what Suelyn and Danny were talking about.

"My gosh, Sue, you look enticing! I can smell your perfume from where I stand! And your dress! It's so sexy. I feel underdressed next to you. But come on over. Let me pour you a glass of Moët." Annabelle's tone was trenchant, perhaps even mocking.

"Is something the matter, Annabelle?" Suelyn replied agitated.

Danny's presence as he reentered the room quelled the brewing tiff.

"So, let's eat. I'm starved," Danny jested.

Lionel set the table, and Annabelle dismissed him for the night.

Suelyn lifted her glass and proposed a toast, "Here's to a special evening—the reuniting of a brother with a long-lost sister and a sister with a long-lost brother." They raised the crystal flutes and gulped down the champagne.

"Don't worry, Danny," Suelyn said, "I filled your glass with soda."

Annabelle sat, quietly stewing with discontent.

Suelyn got up and said, "Danny, would you excuse Annabelle and me for a little while?"

Annabelle followed her into the kitchen while Danny went over to the telephone to make a call.

"What's the bitching about?" Suelyn carped.

Annabelle turned her back toward her and said awkwardly, "It's just that I ... well, I was a little jealous. There he was telling you about his life ... anyway, let's go back in and pretend nothing happened."

The loud sound of laughter filled the room as Danny popped a second bottle of champagne for Annabelle and Suelyn. Annabelle noticed that a spark had ignited between her brother and Suelyn. She should have been happy, but she wasn't—perhaps it was woman's intuition or just sheer jealously, but she was sceptical. Suelyn was her best friend, and the thought of having her as a sister-in-law bothered her. And, although she harboured affection and respect for Suelyn, there was one trait about her that was disturbing. She was temperamental; Annabelle had seen her morph from pleasant to bitchy in an instant, like she did tonight. And she could be bossy and aggressive.

Annabelle masked her disapproval and pretended not to notice the budding romance between them. She placed an affected smile on her face and invited them to the porch for dessert. She sat opposite Danny, still amazed by his radical transformation—he looked so much like Pa, she observed—and was anxious to hear about his life.

Danny sat next to Suelyn and stared endearingly at her when she spoke, which was frequently, as the champagne had released her inhibitions. Her flawless skin, long black hair, oriental eyes, oblong face, and small button nose conspired to make her look like a living porcelain doll—even her slender frame and the dress she wore. Danny was mesmerized by her. And too, she was about his height—all the other girls he had dated before were awkwardly taller than he was. Annabelle engaged her mind in wishful thinking—that it was only a fleeting attraction that would be forgotten with the morning light.

It was well after midnight when Danny asked to use the phone to call his buddy for a lift back to his apartment. Suelyn reprimanded him, "How dare you call for a lift when my car is parked in the driveway?"

Annabelle quickly interceded. "Danny, you can use my car," she said and proceeded to rummage through the drawer for the key.

"I said I'll give him a lift, and that's that!" Suelyn retorted.

Danny smiled awkwardly and said, "If it's not a problem, I'll take a ride with Sue."

Annabelle sneered and volunteered snobbishly, "Whatever you decide." She then looked on with malice as the lovebirds entered the car. Danny opened the passenger door for Suelyn, and he got into the driver's seat.

The quarter moon looked as though it was suspended in the cloudless, starry sky as Suelyn and Danny strolled hand in hand across the lush gardens of the Queen's Park Savannah. When they reached the bandstand, he led her inside and held her tightly; his face pressed against hers. He pulled her forward and thrust his eager lips against hers, kissing her passionately. She eased herself from his embrace and walked to the other side of the bandstand with a worried look on her face. Danny followed behind.

"What's wrong, doll?" Danny asked.

"For one thing, your sister seems to detest our relationship," Suelyn said.

"You know what the problem is? Belle has always been spoiled and, if I dare say, jealous of every beautiful girl. She likes to control, but she'll just have to get used to the idea that we love each other," Danny declared.

"Well, she's my best friend, and I don't want to do anything to hurt her," Suelyn replied.

"What? You will give up your own happiness to please someone else? Let me tell you something—Belle's my sister, but I must say this. She has never found happiness with any man because she doesn't know what love is. She loves money, power, and control; she looks for men who can give her those things. And what is eating away at her is the fact that my younger sis, Rosa, married the only man she truly loved, and they have a daughter—" Danny stopped short.

"I didn't know Rosabelle had a daughter too. I know about Belle's daughter, Joyanne," Suelyn said, perplexed.

"Forget I said that; it's a long story," he said. "Anyway, I was telling you about Belle; she's like a child who doesn't want a toy until another child shows interest in that toy," Danny articulated.

Suelyn pondered for a while; she turned around to face Danny and placed her head on his shoulder. "Danny, there's something else that bothers me; I'm a lot older than you," she blurted.

"I know, and I don't care. Besides, you Chinese don't age. Look at you—you look ten years younger than me," he said. "This is our sixth or seventh date; that should say something about what we feel for each other," Danny replied.

A curious look emerged in Suelyn's eyes. "How did you know I was older?" she asked.

"Belle told me," Danny replied.

"That bitch," Suelyn muttered.

"What?" Danny asked.

"Nothing," she replied.

Danny took her by the hand and led her to a bench beneath a large tree and placed his arm around her shoulder. She responded by resting her face on his shoulder.

"I can sit here until the sun comes up," Danny said.

"Why don't we?" she chuckled.

"What's wrong, my porcelain doll?" he asked. "I know something is bothering you. Tell me what it is."

"Nothing's wrong. The problem is that everything is too perfect. Is this really happening to me, or is it just a dream from which I will eventually awake?" she replied emotionally.

He pinched her on the cheek.

"Why did you do that?" she grumbled.

"Does that feel like a dream?" he jested.

He removed his arm from around her shoulder and reached into his pocket, retrieving a small box which he held between his fingers.

She was choked up with anxiety when she saw the box in his hand. It took her by surprise; there were so many unresolved issues in her mind about marriage.

He got up from the bench and kneeled before her. He opened the box and retrieved a shiny ring, which he placed on her finger.

She covered her face with both hands and began to sob. It all appeared so surreal to her. She removed her hand from her face and looked up at the trees with bleary eyes to see rays of moonlight seeping though the branches of glistening leaves.

He walked to the other side of the tree to give her some privacy to think. A minute later, he returned and stood over her with arms akimbo; she took his arm, and they walked toward the car, arm in arm, without uttering a word.

When they reached the car, she blurted, "Please give me some time to think about marriage."

"Okay," he said. "And I promise I will not bring up the subject again until you do," he whispered passionately in her ear.

"There's one more thing I wish to say," she muttered. "I have never felt this way about anyone!"

He took her gently in his arms and held her forever.

Chapter 36

· ·

Annabelle lay supine in bed, mulling over Danny's life story and her own life. She felt as though life had defeated her—for every step forward, it seemed that life had dragged her ten steps backward. What had she really achieved? She asked herself—money, fabulous houses, and fame—or loneliness, grief, pain, and guilt? If money could buy happiness, she'd be the happiest woman alive, she thought. Life isn't fair!

A trickle of hope came gushing through—at least Ricardo was still there, and she could only hope that he still loved her—and now that Rosabelle was gone … She made an oath to herself to go back to Bristol Village and salvage what was left of the life she once knew. But she knew it wouldn't be easy or even possible. The therapist had told her that too much water had flowed under the bridge.

Danny's account of his recent visit to their old home town echoed through her mind like a poignant song.

"The house is still there," he said, "and so too is the big immortelle tree and the old church. Pa and Ma are buried side by side; I carried flowers for them and told them that they were from all of us—you too. I called your name ... And the small grave ..."

"What small grave?" Annabelle asked curiously, but she was afraid to hear the answer.

"I don't know," Danny said. "Just a small grave."

He wasn't supposed to say anything about the small grave to Annabelle. He had promised Ricardo he wouldn't, but it slipped out.

Annabelle shook her head from side to side in self condemnation. "Rosa and Ma, gone, and I didn't even know. Imagine, I wasn't even at my mother's and sister's funerals. Everyone must think that I'm a bitch! And Pa ..."

"Things happen, sis; it's not your fault. Besides, you all drifted apart; it happens to the best of us. In any event, you did not neglect them; you sent them money," he consoled her.

She lit a cigarette. "You still haven't told me about you! I want to hear what my baby brother was up to!" Annabelle insisted.

He heaved a loud sigh and regaled his life story.

There was no one waiting for him at the institution when he was released. He was now a homeless eighteen-year-old. His first thought was to go back home, but he quickly dismissed that notion. There was nothing to go back to, and in any event, he might have been a burden to his family. The fact that no one even visited him or came to claim him upon his release validated his sentiment.

Institution life had made him callous—he learned that survival was about self-defence, both physical and emotional. He slung his small bag, which contained the only possessions to his name, over his shoulder and headed for Port-of-Spain. Freedom and independence slapped his face like a cool, refreshing breeze; he was dead set on making a new life for himself.

He turned his head in every direction, absorbing the atmosphere of the city. Bent on fulfiling a promise he had made to himself while still in prison, he followed his eyes and headed in the direction of the steepled church in the far distance. He came out of the church five minutes later, beaming with optimism. A sign posted in the show window of a small store—"We Repair Radios"—caught his attention. He pushed the door brazenly and entered. A thin, middle-aged man lifted his head from the morning newspaper.

"Can I help you?" the man asked politely.

"I'm looking for a job and am willing to do anything," Danny said.

"I'm sorry, young man, but I don't need anyone at the moment, but if you wish, you can clean the storeroom for a small stipend," the man replied.

Danny placed his bag on the counter, rolled up his sleeves, and followed the man to the back of the store.

An hour later, the man returned and was pleasantly surprised not only to find the room conspicuously clean but to hear music emanating from a broken radio.

"Did you fix that?" the man asked.

"Yes, sir. I learned the trade at the institution," Danny replied proudly.

"What institution?" the man asked curiously.

"Well, sir, I spent the last few years of my life in an institution for delinquent boys. If you have a problem with that, I will leave, but I wish that you would give me a chance to make a new life for myself," Danny replied.

The man was hesitant and was about to ask him to leave, but Danny's honesty impressed him. He looked

Danny in the eye and said, "Son, I've had problems with workers before—stealing, dishonesty, disrespect—but I will give you a chance to prove your worth. After all, I believe everyone deserves a chance in life. But any hint of wrongdoing, and you're out of here!"

Danny nodded his head and said, "Thank you, sir; you won't regret it."

"My name is Mr Sawh," the man said.

"Danny Castello," Danny reciprocated.

For the next few months, Danny worked diligently repairing radios and doing odd jobs; he was provided with sleeping accommodations on a small bed in the storeroom. Unbeknownst to Danny, Mr Sawh intentionally left money and other valuables lying around the store to test his honesty. Danny would return the money and items to Mr Sawh, whose face would light up in admiration. Mr Sawh was pleased with Danny's work and often left him unsupervised while he was away. But Mr Sawh's affection for Danny peaked one Christmas morning.

It was around 7.30 when Mr Sawh went over to the store to deliver a special Christmas breakfast, which Mrs Sawh had packed for Danny. He opened the store to find Danny holding up a small, neatly wrapped present, which he handed to Mr Sawh.

"Merry Christmas, sir," Danny said.

The gesture brought tears to Mr Sawh's eyes. He had no children of his own, and no one except for his wife had ever given him a present.

"What's this, son?" Mr Sawh asked emotionally.

"Oh, just a little token of appreciation," Danny replied.

Mr Sawh sat down and opened the present. "My goodness, son, this must have cost you a fortune!" Mr Sawh exclaimed as he retrieved the shiny gold watch from the box. He got up from the chair and patted Danny on the shoulder. "You spent all the money you earned on this present, boy. Why?" Mr Sawh asked.

"You're kind of like a father to me, sir," Danny replied.

Mr Sawh could not hold back the tears; he turned around and walked away clutching the watch in his hand.

A few days later, when he was about to close the store, Mr Sawh turned to Danny and said, "Pack your things, boy; my wife wants you to move in with us."

Danny was choked up with emotions as he followed Mr Sawh home.

Sheila Sawh was a plump woman in her mid-forties who spent her day taking care of Mr Sawh and the large house. She was an excellent cook and master of most domestic crafts—sewing, cake decorating, knitting … She was a compassionate woman who went out of her way to make Danny feel at home; he repaid her generosity by helping out around the house. Sheila had confided in him that Edmund suffered from a heart condition and should not be doing any strenuous work. "But he's as stubborn as a mule!" she chided.

Sheila insisted that he call them by their first names, but Danny found that inappropriate. After all, they treated him like a son, so instead, he called them Auntie and Uncle.

One slow afternoon at the store, Uncle called Danny into his office. "Son," he said, "it's about time you learned to do the books." He noticed a distressed expression on Danny's face. "What's wrong?" Uncle asked him.

There was no reply from Danny; he bent his head down.

"It's okay, son, I don't expect you to learn all of it right away," Uncle said compassionately.

Danny got up and left the office.

Uncle was surprised, as he had never seen Danny look so dejected before.

He went outside to find Danny propped against the wall.

"What's wrong, son?" Uncle asked.

There was no reply from Danny.

"Come on. You can tell me," Uncle insisted.

"I can't read and write very well, sir," Danny muttered.

"I'm sorry, son, I didn't know," Uncle replied and held Danny by the arm and led him to the office.

A month later, Danny rushed into the office beaming with pride. "Let me read you the news on the front page of the newspaper!" he gushed.

Uncle smiled as Danny read him the news fluently. The many evenings he and Auntie had spent with Danny were not wasted.

Weeks later, Danny was writing entries in the ledger.

A year after, Danny stood in front of the mirror, fumbling to tie his necktie the way Uncle had taught him, but he had to eventually call Uncle to do it for him. At first, he felt silly, but after looking at himself in the mirror for the third or fourth time, he felt dignified. It was the first time he had worn a suit and tie in his life. He held on to Auntie and Uncle and mumbled emotionally, "I'll miss you. Take care of yourselves."

"Four years will fly by quicker than you know. Besides, you'll be home every vacation," Uncle replied. "All we want you to do is study hard and earn your diploma."

Auntie dried her eyes with a damp handkerchief she clutched between her fingers. She was too choked up with emotions to say anything, so she hugged him tightly and kissed him on his forehead.

Four and a half years later, a mild drizzle greeted the passengers on the flight from London as it touched down in Trinidad. Edmund Sawh held an umbrella high above his head to shelter Sheila and Danny from the rain, which poured heavily. When they reached the lobby, Sheila retrieved a camera from her handbag and handed it to a man, asking him to take a picture of the three of them.

"Not again, Auntie!" Danny protested as she insisted that they pose for another picture.

Edmund scolded her, "The boy must be tired, dear!"

Danny's callow glow had faded and was replaced by features of a mature young man—manicured sideburns edged his round face, a trimmed moustache lined his small pouty lips, visible laugh lines creased his flat forehead, and there was a horizontal scar on his round nose. Although he was no taller than five feet four, his muscular arms and broad chest conspired to give him a tough appearance.

Sheila stuck more than a dozen photographs of Danny's graduation in the store. He was, however, against her hanging a framed copy of his certificate; he told her that it would make him seem boastful. She, however, hung it conspicuously in the living room and boasted to everyone who visited that her son was now a qualified electrical engineer.

Danny worked with a large international engineering company in Port-of-Spain, but following the death of Uncle—and then Auntie, eighteen months later—he took up a job offer at the company's New York operations.

He returned to Port-of-Spain nine years later to open his own business with two partners he had met in New York. There was food and drink for everyone: friends, well-wishers, and business associates. The new, modern building with a large sign—"DES Engineering"—which sprawled across its façade, contrasted with the old colonial architecture of Port-of-Spain. He dedicated the business to Uncle and Auntie and spoke endearingly about them in his opening speech.

"Why did you come back to Port-of-Spain, Danny?" Annabelle asked.

"Since we're sharing each other's innermost secrets and since you were honest to tell me that you were jealous of my relationship with Suelyn, I'll tell you the God's truth. I met a Puerto Rican woman and had a fling with her; she told me she was having my baby. I know it wasn't mine. Turned out her brother was a hit man. He threatened to execute me if I didn't marry his sister, so here I am," Danny blurted.

"That's not true, Danny. You made that up," Annabelle said.

"Well, believe what you want. Your brother's a thug!" he jested. "So you're okay with Suelyn and me getting hitched?" he asked.

"Yes," Annabelle replied.

She escorted him to the door and went to bed, still unable to quell the doubts in her mind about Danny and Suelyn getting married. But she'd have to pretend to be happy for them.

She went to bed, reminiscing about her years in Bristol Village, trying hard to shrug off pessimistic thoughts. It was good to have her brother back after all these years. She smiled.

Chapter 37

•••

The bright sunlight seeped through the bedroom drapes as Annabelle opened her eyes. She frantically pulled the sheet aside and jumped out of bed, chiding herself, "Oh my gosh, I've overslept!"

She pulled a duster coat over her nightgown and bolted through the doorway, fixing her hair with her hands as she hurried down the stairs. The men who were setting up the tents were almost halfway through when she reached the backyard. She pulled the foreman aside and said, "I'm sorry I wasn't here when you arrived. You see, I've hired a decorator who has proposed a total rearrangement of the layout. I hate to sound bothersome, but I need everything to be perfect for my brother and my best friend's wedding," she insisted.

"Good heavens, sis! This is too much! This decor is fit for a king!" Danny declared as he walked up the driveway and stood next to her, staring at the garden in amazement.

"That's not your concern, little brother; both you and Suelyn promised to leave the planning to me. Anyway, that's not what I called you about," Annabelle replied. She retrieved a brown envelope from her pocket and handed it to him.

"What's this?" he asked.

"My wedding gift to you and your bride," she gushed.

Danny opened the envelope with a curious look on his face. "This looks like the deed to a house," he said.

"Yes, it's the deed for this house. I want you to have it. I thought I'd give it to you now, just in case you were thinking of making other plans," she said.

"Belle, this property is worth quite a lot of money, and besides, I have already rented a home for us," he replied.

"Well, you will have to change your plan," she demanded.

"I don't understand; I'm confused," Danny said.

"Remember the talk we had the other night? Remember I told you I needed a change of environment? Well, I'm going abroad for a while, and if and when I return, I'll buy a beachfront property, perhaps in Mayaro. If I stay here, I'll go mad for sure!" Annabelle shrieked.

"Sis, this is too drastic. Could we talk about this after the wedding?" he asked.

"Nothing to talk about," Annabelle retorted. "Now go! You have a wedding in a couple of hours, and you're the groom. Besides, Aunt Catherine's son wrote, offering me his mother's old house in St Clair at a good price. He doesn't want it to fall into ruins or to some stranger who might tear it down."

Danny walked away slowly with a baffled look on his face.

Annabelle threw her tired body onto the sofa and called out to Lionel to fetch her a glass to water.

"Ma'am, the wedding's an hour away; Miss Suelyn's waiting for you, and you need to get dressed," Lionel said.

She heaved a long sigh and forced herself off the sofa.

Annabelle hurried to the bedroom with a glass of brandy in her hand. "Here, sip this. It will help you to relax," she said exhaustedly.

"You've been working too hard!" Suelyn snapped.

"I want everything to be perfect!" Annabelle insisted.

"I'm glad that you're okay with Danny and me getting married," Suelyn uttered.

"Well, guess I was being selfish," Annabelle replied.

Suelyn retrieved the glass from the dressing table and gulped down the contents, grimacing her face as the pungent drink hit her throat. She slipped a duster coat over her lace underwear when the hairdresser arrived. She sat in front of the mirror, fidgeting with a rubber band in her hand.

"Annabelle, has Mother called?" Suelyn asked with a pang of anxiety in her voice.

"Not since yesterday. But don't worry, she'll be here soon. The driver left for the airport an hour ago," Annabelle replied.

The clock on the wall struck 2.30 as Suelyn slipped into her dress, preening herself as she twisted from side to side in front of the mirror.

Annabelle returned with another glass of brandy. "This is the last drink I'm pouring you; another drink and you will not be able to stand up at the altar," Annabelle joked.

Suelyn sucked the rim of the brandy snifter and handed it to Annabelle. "I best not drink any more," she said. She retrieved Annabelle's shimmering tiara from a velvet box and placed it on her head and stared at her bleary image in the mirror, blotting the tears with her finger. "This takes care of something borrowed," she said to herself.

Her heart skipped a beat at the words, "Oh, you look like a princess, my child." It was unmistakably the voice of her mother. She turned around and rushed into her mother's arms. They both burst into tears. A flash of light illuminated their emotional faces as Annabelle took a picture.

"This is undoubtedly the happiest day of my life, Georgia," Suelyn's mother repeated over and over until her voice grew muffled with emotions.

She dried her eyes and retrieved a string of stained, white pearls from her handbag. "I want you to wear this, Georgia," Suelyn's mother said.

Suelyn took the string of pearls and placed it around her neck. "It's gorgeous, Mom; I'll be proud to wear it," Suelyn replied emotionally. "That takes care of something old," she quipped. They both laughed.

Their laughter was cut short by Annabelle, who stood at the entrance of the door and announced, "Another surprise awaits you, Sue." She led an old Chinese man by the hand into the room. Suelyn hurried toward him and threw her arms around his shoulders, causing him to lose his balance. Annabelle rushed over and placed her hand against his back to prevent him from falling.

"You're my uncle Ed," Suelyn said, excited. "My wedding day is perfect—like a dream."

Annabelle showed Suelyn's mother to her room. "You may change in here," she said and hurried back to show Uncle Ed to the guest room. With utmost urgency in her voice, she clapped her hands and announced, "We will be leaving for the church in thirty minutes!"

The cars drove past Annabelle's enchanted garden with its newly painted gazebos in lime green and white and enormous floral arrangements towering over latticework panels. Gaily decorated tables and chairs were meticulously placed beneath white tents with festoons of pink and white balloons sailing in the breeze. A large, white, heart-shaped motif with the names Suelyn and Danny topped the ornate, tiered cake. Hundreds of lights were strung on every tree and shrub in the garden.

Annabelle turned to Suelyn's mother, who sat next to her in the car. "How do you feel, Ma Ling?" Annabelle asked.

The question incited tears to roll down her wrinkled face. "I feel happy. You are good friend to my Georgia," Ma Ling replied.

Ma Ling, as she was affectionately called, was an emotional woman who cried at every occasion—happy or sad. Her coarse grey hair with streaks of black fell below her ear, framing her broad, flat Chinese face, with round nose and small eyes, which looked like thin lines below her white eyebrows. The blush of red rouge on her cheek barely concealed the age spots on her face. Her lips were two tiny strokes of red lipstick, dotted by a large mole just above her top lip. She was a short, thick woman with a slightly curved back but was surprisingly agile. She glanced at Annabelle and with her witty repartee said, "I tell Georgia I will die before she get marry." She laughed heartily.

The first time Ma Ling met her brother was ten years before when he wrote to say that he had left China and moved to Canada. His mother, he said, had remarried in China, and as a child, she told him that his father had died in an accident in Trinidad, eventually disclosing the truth about his real father and sister on her deathbed. He said he must have been no more than two years old when his mother took him to China and never returned to Trinidad. Ma Ling had tried in vain to locate him after her father died, even writing to the Chinese embassy in Britain. Though this was his first visit to Trinidad, she had visited him in Canada almost every year since their first meeting. At times, she spent months in Canada and returned to Trinidad when it grew uncomfortably cold. Georgia, her pet name for Suelyn, never met Uncle Ed, although she sent him Christmas cards and spoke to him on the phone.

A cloudless Saturday afternoon sky greeted the bride and her entourage as they arrived at the church twenty-five minutes late. Lionel alighted from the car and opened the door for Annabelle and Ma Ling, while Suelyn and Uncle Ed waited in the limousine for their cue.

The bridesmaids and groomsmen shuffled around until they were appropriately matched with their partners, while all eyes in the packed church were riveted toward the entrance as the sound of antiquated pipe organ belched out the wedding march.

A volley of camera flashes greeted the bride as the chauffeur opened the door of the black limousine and offered his arm to her. Annabelle and Ma Ling assisted in fixing the lace dress and long, flowing veil, which Annabelle had imported from Paris. Ma Ling's eyes over-flowed with tears as she hugged her daughter.

"Good luck, Georgia," she said before clutching her large blue handbag and following Annabelle inside the church.

Uncle Ed straightened his navy-blue suit and offered his arm to Suelyn. All eyes fixated on them as the bride sauntered up the aisle on the arm of Uncle Ed. She glanced at the gaily attired congregation and the bouquets of white lilies and lit candles which decorated the church.

Suelyn's heart throbbed against her chest as she neared the altar and caught a glimpse of a smiling Danny in a grey suit and burgundy tie. A tingling feeling engulfed her as the organ stopped playing and the priest recited, "We are gathered here in the name of God the father, to witness the union of these two souls." The choir rose to its feet and belted out "O Perfect Love".

The reading of the scriptures and singing of two hymns followed, as well as another rendition by the choir. Twinges of excitement filled Suelyn's stomach as the priest recited the vows: "Do you take Danny to be your lawful husband, to love and to hold ..."

"Yes, I do," she repeated with a nervous slur in her voice.

"The rings, please," the priest requested. He blessed the rings and said, "Repeat after me. With this ring, I thee wed ..."

Danny slid the shiny gold ring on her finger, and she in turn placed a ring on his finger. Before the priest could finish the statement, "I pronounce you man and wife", a distant but conspicuous echo grew louder and louder and diverted the attention of the congregation to the back of the church. All eyes turned around to see an old man decked in a dark suit hobbling up the aisle with a walking stick. The priest ignored the commotion and continued, "I now pronounce you man and wife. You may kiss—"

The man was now halfway up the aisle. He pounded his walking stick against a pew as if to stop the priest.

The priest looked at him curiously but continued, "You may kiss—"

The old man pounded his walking stick louder, and in a weak voice that struggled to speak, he managed to say, "Stop this wedding!" his voice fading into a whisper. "Stop! Stop! Now!" he demanded.

The members of the entire congregation, some standing to gain a better view of the old man, the priest, the bride and groom, and the wedding party were riveted on this old man.

Mustering all the strength he could, he forced himself toward the priest, muttering, "These people can't—" He paused to catch his breath. "These people can't marry. Stop now. These people have the same blood. These two people have the same blood flowing through their veins," he said before collapsing on the floor.

A deafening silence ensued.

Chapter 38

1995

Annabelle was startled from her state of reverie by Joyanne, who had just entered the gallery of the small, wooden house in Bristol Village with a cake which she held delicately with both hands. She placed it on the table and rushed inside, returning soon after with a candle, a box of matches, and serving implements. She stuck the candle in the middle of the pink-and-white cake, making several attempts to light it amid strong northeast trade winds. Annabelle looked on with a tender smile on her face.

"Happy birthday, Auntie Annabelle!" Joyanne said in a soft, elated tone.

Annabelle's tender smile turned into a broad grin. "Oh my gosh, Joy, you remembered my birthday!" Annabelle said, excited.

"Yes, I did," Joyanne replied.

Annabelle leaned over and kissed her gently on the cheek. "Thank you, Joy. You don't know how much this means to me," Annabelle replied while passing her finger below her eyes to wipe the tears.

"I'm sorry it's so crude looking, Auntie; I'm not very good at icing," Joyanne said.

Annabelle stared her in the eyes and said emphatically, "Joy, you may not fully appreciate what I'm about to say, but this crude cake means more to me than the most expensive cake in the world."

Joyanne blushed and said, "Thanks."

Joyanne went inside and returned with two cups of steaming-hot coffee.

After sipping the coffee, Annabelle turned to Joyanne and enunciated, "This is the best birthday I've had in sixty-five years!" An immense glow on Annabelle's face validated her sentiments.

It was two years since Annabelle had abandoned her eminent life in Port-of-Spain. She now shared her time between the old house in Bristol Village—now Joyanne's home—and her beachfront estate in Mayaro. For the past two years, on the anniversary of Ricardo's death, she convened a thanksgiving service at the house in Bristol Village in memory of all her dearly departed relatives: Ricardo, Rosabelle, Ma, Pa, Troy, and Aunt Catherine. At the last service, she said a silent prayer for Joyanne, her firstborn child. After the service, some of the villagers approached her in a servile manner, addressing her as Mrs Johnson, Miss Annabelle, Madam, or Miss Castello and extending congratulations to her for being a famous carnival queen. She told them that she had given up that aspect of her life and to please call her Annabelle or Belle and that she had returned to Bristol Village to be with Joyanne and the folks she grew up with. She invited them to visit her at her old home and her beachfront estate in Mayaro. Her manner was no longer condescending, and she traded in her swanky wardrobe for simple clothing. She, however, still dyed her hair to conceal the greys and applied powder and creams to conceal her age marks.

A week after the thanksgiving service, she returned to her estate in Mayaro, accompanied by Joyanne, who was now well into her forties—pudgy, emerging wrinkles and laugh lines, and greying hair. It had taken awhile, but Joyanne had finally opened up to her. When they were through with breakfast, Joyanne turned to her and asked, "Auntie Annabelle, can we talk about something that has been bothering me? I have a decision to make, and I honestly don't know what I should do."

Annabelle's face lit up; she was delighted that Joy felt comfortable enough to seek her advice.

Joyanne was as at first timid to share the intimate aspects of her life with Auntie Annabelle, but there was nobody else to talk to about personal matters, and besides, Annabelle was well learned.

She began her discourse while Annabelle lit a cigarette and listened attentively.

"There is this guy I used to know a long time ago; his name was Peter. He stood me up at the altar when I was eighteen. Now he has returned after all this time and asked me to marry him again. I told him that I never wanted to see him again. I continue to chase him away, but he will not go. The problem is I think I still love him after all he has done. What should I do?"

"First thing—did he give you a reason?" Annabelle asked.

"Yes," Joyanne said, "but …" Her face morphed into a reflective expression as she replayed the incident in her mind.

She was eighteen when she was stood up at the altar and had not until a few months ago seen or heard from Peter. At first, she did not recognize him when he came to the house. Like her, he too had aged. But when he spoke, she stared him in the eyes and began to tremble. She wanted desperately to hurt him as much as he had hurt her, but she was intimidated by his presence. The hurt she felt decades ago came surging through the years. Instead, she ran into the house and began to sob. She did not see him again until three weeks later when he approached her on the streets in Rio Claro. This time, she was more composed.

He said, "I don't blame you for hating me, Joy, but I would do anything if you would just listen to what I have to say."

She scoffed at him, "Look! Go away! I don't need you or anyone else."

He fell on his knees in the presence of everyone.

She looked around and was mortified to see a crowd staring at the spectacle. "You're embarrassing me," she said, "and besides, you look ridiculous. All right! All right! I'll listen to what you have to say! But be quick. I'm busy!"

Peter's father owned a large transport business and, being the first of three sons and one sister, he was the heir to the business and was groomed from a tender age to assume the leadership position. As he grew older, he found out that his father controlled every aspect of his life. Although he worked hard for his money, he did not have the independence to do as he liked. He had to account to his frugal father for every cent he spent. He was told how to dress, which functions to attend, what time to return home. His father even approved or disapproved of his friends. He felt like a prisoner but was afraid to confront his father for fear of being disinherited. His father often said to him and his siblings, "Either you comply or leave my home!"

But with all the restrictions imposed on him, Peter never felt the urge to move out of his father's home. At least he felt a sense of security. But his real challenge came when he approached his father about getting married.

"She's a nice and decent girl, Pa," he said to his father. A few days later, his father barged into his room like a raging bull.

"You cannot marry that girl, Peter! She's below your class!" his father said vehemently.

"But I love her, Pa," Peter pleaded.

This angered his father. "Love! Love! You stupid ass! Love is for foolish people. Marriage is about opportunity. I have arranged for you to marry my associate's daughter. This is about matching money, not about love, you idiot!" his father retorted.

But Peter was adamant about marrying Joyanne; his mother and siblings pleaded with him, but to no avail. A week before the wedding, his father issued the final warning to him. He consoled himself with the thought that his father would be angry for at least a few weeks but would eventually come around. After all, he was his oldest son and was trained to take over the business.

At first, he thought it was just a bluff until the morning of the wedding when he realized that he had nothing. His bank account was closed, the locks on the door were changed, and he was refused entry into the house. He was humiliated and was not about to go crawling back to his father. With the help of a few friends, he boarded a flight to Miami.

"I know I have no excuse for not contacting you, Joy, but I was embarrassed. I had nothing to offer you. My father even took the suit I had bought for the wedding and burned it. You deserved the best, and I just couldn't provide a life for you," Peter said.

"Did it ever dawn on you that all I really wanted was you? We could have survived somehow," she lamented.

"Joy, when you are a woman, you see it that way. But a man sees things differently," he snapped.

When she was through, Joyanne looked at Auntie Annabelle and asked, "What do you think I should do?"

"I can offer my advice, but the decision should be yours and yours alone," Annabelle replied tenderly. "But do you love him?"

"I think I still do. I wish I could hate him, but I don't," Joyanne said.

"Do you believe that he is sincere?" Annabelle asked.

"I don't know what to believe. I keep asking myself, why did he come back after all these years? What does he want from me? The only answer I could come up with is that he still has guilty feelings and probably wants my forgiveness," Joyanne cried.

"Do you honestly believe that, Joy?" Annabelle asked.

"No, I don't, but I'm so scared that I might make the wrong decision," Joyanne replied.

"Did he ever marry?" Annabelle asked.

"I don't know; I didn't ask him," Joyanne replied.

"Well, ask him. Depending on what he says, you will know the right thing to do or whether or not he has an ulterior motive," Annabelle said.

Joyanne was at first confused by Auntie Annabelle's statement but soon realized what she meant.

A week later, they returned to Bristol Village and were sitting in the gallery, absorbing the rural ambiance, when

Joyanne turned to Annabelle and asked, "Would you help me plan a small wedding?"

Annabelle's face lit up. She hurried over to Joyanne and wrapped her arms around her. "Are you sure you trust me with planning your wedding?" Annabelle jested.

Joyanne was confused by Auntie Annabelle's reply. "What do you mean?" Joyanne asked.

"Oh, it's just a joke. The last time I planned a wedding … Oh, never mind," Annabelle said, but Joyanne's interest was piqued.

"Get me another cup of coffee and my cigarettes, and I'll entertain you with yet another story about my life," Annabelle said.

"It's amazing how you can see the funny side of a tragedy in retrospect." Annabelle smiled as she twisted her head from side to side.

The piercing silence which fell over the church when the old man revealed that Danny and Suelyn had the same blood flowing through their veins was eventually replaced by gossip and speculation. At first, she thought that he was just an old, senile man, but something about him seemed very familiar. Annabelle searched the far corners of her mind but could come up with nothing. Then it struck her like a bolt of lightning—the large scars on his face took her wandering mind back to Bristol Village and a distant memory of a man who had spent some time at their home assisting Pa with the garden. What was his name again? she asked herself. Then it came to her—Sticks. He was called Sticks. Hard as she tried, she could not recall his given name.

In the melee, no one noticed that Ma Ling had fainted. Seeing Ma Ling's plight, Annabelle called out for help, and a doctor in attendance rushed to revive her. He ordered her to the hospital for observation. Before she left, she asked to see Danny. She stared at him curiously and mumbled, "Sticks know … you, you … George son. Doh, don't marry my Georgia."

Danny was bewildered into silence. *This must be a bad dream,* he thought. Annabelle trotted behind him as he dashed out of the church. "This is all a misunderstanding," she said.

Ignoring her, he headed for his car. She looked on helplessly as his car sped from the churchyard. Suelyn had earlier scampered out of the church and ordered the limousine driver to take her home.

A week later, Annabelle went to visit Ma Ling, who was released from the hospital and ordered by the doctor to stay in bed.

Pangs of anxiety enveloped Annabelle as she climbed the stairs to Ma Ling's home.

"Can I help you?" an austere Chinese woman asked.

"My name is Annabelle; I'm a friend of Suelyn, and I would like to see Ma Ling," Annabelle replied.

"You no see she," the woman said in a stern and abrupt tone.

"Please, Suelyn asked me to visit her mother," Annabelle pleaded.

"Where Suelyn?" the woman asked.

"She's with her uncle in Canada," Annabelle replied.

"Come inside," the woman mumbled. "Don't know what good it do. Follow me."

Annabelle followed the woman to a closed door.

"In there," the woman gestured. "No stay long!" she warned.

Annabelle pushed the door and cautiously entered the smoky room which reeked of burning incense. Ma Ling was seated on a creaky rocking chair next to the bed, humming to a familiar melody which emanated from an antiquated jewel box which she clinched tightly in her hands. An old, white veil was draped around her head.

"Is it time for the wedding, Agatha?" she turned to Annabelle and asked.

"I'm Annabelle, Suelyn's friend," Annabelle replied.

"Is he at the church? You go ahead, Agatha! Tell him I'm coming. Go on! Go on! I'm coming!" Ma Ling shouted.

Annabelle gently took Ma Ling's hand and looked her in the eyes. "Ma Ling! Ma Ling!" she repeated.

"Agatha! What you still doing here? You go right away! Tell him I'm coming! I'm coming!" she blared.

"Oh my gosh! She has gone mad!" Annabelle observed.

She threw the music box on the floor. "Get out! Get out! Tell him I'm coming!" Ma Ling bawled.

Annabelle wondered whether Ma Ling was speaking incoherently or whether she was recalling some incident from her past.

"Agatha! Agatha! Where's George? Where's George? Tell him I'm coming!" she screamed louder.

The Chinese woman hurried into the room and said, "You go now."

"Oh my gosh, it must be true," Annabelle exclaimed, "George, Pa, was Suelyn's father? That's what the old man was trying to say? Impossible! Can't be!"

Annabelle left. She had an urgent need to speak with Sticks. The priest told her that he was recuperating at a convalescent home run by nuns.

Annabelle was turned away by a nun who said that Mr Ransome was in no condition to receive visitors. She was told to come back in a week, which she did.

The name Mr Ransome sounded strange to her, but a man who sat on a chair in the room called him Sticks.

Annabelle learned that both he and Sticks regularly visited the clubs with her father.

"You look a lot like old Georgie," the man said.

Sticks was asleep, so Annabelle got to talking with the man, who told her that his name was Robbie.

"But your old man knew me as Smart Man," he giggled.

Annabelle told him about the incident at the church; but before she could say another word, he became excited and bawled, "Oh yeah!" He proceeded to retrieve a newspaper from the nightstand. "It's a good thing for this report in the paper that your brother didn't marry his sister. Me and Sticks got around to talking 'bout Sam's granddaughter getting married, and Sticks turn to me and said, 'Wait, nah. Just one minute, Smart Man. Danny Castello, Danny Castello, Danny Castello.' Then he noticed, son of the late George Castello. 'I wonder if that is the same George Castello we knew.' So, we decided to go in front the church. We didn't know what he look like, but when Sticks saw April, he bawl, 'Oh God! Nah, this can't happen!'"

"My gosh," Annabelle said. But she was happy to meet George's old friend from way back. They sat chatting, and Smart Man regaled her stories from George's past.

It was 1921. Wanted by the police for a murder he presumably committed together with Sticks, George Castello was forced to leave Port-of-Spain. He returned a week later to Sam Lee, the Chinese proprietor with whom he had worked and developed a close kinship. He narrowly escaped being captured by the police. Thanks to Sam's tactfulness, he evaded capture. Left with no other choice, he returned to Mayaro to marry against his will the daughter of the coconut vendor who had helped him to escape to Mayaro in the tray of his truck. He left his heart with Sam Lee's daughter, April. A month later, Sam found out that his daughter was carrying George's child. He immediately sent a request to China for a man to marry her. In exchange for saving his daughter's reputation, Sam offered the young Chinese man the grocery store. April was adamantly against marrying a man she did not love; the only man she wanted was George. Sam tricked her into going to the church by telling her that he had sent for George to marry her. She was devastated.

Seven months later, she gave birth to a beautiful baby girl who was named Suelyn. No one else except Sticks and Sam knew that George Castello was Suelyn's father. Unknown to Sam, April visited Sticks in prison with the hope of finding George. When the child was about a year old, April said that she looked like George and called her Georgia.

"That's an amazing story, Annabelle!" Joyanne declared. "To learn that your best friend was also your sister! When last have you heard from her?"

"Oh, not since the wedding," Annabelle replied in a soft, wistful tone. "April passed away a few weeks later. I feel sorry for her; she was denied true love, and so too was my father. The same can be said of me. The only man I ever loved was your father. Fate can be so cruel!" Annabelle lamented. "Don't allow foolish pride to rob you of the chance to find true love. It's life's ultimate achievement," she said.

She took Joyanne's hands gently in hers. "At least we have each other, Joy," Annabelle cried.

Joyanne looked at her with pity.

It was raining incessantly in Bristol Village when they retired to bed. Joyanne whispered, "Auntie Belle, what became of Suelyn and Danny?"

"Well, my sister, or rather half-sister, Suelyn, went to Canada with her uncle Ed, and my brother Danny went to England," Annabelle replied. "Now go to bed."

Chapter 39

· ·

The morning sun showered its warmth on Bristol Village as Annabelle strolled alongside the almost-deserted road, accompanied by Joyanne, who was bursting with the joy of expectant motherhood. The brilliant orange blossoms of the towering immortelle trees, the warbling birds, and the serene ambiance conspired to create the quintessential rustic idyll, stirring a light and airy feeling in Annabelle.

She held a bouquet of pink and white flowers in her hand while Joyanne carried stems of blazing red bougainvilleas in hers. It had become somewhat of a ritual for Annabelle to visit the cemetery at least once per week to place flowers on the graves of her loved ones.

Joyanne began accompanying her when she found out she was pregnant. The doctor was concerned about her conceiving a child so late in life and advised her to take regular walks. Annabelle took the flowers from Joyanne as they neared the crest of the narrow track in the cemetery. Joyanne propped herself against the pillar of the shed as Annabelle placed the flowers on the graves. She bent over and rested a branch of flowers on George's grave and one on Rosey's, which lay side by side. She bowed her head in prayer for a moment before proceeding downhill to Rosabelle's grave, where she laid a bunch of pink flowers and bowed her head in reverence. Then she walked a few steps and placed a few bunches of red foliage on Ricardo's grave where she spent more than a minute. From a distance, Joyanne could see her lips moving.

Joyanne looked on curiously as Annabelle returned to George's grave, from which she retrieved a small bunch of white flowers and placed it on the small grave between George and Rosey.

When Annabelle told her to destroy the letter that Ricardo had dictated to give to her, Joyanne was more than convinced that Annabelle knew. Perhaps someone told her, perhaps it was intuition or logical deduction, but Auntie Annabelle knew that she was not the child she had given birth to and not the child she kissed goodbye at the train station in Rio Claro eons ago. Come to think of it, she only now understood what Auntie Annabelle meant when she said, "Sometimes it's best not to know the truth; ignorance is bliss."

Joyanne went home and tore the letter in little pieces and scattered the pieces in the wind. She was convinced that Ricardo would have wanted it that way. But she could still hear her father's voice as he dictated the letter. Between a dry, nagging cough, he insisted, "Please, Joy, this is for Annabelle's eyes only. You will know when the time is right."

Rosabelle was eight months pregnant with Ricardo's child, and she questioned whether Ricardo had any love left to give to her baby. He had an unnatural obsession with Annabelle's child, Joyanne. She had become the world which Annabelle had taken away from him when she left Bristol Village. He practically worshipped that child, and Rosabelle was insanely jealous. He reacted violently when she told him to send the child to Annabelle in Port-of-Spain. He tossed any object he could lay his hands on at her. When he was through, the house looked as though it had been ravaged by a storm. He took the crying child in his arms and began to sob. "I'll never leave you, Joy! Never!" he said.

Rosabelle ran out of the house, shouting, "He gone mad! He gone mad!" From that day, she was cautious about what she said about Annabelle and Joyanne.

One night, Joyanne's persistent cry awoke both Ricardo and Rosabelle. He sprang out of bed, hurriedly lit the lamp, and took the child in his arms and began patting her back when he discovered that she had a high fever. He became profoundly worried and said that he had to take her to the doctor right away.

"But it's the middle of the night; the doctor's more than ten miles away!" Rosabelle chided.

"So you expect me to do nothing!" he shouted.

"Rub her down with some oil; that will cure her," Rosabelle said. "It's not the first time she came down with a fever!"

He took the child back to the room and applied some oil to her hot skin, and she stopped crying.

They both went back to bed.

Ricardo got up at four in the morning, as he could not sleep. He looked in at the child, who appeared to be peaceful. He took a shower and dressed himself for the journey to the doctor's office in Rio Claro.

"Oh my God, she's hardly breathing!" he shouted.

Rosabelle got out of bed. "What's wrong? What's wrong?" she asked.

"Get out of my way!" he shouted as he bolted out of the house with Joyanne wrapped in a blanket.

He flagged down a taxi. "Driver, please hurry to Rio Claro! I'll pay for the entire car!" he demanded.

Hours later, a tearful, self-absorbed Ricardo returned home. He sat on the bed and stared as though he was in a trance. For days, he did not speak a word. He stayed away from Joyanne's funeral. "If I go to the funeral, it would mean that I believe that she's really dead. I know she's not!" he told Rosabelle.

He harboured a desolate frame of mind until Rosabelle's baby was born. At first, he refused to even look at the child. Then, one morning, he got out of bed and retrieved the baby from Rosabelle. She became scared that he might hurt the child. Instead, he placed the baby to his chest and began to sob, "Oh, Joyanne! Joyanne! I knew all along that you were not dead!"

On his insistence, the child was christened Joyanne.

The reaction of the mild shower on the warm earth incited a refreshing scent. Annabelle rested her cigarette in the ashtray and took a deep breath to absorb the scent of the fresh earth. "This is the life!" she exclaimed. A smile emerged on her face as she recalled a most pleasant discovery earlier in the week. She was gathering flowers in the backyard when she strayed toward the large immortelle tree where she had lost her virginity to Ricardo. While staring at the tree, she noticed a faded inscription. She rubbed her hand against the trunk of the tree to clear a veneer of moss, and to her astonishment, an inscription which Ricardo had carved on the tree with his penknife was still visible—a heart encircled "Ricardo Loves Annabelle—21/08/1947". Tears filled her eyes as she stared at inscription. A chill ran through her body and caused her to twitch. She was convinced that it was the spirit of Ricardo. She hung a bunch of white roses on the inscription and said a prayer for Ricardo and Joyanne. She placed a bench beneath the tree where she sat most evenings, quietly sipping her coffee and conversing with Ricardo.

The loud cry of the newborn child caused Annabelle's heart to jolt. She hurried to the room, took the baby boy from the midwife, and smiled endearingly at him. "Ricardo! Ricardo! You have come back to me!" she whispered. She saw Ricardo in the child's face while Joyanne saw his father, Peter. Six weeks later, he was christened Peter Ricardo.

"My grandson is going to grow into a happy and humble man," she declared.

She sat in the gallery, absorbing the Bristol Village atmosphere, staring at the phenomenon of rain and sun occurring at the same time, and she chuckled at the recollection of the village folklore: when it rains in the midst of brilliant sunlight, it means that the devil and his wife are fighting for a ham bone.

The light of the sun shone through a layer of gauzy clouds and illuminated the pouring rain and droplets of water on the trees and vegetation, creating a magical illusion. It was as though the water had crystallized on the leaves. Annabelle stared in awe at this wonderland, as though her mind had wandered off into another time. Her face periodically twisted into sentimental smiles. She felt light and airy, as though something sinister and burdensome had departed from within. Life had finally given her the absolution she craved. A rainbow appeared above the trees as if to culminate nature's resplendent finale. She continued to stare at the rainbow until it faded into obscurity. Her mind drifted off into a sanctuary of sweet oblivion.

Conclusion

• •

The events of 1970, referred to as the Black Power Movement, had brought about a new dawn on the Trinidad and Tobago landscape. A new ethos prevailed— complacency had vanished forever. "Power to the People" became a mantra, and mental lines of divide along racial and social status were established. The rainbow which reflected the eclectic races and cultures was no longer viewed as a single entity; its individual colours became apparent.

This new ideology had not yet infiltrated the minds of rural folks. Racial harmony and simple values and virtues continued to flourish in communities like Bristol Village. In a way, these people became the keepers of the rainbow and the messengers of peace and tolerance. Free from the burdens of competitiveness and the power struggle which have enslaved urban man, they continue to enjoy the quintessential life.

Annabelle assumed the role of matriarch of the Castello family and continues to enjoy peace of mind with her new family and has once again assimilated herself

Roland P. Joseph

in the serenity of Bristol Village. Joyanne, Peter, and her grandson fuel the burning fires of the happiness within her. She harbours no urge or desire to return to Port-of-Spain; as far as she is concerned, that era of her life is just a faded memory.

She convenes regular memorial services in honour of her dearly departed ones and is convinced that the tingling feeling which at times envelops her is the spirit of Ricardo. She sees his face and hears him in her grandson. Premonitions regarding the daughter she had given birth to were forever banished from her mind. As far as she is concerned, the child she had kissed goodbye at the train station in Rio Claro many moons ago and the Joyanne with whom she is now reunited are one in the same person. She continues, though, to place a bouquet of flowers on the small unmarked grave in the Bristol Village cemetery.

END